(Un)wise

Melissa Haag

(Un)wise
Copyright: Melissa Haag
Revised Edition

Published: September 5, 2014
ISBN: 978-1-4929610-8-6
Cover Design: Indie-Spired Designs

Titles by Melissa Haag

PROLOGUE

I woke with a start, the terror of the dream still gripping me. Sweat coated my face, and my soaked shirt clung to my skin. I looked around the room. My room. Safe. I let out a shaky breath and tried to convince myself that the dream had only been a product of my imagination. Nothing more.

The alarm clock next to my bed showed just after five a.m., but it felt like I hadn't slept at all.

Kicking off the covers, I got out of bed. Clothes lay scattered on the floor, shadowy lumps that I stepped over on my way to the bathroom. I turned on the light and scrunched my eyes against its bright glare for a moment.

Scrubbing my hands over my face, I leaned against the sink trying to shake the dream. It just wouldn't fade. I dropped my hands to study myself in the mirror. Dark strands of hair stuck to my glistening pale face, an unnatural flush on my cheeks the only splash of color. Even my lips, usually a warm full pink, matched the surrounding colorless skin. Glassy bloodshot eyes, too wide and filled with lingering panic, stared back at me.

I took a deep, unsteady breath. It wasn't real. I was still me. I let my breath out slowly with a self-deprecating laugh. I looked like crap and needed a shower. Great way to start my senior year.

The details of the dream continued to swirl in my head as I stepped into the shower. The lingering sensation of fur hides brushing against my legs scared me. It made it all seem more like a memory than a dream. A memory from an era long past, seen through the eyes of a woman who wasn't me...yet she was.

She wore animal skins and stood outside her mud and grass hut. Other huts surrounded hers. The heavily clouded sky cast a grey gloom on the primitive village. Fear swelled within her. Her fear filled me as if it were my own. I saw what she saw. I was her...yet not.

People ran past her, sprinting between huts, terror in their eyes. Her stomach turned sour with panic. Her vision suddenly changed. The world disappeared, replaced by nothing but tiny sparks floating in a vast darkness. The sparks moved, flying past her in time with the sound of running feet. After a moment, I understood what she saw.

She had an amazing ability that enabled her to see the locations of people. The sparks shrank in size as the view expanded. Not just the location of those around her, but anywhere in the world. She focused on the immediate area worried about her family, using her gift to try to find them. She ran to check each spark. The tang of smoke drifted in the air. Her despair grew, and she ran faster.

All of the tiny sparks looked the same, making it difficult to find the right ones. Too soon, an orange glow illuminated the dark sky. Smoke burned her eyes and nose.

Close by, a different color appeared in her mind. Panic flared within her when she spotted the blue-grey sparks. She stopped running and stood still for a few seconds, terror squeezing the acrid air from her lungs. One heartbeat. Two. She hesitated. Despairing over her family, she spun away from the unique sparks. Her heart clenched, and tears clogged her throat. She left behind those she loved, hearing their dying screams as she ran.

The smoke masked her direction until the yawning abyss of open air loomed before her. Skidding to a halt at the edge of the cliff near her village, she watched dirt tumble over the ledge. She leaned forward, peering over at the broken rocks below. Hopelessness and despair filled her. There was no escape. Her thoughts filled me. Die as they had or die her own way? She continued to stare at the rocks below as she made up her mind.

I struggled to separate myself from her, to scream at her to stop; but inside her own mind, she couldn't hear me.

She glanced over her shoulder and saw a huge beast running at her. A strange calm filled her.

I finally understood the fear and stopped struggling.

It looked like a wolf on steroids and had blood covering its muzzle. As she watched, it changed midstride from beast to man, never pausing.

She turned and flung herself from the cliff. As she fell, she twisted midair to look back at the fate she'd escaped. The man stood naked at the cliff's edge, blood smeared across his face. He yelled in a language I couldn't understand, but she did. He cursed her, saying they would never give up. They would wait as many cycles as it took until we were all theirs.

I woke before she hit the ground; but the fear, the feeling of freefalling, the willingness to die rather than to fall into the hands of that *thing*...it all stayed with me.

ONE

I needed a fix, and I needed it bad. Standing in the mall, I reviewed my options while nervously tugging the long sleeves of my shirt over my wrists to hide the scars there. Since it was a Sunday afternoon, nicely dressed kids trailed behind their equally neat parents in the packed mall. In my worn, dirty clothes from the day before, I stood out. The clerk in the drug store would certainly remember me from yesterday. I'd almost tipped over while waiting in line. When my turn came at the register, he'd looked me over and asked for my ID. His doubtful, long gaze at it had made my palms sweat. When he'd finally glanced up at me, he'd asked, "Are you sure you want these?"

I couldn't go back to the same clerk. My ID was okay at a glance, but it wasn't a great fake ID. And he'd wonder why I was back for more pills when what I'd purchased yesterday should have lasted at least three days.

Shifting from one foot to the other, I chewed on my nail knowing what I needed to do but hating it.

Dani and her friend, Cadence, loitered near the food court, talking. Dani stood six inches taller than me, had multicolored hair (pink and red today), and a cheek piercing to enhance her classic features. She'd get what I needed if I asked. I knew she had a soft spot for me despite her slightly tough appearance. She wouldn't even ask for money though I did have it crumpled in my pocket. No, she was interested in something else as payment.

Everyone knew Dani swung the other way. Just like she knew I didn't. But it didn't stop her from asking for a kiss anyway. She didn't demand a kiss from anyone else. The first time I'd asked for her help, I thought she was doing it to test me. To see if I was really serious about what I wanted her to buy. I'd been desperate. Yeah, I kissed a girl...and I didn't like it.

If I was careful about when I bought, I didn't need to ask her. I'd learned to be careful. I tried to wash up, change my clothes if there were any to change into; and I tried to close my eyes. Not to sleep. No, not that. I just tried to relax so I wouldn't look like a troubled kid strung out on drugs. And I wasn't. Strung out on drugs that is. I was definitely troubled. More troubled than anyone around me would ever guess.

I realized my train of thought had drifted and reined it back in. I needed caffeine, stimulants...whatever I could get my hands on over the counter to stay awake. Not forever. No. I tried to take thirty-minute naps throughout the day and night. If I did that, I could still function. Sort of. Not really. But it was better than the dreams.

Last night I'd finally succumbed. I'd slept twelve hours. I felt like crap today. I'd died again. Several times actually. I hated dying. The last one had been violent. Dogs that looked very human had torn me apart. They'd talked. Well, yelled really. They'd wanted me to choose. I didn't know what.

A shiver ran through me. Just thinking about the dream

made me tired. I ran my fingers through my oily, dark hair to comb it out, hoping it looked decent. I couldn't remember my last shower and cringed at the thought of my mom seeing me like this. Thankfully, she worked. A lot. We communicated via notes left on the fridge. Mostly she told me to clean my room. I kept it strategically messy to help hide whatever it was I bought that week, day, hour, whatever... I sighed and rubbed my head. It ached constantly.

My wandering eyes shifted back to Dani. She watched me with a slight smile. She knew. I didn't know how she could stand kissing me. I looked and felt like crap. At least I'd brushed my teeth before leaving the house. Stuffing my hands into the pockets of my faded, ripped jeans, I started making my way to Dani and the next torturous kiss.

"Bethi Pederson," Dani said, flashing her straight white teeth at me. A smile. Friendly, but the sight reminded me of the snarling gleam from my dream. I fought not to cringe.

"I didn't think I'd see you any time soon." Her eyes roved my face, and she angled her head. "You don't look so good, hun. What's up?"

"Same clerk as yesterday. Can you—"

She didn't let me finish.

"Bethi, maybe you'd be better off coming home with me and sleeping for a few hours."

Cadence rolled her eyes at Dani's comment but said nothing. I could just imagine what would happen if I went home with Dani. Though, looking into her soft brown eyes, the concern there made me hesitate. Sure, she'd probably put a move on me, but I knew she'd also try to get me to rest. To help me. I really did like Dani, just not *that* way. If only she knew sleeping was the last thing I needed. I needed peace. Two totally different things. The thought of someone helping me was tempting, but I knew I had to deal with this on my own.

"Thanks, Dani, but I can't." I pulled my hand out of my pocket and tried giving her the money.

She didn't move to take it. "You know the price." Her smile was gone.

"Why?" I partially whined unable to keep the anxious uncertainty from my voice. "You know I like guys, Dani. Plus, I look like hell. Probably smell bad too."

She studied me for a moment. I tried to look confident, but my arms wrapped around me so I hugged myself.

"It's your eyes," she said, taking pity on me but shrugged away any further explanation.

I averted my deep blue eyes, which looked violet in certain light or on days when I got very little sleep. Against my pale skin and dark hair, they startled people with their naturally vivid coloring.

"As far as liking guys goes, I'm hoping you'll change your mind." Her lips curved in a soft smile.

I was glad she didn't mention my smell. It would have hurt. I wanted to shower, but the warm water put me to sleep, and standing tense under a jet of frigid water wasn't worth the pounding headache afterward.

Exhaustion made the floor dip and crest under my feet. Enough playing around. We both knew I didn't have a choice. I closed the distance between us, fisted my hands in her hair, and pulled her down for a kiss. Her lips were soft and warm against mine. My stomach turned sour as memories swamped me.

This wasn't the first life in which I'd kissed a girl. There'd been so many dreams since the start of the school year. In each dream, I starred as the leading lady. I felt what she felt, saw what she saw—her, but not her. After a while, I began to notice similarities. The dreams themselves didn't repeat, but it often felt like I dreamt of the same person even though their appearances changed from one dream to the next. Each time I closed my eyes and dreamed, I had a unique ability. In all the dreams so far, there had been six distinct abilities...six unique women. Learning about them and what they could do was by far the most interesting portion of the dream. If only the dreams ended there. The appearance of the beasts and what they did made me shudder. But worse still were all the deaths I experienced.

Dani misunderstood my shudder and lifted a hand to my cheek as she kissed me sweetly in return. After counting to four in my head, I pulled back hoping it'd been enough.

The dream kiss had been just as chaste. But it'd felt different. I'd been saying goodbye to someone I loved dearly. Maybe a sister or best friend. The girl in my dream hadn't spoken. She'd simply turned and calmly pushed through the fleeing crowd, people running from the beasts who screamed in their guttural voices for me to step forward. In that dream, my life had been spared...for a while. Hers had been taken.

"Kay. I'll get you what you need." She walked away leaving me standing with Cadence.

My hot, gritty eyes tracked her progress. How could I feel this tired after sleeping twelve hours? My life hadn't been like this for long. After the first dream almost three months ago, I'd slept fine for several nights before figuring out the dreams were skipping nights here and there. On the nights I had those dreams, I woke as tired as I'd been when I went to bed. Too soon, I started having them every night. Sometimes several dreams a night if I managed to fall back to sleep. So many dreams. But, I'd learned something.

Without a doubt, each dream played a scene from a past life, an echo of memory. The surety that I was remembering, and not just dreaming made me doubt my sanity. Some *thing* throughout history continued to hunt me...and others like me. Yeah, I wasn't alone. Sometimes the women looked similar to how I appeared now. Sometimes I wasn't me, but a completely different person, one of the other five. Often names repeated in different lifetimes, or we had family members with the same names. But, it was the lingering details of the life after waking that convinced me they were surfacing memories and not just random dreams.

Usually I died young, unaware of the danger. Sometimes, the dreams came and helped me to prepare. To run. Either way, I never lasted long. They could track me by my scent. Back then, though, there hadn't been cars or other ways to travel fast. I hoped this time would be different. I had no doubt...they would come. But maybe I could finally out run them.

I closed my eyes for a second to relieve the hot sting. They stayed closed and wouldn't open no matter how hard I tried. My legs felt weak, and I knew I'd crumple to the ground any moment. In a distant part of my mind, a dream gathered, an angry storm of memories, swirling and gaining speed.

Cadence's voice and rough hold pulled me back from the brink of sleep.

"Geez, Bethi. Get a grip. People are staring."

Paranoia fueled an adrenaline spike. My eyes popped open.

My knees kept shaking, but no longer from sleep. Flight or fight mode. I was ready to fly. Controlling my breathing and relaxing my shoulders, I glanced around. A security guard watched me. My relief sprouted a genuine smile on my face. The woman looked confused for a moment, then shook her head and turned away. I could only imagine what she thought of my odd behavior.

"Thanks," I mumbled to Cadence, thinking of the adrenaline rush. Maybe that was the way to go. I fingered the scars on my arms. Pain, though effective, was a pointless method to stay awake. After all, it was the pain in my dreams I wanted to avoid.

Adrenaline might be the answer. I'd watched myself and others do amazing things in my dreams because of it. Although, there were times it didn't work. The phrase "flight or fight" should really be "flight, fight, or freeze." So many times the surrealism of the situation shuts down a person's brain even though the body is pumped full of that magic juice.

Fingers waggled in front of my eyes, and I realized I'd been drifting in my own thoughts. Dani stood in front of me with an amused smile, one that didn't reach her eyes.

"I got you some caffeine pills and a Monster, but rent-a-cop over there is watching us. So how about you tell us what's got you so messed up. And don't say no sleep, we got that."

Dani's eyes pulled me in, encouraging me to let someone help. I'd tried talking to my mom about the dreams, but her answer had been to try sleeping pills. She didn't really hear the problem within my dreams even though she listened to my whole explanation. Since I already questioned my sanity, I hadn't wanted her to start questioning it too so I let it drop. Last thing I wanted was a padded room and an IV cocktail. No, better keep my crazies to myself.

"Haunting memories. Let's leave it at that," I said with a smile I didn't feel. We were getting too serious, and I needed to break the mood somehow or pretty soon Dani wouldn't be so willing to help me. Not even for a kiss.

Cadence cleared her throat. "Hottie approaching."

Before I could turn to look, I felt a light tap on my shoulder.

"Pardon, do you know where the loo is?"

Loo? I turned to look over the owner of the clipped British accent. Holy, hotness. Shock and awe filled me. My heart stuttered out a beat as my mind went blank. It did that a lot lately.

The man stood well over six feet. Lean and long, his shoulders filled out his worn, brown leather jacket. The mall lights glinted off his bronzed, mussed hair and highlighted the amused twinkle in his hazel eyes. Eyes a girl could lose herself in. Why couldn't I have kissed him instead of Dani? The wayward thought bounced around in my head for a moment as I stared at his dark brown lashes and tried not to sigh. Or drool. I reined myself in not wanting to hurt Dani's feelings. She still had what I needed. I blinked at him while trying to think. His lips twitched as he waited for me. His gaze skimmed me, not settling anywhere, just taking me in the same as I was doing to him.

A sense of familiarity settled over me, and my stomach did a weird little flip. I tried to study him with indifference. Was this someone I knew but my sleep deprived brain had forgotten? Embarrassing.

I closed my mouth, swallowed hard, hoped I wouldn't blush, and tried for cool-sarcastic, "Oh my God, an accent. Take me, I'm yours."

Dani and Cadence sniggered. I curved my lips in a smile as I waited for him to go away. I just wanted to get my stuff and leave.

Something in the man's expression changed. He tilted his head and took a slow deep breath. I thought for a moment he had a witty reply or would say something rude. Instead, he leaned toward me, his eyes locked on mine, and murmured, "You smell amazing."

My insides froze and, for the second time in five minutes, adrenaline spiked through my veins. He pulled back, his intense gaze never leaving mine. I struggled to contain my panic and to think clearly. I did *not* smell amazing.

His pupils dilated as he continued to watch me. A smile tugged at his lips.

A small sound escaped me somewhere between a whimper and a throat clearing. Dani moved beside me. I knew she was trying to figure out my reaction, but I couldn't spare her more than a passing thought.

He caught the noise. Awareness crept into his eyes almost as if he'd emerged from a trance. His smile faded, and he began to look troubled. It didn't matter. I'd witnessed that concentrated look before and knew what he meant, what he was.

I didn't want to die, but all those dreams had prepared me for what would come next. Dani and Cadence needed to get out of range. Now. Memories of blood and carnage, of the gory ending of past lives, flitted around in my mind. My heart tripled its rhythm at the remembered pain.

"I need a minute," I said to Dani and Cadence. My voice remained calm and steady. Weary acceptance filled my lungs and radiated throughout me.

They nodded and moved a few feet away. I glanced at the rent-a-cop. Her attention once again rested on me. I knew better than to try calling for her help but still felt a small glimmer of hope. Maybe I was safe. Maybe the crowd was enough.

He watched me expectantly, his eyes causing my stomach to do erratic flips of joy. One of their kind always called to me like that. Messing with my insides, my emotions, pulling me to them like a moth to a flame. Just like the poor winged creature, it never ended well for me.

"I do *not* smell amazing," I said softly, trying to keep anyone from overhearing. "I smell like I need a shower. Badly."

He frowned, held up his hands in a placating manner, and said, "No offense, luv. I'm just looking for the loo."

I stared at him for a moment, the wild beat of my heart pounding in my ears as I tried to decide what game he played. Barely lifting my hand, I pointed to the right near the rent-a-cop wondering how long he'd keep up the pretense.

He nodded his thanks, but didn't move. He hesitated. His eyes swept my face. He opened his mouth as if he wanted to say more. Instead, he jammed his hands into his pockets and walked away.

Stunned, I watched him leave. My mind tried to keep up with what my eyes processed. One of them was walking away from me. What did it mean? It meant I wasn't dead. Yet. I knew what I needed to do. Wait...wait for it. He kept walking away. I felt Dani join me as my eyes remained riveted on the man. He didn't glance back, not once, before rounding the corner to the bathrooms.

"Don't come back here," I whispered to Dani.

Then, I ran.

* * * *

The overgrown, low border hedges lining the sidewalk of my house loomed ahead. I hurtled them neatly, not knowing I had it in me. Palming the key from my pocket, I slid it into the lock of the front door entering the house only seconds after leaping into the yard. I slammed the door behind me and didn't bother looking out the window to see if I had been followed. Either he would break down the door or not. Looking wouldn't change the outcome, and I couldn't waste time. Not a second.

My bedroom slowed me down a bit as I waded through the ankle-deep clothes swamp. Snatching the grey duffle from under the bed, I crammed in whatever lay nearby until I couldn't fit more. I struggled with the zipper, and the harsh panting of my breath filled the room.

Could he follow my scent even though I had taken the bus most of the way home? Would it slow him down?

I grabbed the dwindling supply of money I'd stashed away for a car and stuffed it in my bra.

Was I taking too long?

Hands shaking, I hefted the duffle. Its heavy weight settled on my shoulder anchoring me to the reality of here and now as I left my room. I needed to catch another bus. This time it would need to take me much further.

Mom's note on the refrigerator caught my eye. I stopped moving and stared at it. My throat tightened. She wouldn't understand why I'd left, and I would never be able to come home. The grief turned into fear when I thought of what she would do after she realized I was gone. She would do *everything* she could to find me again. Police. Newspapers. Radio. If she called too much attention to herself, to me...I shuddered at the possibilities.

I hastily searched for paper and a pen. I had to give her a reason for disappearing. The message hurt to write. My hand shook as I signed it. Then, I pulled out my cell phone and set it on the kitchen table along with the note.

Mom,

School's not for me. I want to see the world. I'm sorry for leaving like this, but hope you'll understand someday.

Bethony

The words screamed at me from the paper. Lies. She'd be hurt and confused, but what else could I say? Tell her about the monsters who would come and threaten her for information? No, she'd go to the police with whatever I wrote. They'd think I just needed a padded room for a while.

But the people looking for me? When they came—and they *would* come—she would probably show them the note hoping they might help find me. If they thought she knew something more, they would hurt her to get it. Keeping her in the dark might help keep her safe. I didn't even want to tell her that I loved her, fearing they'd see it as leverage.

I left my house, jogging toward the bus stop I knew had pickups heading out of town. I didn't turn to look at my house one last time, though I wanted to. I kept focused on what I needed to do.

Several people stood waiting when I got there. After asking, I found the next bus wouldn't arrive for at least another fifteen minutes. Time enough for the adrenaline, which had been keeping me going, to ease out of my system. Time enough for the man with an accent to catch up to me. Time enough for me to give in to the ever-present urge to sleep.

I eyed the people around me. An older crowd, geriatric types. Generally safe. But with that man, that thing, chasing me, I couldn't risk sleeping.

Easing into a squat and leaning back against the pole of the bus stop sign, I struck up a polite conversation with an elderly lady. She introduced herself as Willa Delson and didn't seem to mind when my attention wandered or I slurred a few words between yawns. By the time the bus rolled up, I'd looked at all of the pictures of her grandkids and great grandkids. Very cute, happy kids. I hoped they never learned the truth: monsters were real. If they did, they would never smile at a camera again.

I paid the driver for the farthest stop on his run, a three-hour drive that would take me north. Having found a friend in Willa, I asked to sit next to her. Her ticket took her to the same town, so we settled in for a long ride. She shared the snacks she'd stashed in her handbag and chatted about seeing her newest great grandchild. Six pounds and seven ounces, Joy Marie Delson wailed her way into the world only a week ago. My desperation to stay awake had me absorbing Willa's every word. At the end of three hours, I could have pretended to be a member of the extensive Delson clan. My legs twitched with pre-sleep spasms several times, but I didn't succumb.

The bus dropped us in front of Chris's Cooking Café. A sign in the window advertised CCC's specials at very low prices. My stomach rumbled. I couldn't remember if I'd had anything for dinner. My days blurred.

Willa waved goodbye as she spotted her daughter-in-law, the new grandmother, waiting for her. My stomach growled as I smiled farewell. Tired was bad enough. Tired *and* hungry wouldn't work. I couldn't run—not far anyway—if I didn't eat. I strode to the restaurant. The smell of fryer oil greeted me. Their prices were low, as advertised, but not fast food low. Who knew how long I would need to keep moving. My money wouldn't last. I settled on a plain burger from the kids menu. The waitress gave me a look but let it go.

After devouring my baby burger, I walked to the only motel in town where the waitress said I could find a bus schedule. The posted schedule showed that the same run that had dropped me here would take me back at the same time the following day. *No thanks.* Other than packing before running, I hadn't thought very far ahead. Too tired to concentrate, I decided to sleep a few hours and then think of a plan.

The man behind the desk eyed me when I asked for a room. The need to sleep coated me in a thick film giving the world a surreal quality. I knew I'd fall hard and worried what would happen if I started screaming. I decided to tell him that I suffered from night terrors. The clerk stared at me and took a second look at my fake ID while I tried not to fidget. Finally, he gave me a bill along with the key.

I needed to plan where to go from here, but the bed swallowed me whole as soon as I closed the door. My exhaustion didn't give me a chance to enjoy the feeling. Immediately, images of a dark haired girl surfaced behind my closed eyes. Crap. I didn't want to die again.

She stood panting at the edge of a cliff, staring straight ahead at nothing. The craggy face of the rock dropped steeply to the tree-filled valley below. Moonlight highlighted each rock and scrub brush.

The details soaked into me, and the perspective shifted as

usual. I slipped further into the dream, becoming her.

Clutching my hands together, I could imagine each scratch and break my body would suffer. I looked down at a large rip in the forearm of my leather tunic. Dark clotting blood from a vicious bite glistened in the silvery light.

An eerie cry echoed behind me. My panicked heart slowed as I made a decision. I turned from the cliff to watch my pursuers silently emerge from the trees and close the distance. Sleek, furred heads rose to howl together in triumph.

The leader slowly loped forward, shifting forms as he approached. His paws widened and fingers emerged where pads once existed. Black claws shrank and flattened into human nails. Fur receded into skin as bones popped and reshaped giving the forelimbs a human appearance. As soon as his feet developed, he reared back to stand on his morphing legs.

Snuffling through his shrinking snout, he spoke before his tongue fully changed. It garbled his words, but I still understood him.

"Amusing chase, but it is time to choose. We will keep you safe as they couldn't."

Safe? Rage boiled in my heart. One of them had bit me during their attack on my village, a poor example of their care for me. Did he honestly think he could persuade me to go with them? They were unnatural. Evil. The dark glint in his eyes showed it. I saw only one outcome.

"I choose death," I said savagely as I pushed off with my feet doing a backward dive off the cliff's edge. Inside I screamed with fear.

I felt each bounce against the rocky surface until my neck broke bringing dark respite.

(Un)wise

Warmth blanketed me, weighing me down comfortably. Something gentle pressed briefly against my forehead. I felt comforted as the dream shifted. I didn't want to witness another death. I tried to surface, but I was in too deep.

Tall stalks of grass and wild flowers swayed in the gentle breeze. To the west, the sun's dying rays painted the sky. A single furrowed dirt track, perhaps made by game, followed the edge of the woods to the east. The air smelled fresh and crisp with no hint of pollution.

In this dream, I drifted as a bodiless bystander without someone else's thoughts or feelings pushing into me as if my own. I observed the area, curious about the change in perspective.

A circle of stones crowned a patch of barren earth in the middle of the wind-ruffled grasses. Seven women stood within. I could see them clearly. One of them had a round, distended stomach, very large with child, and she was dressed better than the rest. Her taupe gown, a thin flowing material, molded itself to her belly in the breeze. The rest knelt in a half circle before her, dressed in rough skins and furs. Dirt dusted their skin and matted hair.

The pregnant one spoke in a guttural tongue. It took a moment for her words to make any sense.

"These I give onto you for your protection."

The speaker motioned for the woman to her right to come to her. The woman stood and approached the one in the taupe gown, her steps hesitant. The woman in taupe gave a small encouraging smile. Her eyes held so many emotions: concern, sadness, hope...

Placing a hand on her swollen belly and the other on the

coarse woman's flat stomach, she spoke a single word, "Strength." Immediately, her roundness decreased while a bump formed on the other woman's previously flat stomach.

The woman gave a startled yelp and quickly moved back to her kneeling position, her hand protectively cradling her newly rounded middle. The woman in the gown motioned to the next primitive and repeated the process. It continued until the stomachs of those kneeling were all rounded with child, and hers showed no sign of inflation.

"Go," she said softly to her group. They stood and parted, each heading in separate directions.

Two

I woke feeling rested, but cranky. I wanted just one night without dreams, not that I wasn't grateful for that last dream. At least no one had died. Struggling out of the bowl my body had created in the mattress, I checked the clock and flew into panic mode. Fourteen hours had passed! Too much time in one spot.

Scrambling to the window, I peeked around the curtain. The sun barely rimmed the horizon. Silence still claimed the morning—but not my thundering heart. My eyes darted around the street, searching for anything out of place. Nothing. I moved away from the window and slid my feet into my shoes.

Grabbing my bag, I eased out the door. The motel office waited a few feet away. Down the road, several trucks stood in front of the restaurant.

I hurried to return the room key. I needed a ride. I needed to move. The man from the night before took the key from me and returned the small cash deposit he'd required since I didn't have a credit card. With a fake smile, I stepped back outside. The bus would bring me back to where I'd started, and I couldn't go back home. I paused looking for options on the very dead street.

An early riser stepped out of the CCC. A dirty green knit cap covered his head and a brown scarf insulated his neck. Grey whiskers protected his cheeks. This far south winter rarely had a bite, but today would be one of those days.

He strode to a late model Chevy truck. Rust and mud speckled the back fender, but I didn't care about that. He was just the option I was looking for. Waving to catch his attention, I hurried over to ask if he'd give me a ride out of town. He looked me over, eyeing my thin long sleeved shirt and asked me a few questions about where I was headed. Satisfied with my answer, a better paying job in a bigger town, he agreed to give me a lift.

"In the bed, 'course. Can't be too careful. Sorry," he said, getting into the truck cab.

I didn't mind the conditions. A ride was a ride, and I needed it desperately.

Using the bumper, I vaulted into the bed and hunkered down near the cab. As I'd expected, the cold pierced my skin as soon as we started moving. At least, the cold would help keep me awake.

I dug in my bag looking for something warmer. My hand brushed against a zipper. Carefully, I pulled a hooded sweatshirt out of the grey duffle. I frowned at it, puzzled. It didn't look familiar. I turned it in my hands for a moment before deciding I didn't care. Nothing seemed familiar anymore. I pulled it on and zipped it up. It smelled good, clean, unlike most of what I'd crammed into the bag, and it helped a bit against the wind.

The panic and need to move calmed as the driver kept a steady speed heading northwest out of town. It gave me time to think. Fourteen hours was crazy long for only one death dream. Since they had started, they had varied little. Discovery, then death. Like an alarm clock, they woke me to the truth: the beasts were coming, and I needed to run to save those I loved. Unfortunately, like those past lives, I hadn't truly believed the dreams until one of those *things* actually arrived.

I rubbed my nose trying to warm it. At least I'd gotten away...this time.

The second dream about the women puzzled me. It was nothing like the other dreams. What did it mean, and why did I dream it right after that man found me? With a sigh, I leaned my head back and stared at the sky unable to answer my own questions.

I wasn't sure if it was pity or his true destination, but the man drove an hour to the next big town with a bus stop. Discreetly digging in my stash of cash, I offered him a twenty for gas, but he waved it away with a gruff, "Take care."

Looking at the schedule, I studied my options. There were several buses departing within the next hour. Only two general directions, however. North and west. Though I'd tolerated the cold, I didn't want to push any further north in November without a decent jacket. West seemed like a good enough choice.

* * * *

The dark circles under my eyes, a constant presence for the last few weeks, stood out vibrantly as I stepped off a bus in Springfield, Illinois twenty-four hours later. Wearily, I shuffled away from the drop-off location. The layovers and transfers had helped keep me awake and prevented a screaming fit while traveling, but I knew I needed to crash soon.

A fellow passenger pointed me in the direction of the nearest motel. Just a few blocks. No problem. Money would be an issue, though. This would be the last room I could afford. I wasn't even sure if the fake ID I'd gotten online would work here. Most kids my age got one for drinking. Not me. As soon as I'd started dying in my dreams, I'd planned to run on some level and bought one just for this purpose. Running and hiding. If only I had a destination in mind. But, how could I when I didn't even know where these things came from? For all I knew, I was heading right to them. Hard to plan when you didn't know which direction was safe. Well, I knew home wasn't safe. One found me there. I thought briefly of my mom and felt a pang. *Please let this keep her safe.*

Checking into the cheapest room I could manage, I headed to my room. I wanted sleep. Bad. My stomach cramped. I wanted food, too. However, both food and sleep would need to wait because I just couldn't stand my own smell anymore. I walked to the bathroom as I peeled off my clothes. The money I had stuffed in my bra fell to the floor. The thin fold of bills worried me. I counted my remaining cash. Less than fifty. Enough to buy a few meals, but it wouldn't get me much further, which meant I needed to earn some more. I set the money next to the sink with a sigh. I was tired, hungry, and poor. Could anything else knock me down?

I looked in the mirror, cringed, and added looking like crap to my list. A poster child for runaway teens stared back at me. I didn't even look seventeen. Most of the makeup I'd worn to the mall had rubbed off. The dark circles, sallow complexion, and weight loss just made me look very young and very sick. Shaking my head at the thought, I picked a few items out of the duffle bag to wash. Since most of the clothes on the floor of my bedroom had been dirty, they needed it. The longer I'd traveled, the more strange looks I'd gotten on the bus. I didn't need to call additional attention to myself by looking like a vagrant.

Back home it'd been part of my act to hide the fact I wasn't sleeping. I didn't need to hide that anymore. There wasn't anyone around who'd care. Besides, staying awake seemed stupid now, anyway. I still didn't want to see or feel myself dying in my dreams, but I didn't like the idea of dying in real life because of tired mistakes, either. And if I kept avoiding sleep, that was going to happen.

The high-pressure showerhead made washing quick and easy for my underthings and shirt. The bar soap smelled okay, too. I rinsed until the water ran clear. The jeans were a pain. Waterlogged, they weighed too much to easily maneuver under the spray of water. Giving up, I stepped in and pulled the curtain closed. Standing under the steamy stream and alternating between rinsing the jeans and washing myself kept me awake until I finished.

Thankfully, towels were abundant in the bathroom. After drying off and wrapping my hair, I used another towel for my jeans. I rolled them inside the towel and stomped on the roll. The towel came away soaked. I grabbed a new towel and did it again. The second time the jeans no longer dripped water. I hung them on the rod and trudged to bed.

The pillows called to me. I tossed back the bedspread. Again, a dream wrapped around me as I climbed under the covers.

Glowing embers floated in the air, red stars against the night sky.

A dark haired girl stood before the blazing huts, facing the fire. The heat curled her hair and burned her skin, but she didn't back away. She screamed a name, searching fruitlessly in the shifting orange flames.

Her desperation crowded into me. My heart stuttered as we merged, her every thought and feeling becoming my own.

Turning, I ran into the darkness only to return a second later with a crude clay container filled with water. I tossed the contents toward the flames, but it fell short. Frustration and terror tore at me. I raced away to try again, this time stepping closer. Water hit the burning grass walls but didn't slow the consuming progress. With a hiss and sputter, the moisture evaporated.

Deep, mocking laughter echoed behind me.

"Child! You are not meant for this. Step away."

I spun toward my tormentors. "Help me! If you care as you claimed when you set the fires, help me put them out."

Auburn-hued from the reflection of the flames, a group of men stood watching. Several wore taunting grins.

The leader tilted his head as he studied me.

"Why? They are all dead," he assured me. "There is not one heart left beating, save yours."

A wall of guilt hit me. My family, gone. I screamed my anguish and fell to my knees. The soles of my feet, still so close to the flames, started to blister. My hair curled back from the heat and started to smoke. I fell silent and looked up with dull eyes.

I knew her choice as it settled in her mind. I fought her, wanting to wake up. Falling had been bad; this would be worse.

"You win. I will choose." I stood, embracing the pain in my feet. It's what my family had all felt while trying to protect me. Searing pain.

"You are indeed wise. Who will it be?" the leader asked.

Several men stood back from the flames waiting eagerly for our choice.

"Not who. What." *I smiled as his triumphant grin fell.* "Death." *I turned and ran into the flames.*

At first, I felt nothing. Then the pain of every blister and crack as I turned into a human candle consumed me. I opened my mouth to scream but nothing came out. There was only pain, everywhere.

I struggled to escape the pain. My heart thumped heavily as I shifted in my sleep, crying out. A hand soothed a tear from my cheek. Lips pressed against my forehead. A voice whispered, "I'm here." I tried to open my eyes, tried to breathe air that wasn't smoke-filled. My fight was in vain. I sank deeper as the dream shifted.

Hidden in the trees, a mother cradled her child in her arms. Sweat still shone on the woman's skin from her recent labor. Birds sang, and sunlit spots danced on the forest floor.

Still matted and slick from birth, the child suddenly squalled loudly.

The mother smiled at her child. "I call you Jin, for Strength, as she promised us. I will keep you as safe as I am able and love you always. Protect us with your strength. Keep them at bay."

She put the child to her breast and laid her head back against the trunk of the tree.

Before her, the taupe gowned woman appeared. "There can be no rest. You must run."

The startled woman opened her eyes and looked down in concern at the infant. "She's so fragile," she murmured.

"If she dies, she will be reborn as often as necessary each cycle. She will know pain and hardship." The gowned woman

knelt to stroke the smooth cheek. She felt compassion and
sorrow seeing the fates of the child. "Balance must be
maintained. The world will burn if they find her."

* * * *

I lingered on the edge of sleep for several minutes before opening my eyes. My stomach churned as I remembered the newest death. I curled into a ball under the covers.

Why wouldn't the dreams just stop already? I'd run like the visions showed me. Maybe too late, though. The face of the man from the mall surfaced in my mind. His warm eyes looked gentle and amused, not malicious like the others. But I knew better than to trust them. I wrapped my arms around my knees. There was nothing gentle about the *things* chasing me. Every memory followed the same pattern. I ran from something that terrified me, the "something" exposed itself as a dog, turned man. The dogs—always a group of them—possessed large sleek heads, intelligent eyes, vicious teeth, and claws, which they put to use. After changing forms, they always talked about choosing. Choosing what? The way they acted and spoke, I guessed they wanted me to choose one of them. But to what purpose?

If I didn't kill myself, they tried forcing me to choose. The methods they used...I shuddered. I wasn't sure whose method was worse. Theirs or mine. In all my past lives I died horribly. I thought I understood the messages of the dreams—run. But if that was it, the dreams should have stopped. Instead, they'd changed. Two now had felt like a memory even though I hadn't merged with anyone. The two about babies.

Last night's second dream made my need to run sound like there was more at stake than just my death. Not that my death wasn't important enough to keep my feet moving. That woman made it sound like I didn't really have a choice.

If I hadn't connected with any of the women, why would it feel like a memory? My brows rose as I realized whom I'd overlooked. The infants in the first unique dream. Of course. Six of them just like the six variations of past lives I kept dreaming about. In the first unique dream, they hadn't been born; and in the second, the newborn hadn't yet experienced her gift, the things chasing her, or much of anything, really. Perhaps that was why I hadn't connected.

So, if those two dreams were still memories, then what that woman said scared me. Would the world truly burn if those dog-men caught me? I shuddered remembering the feeling of the flames consuming my flesh. Thankfully, the searing pain had been cut short.

I stopped that thought and with wide eyes froze under the covers. A gentle hand had soothed me. The kiss. Had it been real? I tried to breathe as quietly as possible as I listened for any strange noises in the room. All I could hear was my own heartbeat. Scrunching my eyes for a moment, I braced myself for the worst. I took a deep breath and quickly sat up, looking around the room.

Everything remained as it had when I'd gone to sleep. The outside door remained securely bolted, and the bathroom door still stood open. I let out a large shaky sigh.

That touch, like the dreams, had felt real yet it hadn't been a part of either dream. Rather, it was a fragment of the shift between them. That was one of the difficulties with sleep deprivation. The confused haziness between reality and imagination was hard to figure out. Well, that plus the headaches...

Flopping backwards, I rubbed my hands over my face. Maybe my first inclination to question my sanity had been right. What if all of this was really in my head? I laughed at myself. Of course it was in my head. But what if it was all just my imagination? That guy in the mall might have really just wanted the bathroom. And my physical reaction to him? Well, he was really good looking, and he had an accent. Who wouldn't suffer a little tummy tickle over that?

What did I really have as solid proof that something was out there? I cringed. I didn't have any. That just furthered my insanity theory. My poor Mom. And school. Exams were in a few weeks. I'd skipped so much school my grades were in the gutter. I had enough credits to graduate at the end of the semester if I passed my current class load. If I went back now and asked for help, I could still do it. Maybe. I'd probably still end up in a padded room for a while. But, the details of the dreams, and my ability to recall everything—touch, taste, smell— bothered me. It seemed so real. What if all those feelings *were* memories? If I went back home, would I be setting myself up for another non-choice...where I sacrificed myself?

With a sigh, I flipped back the covers and got out of bed. No matter what I chose, I needed to get dressed first. Padding across the carpet, I stepped into the bathroom to check my clothes. Dry, but stiff.

Dressing slowly, I mulled over my options. Home called to me. I had very little money left and nowhere to go. But, I needed to be sure. I didn't want to go back and bring trouble with me. This was a big enough town. I could find a job and wait out a few weeks. See if the dreams got better.

Gripping my jeans to pull them up, I felt a crinkle in the front pocket. Odd. I hadn't felt anything when I washed them. Something dug into my hip when I tugged them up the rest of the way.

I reached into the pocket, and my fingers brushed something. Hard plastic. I dug deeper. Paper. A chill swept through me as I wrapped my hand around the items and pulled them out. I stared at the five neatly folded hundred dollar bills, a note, and a cell phone lying in my open palm for a moment before I instinctively dropped them on the tan bathroom tile. Nothing was mine.

The hand wiping the tear from my face...

Icy fear pierced my stomach, and I sat heavily on the toilet seat. With shaking fingers, I tentatively picked up the note. Each crackle as I unfolded the hotel stationery sent a shiver down my spine. The paper had nothing on it but a phone number. No. No way! How had he found me again? Could it be the same guy? I crumpled the paper and threw it in the garbage along with the phone.

The dreams. People chasing me. It *wasn't* in my head. I stared at the solid proof that it was real. I couldn't go back home. I needed to keep running. Move. I eyed the money. I wasn't about to use the phone to call that number, but the money...I'll be taking that, thank-you-very-much!

Wasting no time, I gathered my things. At least, I'd showered and slept. Looking around to make sure I wasn't forgetting anything, I spotted stationery on the bedside table. The pen lay beside it. Lifting the pad to the light, I saw the indentations of the phone number that had been in my pocket. Of course, I already knew someone had been in my room but seeing the used pad of paper gave me the shakes again.

Run!

I didn't look back.

THREE

When I stepped outside the hotel, the chilled air slapped some sense into me; and I schooled my terror-filled expression. I couldn't doubt myself any longer. Not even slightly. The dreams had continued after my discovery for a reason. I had lifetimes of wisdom in me. I just needed to remember it all. Remembering would help me survive. But to remember, I needed a safe place to sleep...I needed a lot of it. Where though? A public place would be good. A place where moaning in my sleep wouldn't be too out of the ordinary. Somewhere low cost. A homeless shelter? I'd never been to one in real life and hoped they offered beds like in the movies.

Decided, I hailed a cab. The driver let me know about an overflow shelter where I'd have the best luck in winter months. After showing the cabbie I could pay, he took me there but dropped me off a few blocks away. I didn't think it would look good if I arrived there in a taxi.

I managed two nights before I admitted to myself I'd made the wrong decision. All of the dreams—each memory—depicted hellish nightmares of brutal past deaths, further driving into me the need to run. I still didn't have a destination. I just needed to keep moving. *They* were closing in. I would die.

Though I'd slept every chance I got, it felt like I'd stayed awake since I left the hotel. Hyped up on caffeine, I caught another bus. This time going south. I didn't pay attention to the destination, nor did I make small talk with sweet old ladies.

On the outside, anyone looking at me would see a calm, sleepy girl. Inside, I twitched and jittered; I moaned and cried as I remembered all the slow tiny cuts from the night before. It had taken a week to die. In that dream, they hadn't meant to kill me...her...us...whoever. A past version of one of the others like me had pretended to be more alert and resilient than she had actually been. When they'd realized they'd gone too far, it'd been too late.

* * * *

The ride left me in a small town with no motel.

I cast my eyes in every direction trying to decide my next move when I spotted an old iron support bridge just down one of the side roads. Its metal skeleton blended with the leafless branches on the banks surrounding it. Trudging in that direction, I kept alert for anyone following me.

Since staying at the shelter, something had changed. The sleep-inducing memories pulled at me even while awake. The pull had an edge to it. It wouldn't be denied for long. I needed a power nap. Thirty minutes tops, I promised myself.

I checked for cars before I stepped off the road and made my way into the ravine that the bridge spanned. The wooden decking provided covering but didn't make a good shelter due to the gaps. Crushed stone had once covered the embankment. Weeds and other growth concealed much of it now. The dry winter vegetation snapped in the quiet as I headed under the bridge and picked a spot where most of the rocks were still exposed.

Peeling off my hoodie, I lay down. The rocks and cold wouldn't allow for a deep sleep. The waiting dream pulled me under before I laid my head on my arm.

I immediately merged with the past.

In this dream, I was myself, or at least a past version of myself, and remembered the man standing before me. He had been responsible for my death twice in the same cycle. He looked much older now.

"This time, we're going to do things a little differently." He *motioned for two of his men to step forward. "Hold her, and open her mouth."*

One man stepped behind me, grasping my already bound arms. Another man gripped my jaw roughly and pressed his fingers inward until I opened my mouth.

My face ached. His fingers left bruises on my skin, but I showed no fear, no pain. I remembered him. I remembered everything. This, however, was new and I wondered what he had in mind.

He motioned for another to join our little group.

This man I'd never seen before. Something about him pulled me, and I felt certain it wasn't good. His eyes roamed over me from head to feet, lingering in any place that caught his interest.

"Her scent is perfect."

"Go then," the leader motioned the man to step toward us.

I braced myself for a brutal Claiming, but the man surprised me by stopping a step away. He tilted his neck to the side. I didn't have time to wonder what it meant. The man holding me shoved my face forward into the man's neck. I pulled my bruised lips back just before the second man holding me moved his hands on my jaw. Instead of forcing it open, he forced it closed so fast and hard that I bit the man's neck. He howled in excitement. I pulled back, stunned and not understanding what had just happened. Both men let go of me and stepped back leaving me with the man I'd just bitten.

He pulled me to him and kissed my mouth passionately. He bruised my lips further. Still, I felt a stirring within me and tentatively responded. His hands tugged at my clothing.

"Stop. You can't mate with her. Not yet."

The man kissing me lifted his head with a feral growl.

The leader didn't back down. Instead, he partially shifted. "She's weak. She's died on us twice already. You need to be in control, not newly Claimed. Wait."

My hands, still bound behind my back, prevented me from catching myself when the man I'd bitten abruptly let go. I fell backward, landing hard on sharp rocks that bit into my thighs and buttocks.

Dream and reality blended in that moment. Rocks still bit into my butt, but they bit through my jeans. I needed to wake up but couldn't open my eyes. The dream still lingered. I hadn't died yet. I always died...except for those dreams with the Taupe Lady. Why hadn't I died?

Something settled over me gently. The physical contact gave me what I needed to pull myself from the dream world. My eyes popped open.

The bronze-haired, hazel-eyed man from the mall swam into focus. He hovered over me. His hands were on my hoodie. We stared at each other for a heartbeat. Then he moved, straightening the hoodie over my shoulder.

I scrambled to my feet. My eyes never left his as he slowly stood from where he'd been crouched on the balls of his feet next to me. How could something so cruel still make my stomach flip in such a toe-tingling way?

We stared at each other for several long moments. His eyes swept over me with a tender look. Concern clouded them when I involuntarily shivered.

He lifted the hoodie still held in his fingertips. "My name is..."

That was as far as he got before I tried to deliver a swift kick to his balls. He dodged smoothly, but his easygoing expression changed to one of wary shock.

I didn't wait for him to recover but turned and scrambled up the embankment to reach the road. It was pointless. I knew he was much faster. Still, I pushed on. Stones slid under my feet. He caught me from behind while I was still scrambling over the loose stones and pinned my arms to my side.

"Easy, luv. Unlike you, I mean no harm," he spoke softly near my ear, sending tingles along my spine. His grip, though firm, wasn't rough. He turned and walked back under the bridge, carrying me easily.

My heart freaked out, going into a very painful overdrive.

He surprised me by letting me go. I spun to face him again with my knees bent and my weight on the balls of my feet, ready to move. His expression seemed more concerned than wary. Probably concerned that someone would hear. We were fairly close to town, no doubt the reason why he'd pulled me back under the bridge.

"As I was saying, my name is Luke Taylor. And you are?"

"Not yours," I answered automatically. "Touch me again

and I'll sac tap you so hard you'll be coughing semen for a week. And this time I won't miss."

I felt a moment of pride at my tough words, but that quickly passed as the details of the life I'd just dreamt continued to filter in. I'd survived the fight, but at only fourteen, I hadn't survived long in the hands of my Mate. He'd been rough and brutish but not completely uncaring. As his leader suggested, my fragility hadn't withstood him.

I was older in this life and determined not to be as fragile. I wouldn't be used that way again. They'd wanted to control me to influence a decision. I wasn't sure what decision yet, but I knew it involved the others like me. The ones who had briefly shared the womb of the Taupe Lady with me, the ones I sometimes dreamed of.

In response to my eloquent threat, his lips twitched as if he wanted to smile.

That gave me pause. Something about this was wrong...

The wind rattled through the empty branches while I tried to pinpoint the problem. I risked looking away to scan the bank and trees behind him.

"What are you looking for?"

It wasn't until I looked back at him that I realized what I'd been looking for—what was wrong. "Your pack of murdering dogs."

Surprise flashed in his eyes. "I'm alone."

I snorted in disbelief. They were never alone. Always in a pack. I stayed tense, waiting for his next move. I knew better than to try running again. Who knew how long his humor would last.

He didn't say anything, just continued to study me. After a

time listening to the dry rattle of barren tree branches and dead weeds around us, he sighed and sat down on the patch of rocks where we'd started.

I flicked the briefest glance at the trees again, puzzled. "What are you doing?"

"Waiting for you to decide your next move. Keeping up with you is exhausting. I thought giving you money would keep you in one place long enough so you could get the sleep you obviously need." He pulled his knees up and rested his forearms on them in a relaxed pose. "So what are your nightmares about?"

The reminder that he'd been in my room had me narrowing my eyes. "All of the ways I'd rather die than bite the neck of a disgusting werewolf who'd be willing to rape a fourteen year old girl just to have control over her when Judgement comes." The lingering memories of my young past life still haunted me, and the words were out of my mouth without thinking.

He flinched as he looked down at the ground. I didn't know what I meant by it all, but the ring of it sounded so right. Something in what I'd said struck a chord in him, too, because with a clenched jaw, he paled. Satisfaction coursed through me. About time one of them felt guilty about what they did. Just as I had that thought, an angry red flush flooded his face.

"Has someone hurt you?" His softly intense words sounded strained. The veins on the back of his hand stood out. This wasn't a mystery to me. I'd witnessed this many times in my dreams. He struggled to contain the beast.

I recalled the word I'd used. Werewolf. So laughably impossible to me a few short months ago, I embraced the truth of it...him...and of the nightmare of my life.

"Tell me who," he demanded. When he looked up, his eyes

were larger in his skull. The pupils dilated as he struggled to maintain control.

I didn't bother wondering why he cared. They were territorial creatures, possessive of their unClaimed women. Even more so of their Mates.

"In this life? No one yet. But it looks like you're about to fix that. In other lives, they've already died." I thought about my dreams and wondered if that was true. Was this my first life in this cycle? I knew I could be born several times in the same cycle, making it possible to meet some of them in more than one life. I'd dreamt that very scenario.

My words seemed to turn off a switch in him. His change receded. "This life?" Confusion laced his voice.

He's good, I thought. The rest had just bullied and beat me. No one had tried acting like they cared.

I narrowed my eyes at him. "Why are you toying with me? We both know what you want."

He shook his head slowly and stood, pulling something from his pocket. Hand outstretched, he offered me the cell phone I'd tossed into the garbage at the last hotel. "Press call. I have a...friend, Gabby. She sent me to look for you. Thought you might be like her."

His words burst a bubble of anger within me. For a moment, I just struggled to breathe. One of my original sisters? This was different. New. Still, I couldn't trust him. They'd talked about the others like me before, but we were never in their control at the same time. Not for very long, anyway. We kept dying on them. The thought made me smile briefly. It faded into a frown. I didn't want to die again.

Looking up at the overcast sky, I decided something felt

different this time. Some balance had been tipped. I just wished I knew in whose favor.

Declining to take the phone, I watched him as I gathered my things and put my hoodie back on. In the distance, I heard the rumble of a car starting up. Slowly, I turned away from him and climbed back up to the road. I reached the top. He didn't stop me. I didn't look back but remained focused forward.

Gravel crunched underfoot as I walked back into town. His steps echoed quietly behind me. I hoped it was well behind me. The car turned onto our road. I didn't change my step, my breathing, nothing. No physical signs to give me away. The car increased its speed.

At the last moment, I stepped into the road waving the car down. My pulse jumped and my hands shook. Kill me or stop. Please stop. I didn't want to die; I just wanted a ride. A fast getaway. It was a risk not just for me, but also for the driver of the car if Luke reached the car before I got in.

The two guys in the car didn't hesitate. The car pulled to the side, and I quickly slid into the backseat slamming the door closed with a breathless, "Thanks."

The car didn't move. I glanced at the driver, but he wasn't focused on me. I followed his gaze and met Luke's eyes through the window. My stomach plunged to my toes. He stood on the shoulder of the road, less than a step away, looking down at the car—at me—through the glass. Though his stance was relaxed, he didn't look very happy. I fought not to give into complete panic as his eyes narrowed on the boys in the front seat. Luke looked back at me, studied me for a moment, and arched a brow.

"Is your friend getting in, too?" the driver asked.

I held Luke's gaze and shook my head. Luke's lips twitched

again as if he fought not to smile.

"A'right." The kid put the car in drive and slowly pulled away.

I kept my eyes on Luke. I'd seen his kind do incredible things and didn't trust him for a moment. From the front, the driver asked where I was headed.

"Doesn't matter. Next town if you're going that far."

Luke faded into the distance along with his last censoring gaze.

* * * *

Though I firmly believed there was nothing worse than facing a werewolf, the two boys in the front seat tested me. They suggestively asked about compensation for the ride they provided. Then, when I feigned ignorance of their innuendos, they flat out asked for head.

"Pull over," I said through clenched teeth.

"Oh, come on," the driver said with a laugh. "We're just messing with you."

The warmth of the car and the soft vibrations weren't enough to keep me lucid, so I rolled down the window. With their current line of conversation, I couldn't afford to fall asleep.

"I've been messed with enough. Just get me to the next town or as far as you can take me."

The conversation silenced for almost a minute, and I let out a slow breath. As if it were a signal, the passenger turned in his seat to watch me.

"So do you have a boyfriend?"

Are you freaking kidding me? I'm on the run from sadistic beasts that actually wear fur and run on all fours, and he wanted to know if I had a boyfriend?

"No." I met his gaze. After a few long moments, his smile faded, and he turned forward once more.

The respite from their inane conversation gave me a moment to consider my meeting with Luke. He was the first one ever to offer his name. Sure, I'd learned a few names over my lifetimes but always by listening to the conversation flowing around me. Not only had he offered his name, but he'd also let me go. I had no illusions. He could have stopped me easily by reaching through the glass and pulling me out forcibly. Why hadn't he?

"Can you roll that window up?" The driver reached over and turned up the heat.

I needed the ride. Though it wasn't a good idea, I rolled up the window. Within a minute, the temperature in the car jumped from cool to goodnight. My eyes blinked closed. In my dreams, I could no longer separate my past-self from my present-self. It was just me...

Several of them gathered where I lay broken at the bottom of a ravine. I'd tried jumping over the gap and misjudged the distance. For once, I had not purposely flung myself over the edge of something. My right leg throbbed painfully; and when I tried touching it, my fingers came away wet before I even got to the spot that really hurt. I shook all over. Definitely shock.

Lying on my back, looking up at the overcast sky and the scrub-dotted crumbling edge of the ravine, their faces danced in and out of my line of sight as each of them inspected me. Finally, the leader came close.

"We remember through stories passed down from each generation which of you is most likely to fight or run. Which has succumbed in the past. Who is born first. Who dies too easily.

We remember." He reached down and smoothed back a strand of hair that covered part of my face. "You, my wise little girl, have given us plenty of trouble because you remember, too. Let us create some new memories, shall we?"

Their hands tugged at my clothes and grasped my arms. Hurt and bleeding, I fought them as they...

...lifted me.

"Never again," a voice said near my head. "She's crazy!"

A hand fumbled for hold on my flailing arm. I stopped fighting and pried my eyes open. The driver had my legs while the passenger struggled with my arms.

"I'm awake," I said. "Stop!"

The driver dropped me when I met his shocked gaze. The passenger was slower to catch on, and I had to yank my arms from his hold. They both stared at me for a second while I quickly looked around. We were still on a straight stretch of country road. I couldn't have slept more than fifteen minutes. We hadn't put enough distance between us and that *thing*, Luke.

"I have bad dreams," I said as I brought my gaze back to the driver. "Night terrors. The car got too warm, and I fell asleep. It won't happen again. Please, I just need a ride to the next town."

Four

The banter suggesting favors changed to worried, darting glances as the driver sped up. I struggled to stay awake—despite my promise—as we drove another twenty minutes in silence. With a sudden jerk of the steering wheel, the driver pulled over to drop me off near a department store. The door had barely closed before the car pulled away. I watched the car shrink in the distance. They were idiots but idiots who may have saved my life. I should be harder to track in a town this size.

Walking a short distance to a sub shop, I ordered food and sat down to plan my next move. I hadn't been eating much since running, so I wolfed the sub down in seconds. People paused in their own eating and stared. Focused on picking the pieces of lettuce off the paper, I stopped paying attention to everyone around me. So, I jumped a little when someone slid into the booth and nudged another sub toward me.

Looking up, I froze with a piece of lettuce still pinched between my fingers. My stomach flipped in a sickeningly pleasant way, and my heart gave an excited beat before I could suppress my reaction.

Luke sat across from me. His hair was windblown, and he

had a thread of worry in his eyes.

"Did they take your money?" he asked with a slight growl.

I flicked my eyes around the small seating area. No other men. Well, a few men sat with their families, but they didn't count. He'd come alone again.

"What are you talking about?" I asked quietly, narrowing my eyes. This cat and mouse game made me edgy. When would the others appear?

"The car pulled over halfway here, and you all stood on the side of the road. Why?" He paused and his jaw clenched briefly before he leaned forward slightly. In a quiet, low voice he asked, "Did they hurt you?"

Hurt me? I frowned at him. He was worried they'd pulled over to what? Have a good time with me? My temper flared.

"Why are you doing this?" I said as I tried to keep my voice down.

My dreams had taught me to stay quiet to save lives. Through self-sacrifice, I saved others. Life after life...death after death, I had learned the people who tried helping me always died. I realized I hated my life as much as I wanted to cling to it.

He leaned back and studied me. "Because I want to help you," he said with a slightly confused smile. He lifted a hand as if to reach across the table and touch me.

I jerked back suppressing the urge to punch him in the face. How dare he mock me by feigning ignorance and sympathy.

"If you want to help me, die." My gaze remained locked on him, ready for anything.

His eyes flared slightly, and he dropped his hand. "You are very hostile for someone your age."

I snorted. "Just how many teenagers do you know?" He

looked like he'd passed eighteen several years ago. I guessed he had to be in his mid-twenties.

He sighed and scratched his jawline. After a moment he said, "Perhaps we started off poorly. I'm Luke Taylor. My friend, Gabby, sent me to find you. She thinks you may have something in common with her."

I felt a tug of sympathy for Gabby. "How is she?" I murmured before I could stop myself. If they had her, she would already be suffering; and I really didn't want to know the extent of it. It would just hurt more.

"Last time I saw her, she was weak but recovering." He nudged the sub toward me again. "Eat. You're too thin, and you'll need your strength."

Weak? I remembered all the torture his kind had inflicted upon me. He wanted me to be strong enough to endure. "You son of a—"

He cut me off by reaching over the table and gently clapping a hand over my mouth. He looked annoyed for the first time. "Hush," he warned when I would have moved away to keep talking. "The decisions you make and the words you speak influence the people around you. Be aware of your influence."

I scowled at him. What was he talking about?

He sighed and answered my question as if I'd spoken it aloud. "There is an adorable little girl just behind you. She can't be more than two."

When I turned, he dropped his hand. Two seats away, an admittedly cute little girl watched us with curiosity. Taking a calming breath, I turned back toward Luke.

He was gone. The cell phone rested on the table, a number already punched in. I stared at the phone for several heartbeats.

What was with this guy? Appearing, disappearing. Letting me go. Giving me money and now food. As much as I wanted to know about Gabby, I wouldn't...couldn't call. They would use her to trap me just like they would use my mom. Besides, she might not even be one of the others I dreamed about.

I ignored the phone but took the sub, shoved it in my duffle, and left. Once outside, I carefully surveyed the light foot traffic around me. Luke seemed to have disappeared, but I didn't believe he had gone far.

Keeping to the populated area, I walked slowly as I tried to figure him out. He had plenty of opportunity to force me to go with him, to hurt me, but he hadn't done either. Instead, he'd found me in the hotels and snuck into the rooms without notice to what? To watch me sleep? To leave me a note and money? But he'd left me alone in the homeless shelter. Why? Probably too many people for whatever he had in mind. My eyes darted around counting as the thought "too many people" stuck in my head.

In all the past lives I'd remembered so far, never had humans gathered in such great numbers. Each time, the dogs had found us in small villages and decimated those around us. No. Not dogs. Werewolves. I needed to face the reality of their existence. The werewolves were vicious and strong, but I'd witnessed them receive injuries. They had weaknesses...and now *we* outnumbered them.

For the first time in days, a smile lit my face. Maybe there was hope after all.

* * * *

I wore a new rough woven tunic that my mother and I had dyed with a red and brown pattern. At almost nine, I was glad to have something that made me feel pretty especially when I stepped out of our sod home and saw the stranger.

A boy on the cusp of manhood stood before me. His sudden appearance surprised me. Winded and shaking, his eyes traced over my tiny frame just as I studied him. His dark hair dripped with sweat and stuck to his olive skin.

My mother and sisters stepped out of our home behind me. I gave the boy a small smile and wondered why he'd come.

The boy fell to his knees before me and brought his face level with mine. His move surprised me, but I didn't budge. I was too curious. My mother made an anxious sound behind me but didn't tell the boy to leave.

His deep brown eyes locked onto mine. "They are coming," he warned with a slight growl in his voice. *"Just behind me. They will kill your family. You need to run—as far as you can—to save them."*

In this life, I remained unaware of the danger of which he spoke. Perhaps this was one of my sisters' lives where I didn't have the dreams to remember. Or perhaps I was too young for the dreams yet. With the boy's shaking, I knew what was coming even if my dream-self did not.

My mother gasped and tried reaching for me. It proved too much for the struggling boy, and he burst into his fur. My sisters screamed and ran toward the field where my father struggled to turn the hard-packed earth. My mother, sobbing and pleading for mercy, followed them.

I stood frozen, watching the wild creature before me. He struggled with himself, slowly pulling back the beast until he was again in human form.

"I'm sorry. I didn't mean to do that. You must hurry. There

are too many of them coming this way." He glanced over his shoulder, looking back at the way he'd come.

He turned back toward me with worry and desperation in his eyes. "Come here," he said.

Heart hammering, I stepped forward. He clasped my hand in his own and looked at me with kindness in his eyes. "I'm going to protect you the only way I know how. After I do, you'll need to run, little one. Go west. Look for my people. We will help you." He tucked a piece of hair behind my ear. "I need you to bite me. It will confuse them and allow you to move away from your family."

It took some convincing, but I did as he asked. He shuddered when I broke the skin, and as I apologized for hurting him, I patted his shoulder.

"Never mind that. Remember, west," he said. He moved back a step, burst into his fur again, and took off at an amazing speed.

By then, my mother and father were running toward me. I waited for them and admitted to biting the boy but forgot about his plea for me to run.

My mother clasped me to her and wouldn't let go. We were still standing like that when a group of men arrived.

I watched as the men attacked my family. Too late, I remembered the boy telling me to run. I screamed my anguish while the leader yelled and cursed.

"Find him. He needs to die so she can Claim another!" the man snarled through his elongating canines.

The dream shifted, but the memory did not fade.

The lady in the taupe gown stood in the circle while watching the women depart. One woman turned back, a worried *look in her eyes and her hand resting protectively on her belly.*

"What is it, dear one?" the Taupe Lady asked softly.

"I will do as you ask and keep her safe. But, who am I protecting her from?"

The Taupe Lady drifted from the circle, her gossamer skirts flowing as if in a breeze. "Not who, but what. Diversity may have gone too far in the beginning and created creatures your fragile race has no hope to withstand during their evolution and their struggles for dominance."

"I do not understand," the woman murmured in confusion.

The Taupe Lady reached forward and touched the woman's cheek gently. "It is not for you to understand, dear one, but for the child you carry. She is wise, and her knowledge will last through the ages."

I woke with a start as a train rumbled to a halt mere feet from my bench. The air swirled around me...reminding me of the Taupe Lady's dress. I stood on shaky legs and glanced around the shelter. A few other people waited with us as several passengers disembarked, no one I considered suspicious. Still my skin crawled.

A man sitting on the bench a few feet away caught my attention. His focus wasn't on me, but on a figure growing smaller in the distance. My stomach did a crazy flip when I looked.

"Nice of him to see you off," the man said as he stood up to get on the train. "Should have stayed just a few more seconds. Boyfriend?"

Instead of answering, I reached into the pocket of my duffle and found my boarding pass along with more cash. He'd put it there. How much did this guy have on him? Ticket in hand, I climbed aboard and chose a seat away from most of the passengers. The ticket would take me two states west, but I wouldn't actually ride the train that far. When I'd closed my eyes on the bench, I'd anticipated he'd find me. And just as I'd hoped, he'd looked at the ticket.

Leaning my head against the glass, I thought of the two dreams I'd just had. Though I'd only dreamt a portion of a past life in the first dream, I recalled how that life had ended.

The boy's arrival before the rest of his pack had been unique and had spared me from torture. Instead, the men had focused their efforts on finding him. After searching for a day, they carried me east to their settlement. There, they shoved me into a rough half-buried hut already occupied with several other young women.

The women had looked up when I'd arrived but made no move toward me until the door closed. When they did approach, they began sniffing me and asking questions. They were werewolves like the men, but not as vicious. I'd lived with them for five years while the search for the boy who'd run continued.

During that time I had feelings that were not my own. Gradually, based on information from my cohabitants, I'd come to understand that it was the boy I felt.

Finally out of patience, the leader had forced me to bite someone else. It was then that they learned something very significant. The bond created with Claiming could be broken without killing one of the pair. You just needed to Claim another.

That memory, along with the latest one of the Taupe Lady, had me questioning what I thought I knew. The werewolves wanted me to bite one of their own and complete the mating bond. Typically, I didn't live long after that so the purpose behind their insistence to choose still remained a mystery.

Likewise, the boy in the dream confused me. He'd been the only one I'd Claimed who had left me. How ironic that I sat on a train heading west...the same direction he'd told me to run. The thought settled over me for a moment before I realized the potential full message of the dream. It wasn't just the direction. Maybe the werewolves that kept killing me weren't the sum of what they represented. Could there be a few of their kind out there different from the rest? Some who were willing to help? Could Luke be like that boy?

I opened my duffle and ate the sub Luke had purchased for me. The same thing I'd ordered for myself. I thought back to the times we'd met while I was awake and the times I slept. He treated me the same as the boy had. With kindness. Sighing, I watched the scenery as the train rumbled west and fought the ever-increasing pull of sleep.

* * * *

I stepped off the train with blurry eyes and scanned the crowd. Thankfully, I didn't see any familiar faces. I'd stayed on the train as long as possible but hadn't even traveled halfway to my destination. I knew I needed to crash soon and hadn't thought my fellow passengers would understand my thrashing and screaming when I did.

Stumbling forward, I left the station as other passengers boarded. This stop, a decent sized town, had several hotels near the station. I picked one at random, paid for a room, and trudged up a flight of stairs. Sliding the room card through the pad, the door clicked open. I didn't look around as I stepped in and closed the door. The duffle, barely clinging to my weary shoulder, fell to the floor.

I fell face-first into the firm mattress. I bounced once but barely noticed. Sleep had already wrapped its arms around me. Fully dressed and lying on top the covers, I gave in.

Absolute darkness surrounded me. A low distant rumble filled the cool, dank air. Lying on my back, I attempted to stretch out my arms, but they didn't move. Bindings bit into the skin of my biceps and forearms. A small noise escaped me.

"She is awake," a voice rumbled nearby.

"Untie her," another voice responded.

My heart hammered as two large hands lifted me and set me on my feet. A light exploded in the darkness, blinding me.

I could remember dogs trotting into the village. They had rolled onto their backs, vying for father's attention. He had laughed and thrown them some meat scraps. They, in turn, had hunted down two rabbits to set at father's feet. He'd piled straw outside the sheep pen, and the dogs stayed there for three nights. On the fourth night, when father sent me out to feed them, they changed into men. One had scooped me up while the other gagged me. Then, they'd run.

But, something had gone wrong. While running, three dogs crossed our trail. The one carrying me had dropped me to the ground as he shifted and launched at one of the new dogs, tearing into it with deadly force. Then, whirling, he had gone after another while his partner fought the remaining one. The fights had inched closer to me, and I'd scrambled to my feet to try to run, but someone had caught me up from behind. When I'd looked up, the man who held me had a horrible gash where his right eye should have been.

The same man stared at me in the dim light while his partner untied me. Dried blood crusted his face, but I noticed the gash had closed a bit. His eye socket, however, appeared sunken.

"Do not dwell on it, child," he said. "Your life is worth an eye and more."

With the simple thoughts of youth, I didn't understand how I could be worth such an injury but kept quiet.

"My name is Roulf, and I have searched for you these last fifty years."

Since I'd just reached my fifth year, I couldn't understand why he'd looked so long. "Why did you bind me?"

"We could not allow you to run. The cycle ends in a few days. They are still looking for the last one. You. This is your third life in this cycle. My son helped you in the last life," he nodded at the man beside him, "and felt when the bond was broken."

His eyes didn't leave mine as if he waited for me to answer. I shrugged at him, my younger-self not understanding while my older, dream-self did. An ache grew within me. I wanted my father.

"You do not need to understand now, just listen. What I tell you will matter later. They must have all of you alive at once. It does not matter to them if you are Claimed. You saw what they did to me. If they take you, they will do the same to you. They will hurt everyone you have ever loved, and people you never knew. You cannot let them take you," he stressed with a slight growl. He sighed and rolled his shoulders. His son set a comforting hand on him. Roulf reached up and patted it as he turned to smile sadly at his son.

"We will stay here as long as we can. If they find us, you must run that way," he said pointing toward one end of the dark tunnel, "and remember my words."

They extinguished the light then, and I sat isolated in the darkness, my little heart hammering, listening for a threat I didn't understand. I shivered and tried to hold in the whimper that wanted to escape.

Roulf's son, who had already helped me once in his life, sat beside me and wrapped an arm around me.

He whispered, "When you need to feel safe, remember this." He gave my arms a gentle squeeze, much like my father might have if I'd woken with a bad dream. I leaned into him trying not to sniffle.

He remained beside me for two days, holding me in the darkness for hours, keeping me safe with his father not far from us. I slept and didn't complain about hunger when I woke. Roulf's words and their cautious silence impressed upon me the need to stay hidden.

In the dark, I lost all concept of day and night, but they never did. Baen, as I heard his father call him, whispered to me occasionally, telling me when a night animal entered the cave.

When I felt Baen suddenly shift into his wolf form, I knew we had been found.

Roulf pulled me to my feet, spun me to the left, and nudged me forward. I didn't say anything. I knew what he wanted me to do. Sticking my hands out, I groped through the darkness, wanting to run but only managing a slow stumble.

"I am proud to call you son, Baen," Roulf said.

The words struck a deeper fear in me than Baen's abrupt shifting had. I tried moving faster. After his words, nothing but silence rang behind me.

Ahead, the distant roar, which had kept us company during our stay, grew gradually louder. Still, I stumbled forward. The thunderous rumble deafened me. The walls of the cave vibrated beneath my hands. Before me, a dim light glowed, a tiny bit of sight in the nothingness. I hurried toward it. The air grew damp. Running now, heart hammering with a mixture of fear—instilled by Roulf—and excitement for the light, I ignored the pain in my feet as I kept slipping on the sharp wet rock.

When I reached a churning wall of light, I stopped in confusion, not understanding what I saw. Mist coated my eyelashes, and I blinked away the droplets. The way Roulf had told me to go was blocked. I cautiously reached out. Water tore at my small hand, pulling me forward and down. Before it pulled me too far, I tugged my bruised hand back and stared at the rushing water. I couldn't leave this way. Turning, I looked into the darkness behind me. Could I go back to Roulf and Baen?

Something glinted in the black tunnel as I considered going back. Two somethings that slowly grew larger. Eyes. Belonging to a dog. I felt a surge of hope until the dog shifted, and I saw it was neither Roulf nor Baen. Blood coated this man, and my heart ached for my would-be friends. The man stretched an arm forward and motioned for me to come to him.

My little heart hammered as I remembered Roulf's words, "You cannot let them take you." My tears mixed with the mist as I stepped into the falls.

I screamed myself awake and heard someone pounding on the door. Pulling myself off the mattress, I quickly checked the peephole. A member of the hotel staff, along with a police officer, stood outside. I debated not answering the door but ended up pulling it open despite my reservations.

After explaining about a bad dream and letting the officer into my room, the hotel very politely asked me to leave as I had disturbed too many of their guests. Just as politely, I asked for a refund since I hadn't even slept an hour.

* * * *

Duffle once again on my shoulder, I walked away from the hotel feeling the eyes of the police officer on my back. At least the hotel had refunded my money. I stopped a passerby and asked for directions to the nearest bus stop determined to keep heading west.

Still feeling exhausted, I climbed aboard the next bus, eyed the other passengers, and wished I knew what to look for. Werewolves looked just like everyone else until they started transforming.

I sat near the window, looked out with a sigh, and thought of the Taupe Lady. If she had the ability to carry six of us within her and send us into different mothers, why couldn't she help us? Why did I have to die over and over? I thought back to the very first dream of her. She'd sent each of us to our mothers with a word: Strength, Wisdom, Hope, Peace, Prosperity, and Courage. From the way some of those things had talked to each of us in past lives, I knew I was Wisdom. So which sister had Luke and his people already found?

Shifting in my seat, I pulled up my hood so I could block out the world as I thought. My damn dreams. They had shown me that the werewolves would come and that I needed to run. And I had. I'd run from my home, my friends...my mom. But the dreams weren't stopping. They had, however, changed. A little. I wasn't stupid...maybe just a little slow, but hey I was sleep deprived. Twice Baen had helped me...or tried to, anyway. Two dreams showing me that not all werewolves were bad. It gave me a tiny spark of hope, and I knew what I needed to do. West, I thought.

The faint smell of soap tickled my nose. The dreams had just pointed out what I was too afraid to believe; someone had already been helping me. I unzipped the hoodie, pulled it off, and studied it. It wasn't mine as I'd thought when I'd pulled it out of the duffle in the back of the truck. Holding it to my nose, I inhaled deeply. It smelled like Luke. He'd also given me money. Several times. Granted, he'd also snuck into my hotel room—several times—and seemed to be following me like a creeper. It would take more than cash and a hoodie to earn my trust, but I would listen to the dreams. I sighed and shrugged back into the hoodie.

My head ached from the need to sleep. After a few torturous hours, the bus stopped for a refuel. Stepping off the bus into the increasingly frigid air, I chose a road heading out of town and started walking.

FIVE

Several hours later, I heard the loud roar of a motorcycle behind me. I looked back, saw it was Luke, and suppressed the urge to run. It wouldn't do any good. He would just chase me. Besides, I'd already decided to talk to him...to see if he really was like Baen. So I stopped walking and waited.

My stomach tugged and twirled as I watched the bike slow. I forced down my physical reaction—it had been used against me in the past—but that didn't stop me from appreciating how good he looked.

He pulled up beside me and cut the engine. His hair was slightly mussed from the ride, and his eyes sparked with annoyance.

"Are you mental?" He dismounted with grace and pulled off his leather jacket.

Too stunned by the sudden display of beautifully defined pectorals beneath his t-shirt, I couldn't answer. Sure, I'd remembered a few Mates from past lives, but none attracted me like this. He was even more dangerous to me because of it.

He stalked toward me, and I didn't even have a chance to squeak in protest when he pulled the duffle off my shoulder.

"You'll freeze out here." He set the still warm jacket on my shoulders and zipped me in without waiting for me to put my arms in the sleeves.

Every time he found me, he helped me. I tipped my head back and stared into his eyes. He watched me intently. Tiny flecks of green and gold peeked through the soft brown of his eyes. Inside, I gave a little sigh of appreciation. How stupid was I to want to trust this man? I needed to be practical. Squashing my tingling awareness, I recalled what had happened in my last dream. Even my help had set me up to die. Wasn't there a way to live that didn't involve torture or forced servitude?

"Tell me about my sister," I said as I shoved my arms through the sleeves. The jacket was better than the hoodie alone.

"Sister?" he asked completely confused.

"The one who sent you to find me." It came out with more force than I'd intended. I knew better than to provoke his kind. I was tired. Trying again in a softer voice, I said, "You said she was weak. Did you hurt her?"

He snorted. "Not a chance. Her guard dog doesn't let anyone near her." He smirked and added, "Well, he tried to keep us away."

What was that supposed to mean? She was being guarded, and he'd found a way to her. But, which side was guarding and which side was going around the guard?

I eyed him as he stood before me. In just a shirt, he didn't seem bothered by the cold. They never really did. I needed to know his intentions. Did he really want to help me like Baen, or was he like the rest? I couldn't ask him outright. These creatures were never honest. But, they were easy to provoke.

Calming my overly attentive physical awareness, I stepped toward him. He watched me with cautious eyes, no doubt remembering my attempt to knee him. Placing my hands on his shoulders, I stood on my tiptoes stretching to get as close to his height as possible. His heat warmed my palms, and my stomach went crazy. The muscles beneath my fingertips twitched, and a shudder passed through him. His pupils dilated. His attention intensified, and I doubted he heard anything around us. His reactions affirmed what I already knew. We had a connection. But what would he do about it?

I leaned in further and let my cheek touch his jaw. His tremors grew. I knew I was playing a dangerous game. His hands settled on my waist, and the touch spiked my heart rate despite my efforts to control myself. I couldn't be sure whether my reaction was fear or excitement, and it worried me. I needed to stay strong. I knew that a sliver of weakness could bring my downfall.

Against his ear, I whispered, "I will not choose you," as a test—as a statement of truth.

When I pulled back, his eyes were closed and his jaw clenched. As slowly as I'd approached him, I eased away. His hands dropped from my sides without a fight. My throat tightened as I watched him struggle. Fear pooled in me. He inhaled deeply, and I knew he smelled it on me.

After a moment, he calmed and opened his eyes.

"Good," he agreed amicably. "Someone your age shouldn't be choosing."

My age? His words confused me as much as they comforted me. He hadn't grabbed me or insisted I was wrong, and I hadn't died. Still, I'd never met one of them that didn't insist on biting.

Even Baen had asked me to bite him the first time I'd met him, and I'd been nine in that life. Things might just be looking up.

He turned away from me and mounted the motorcycle. Then, he held my duffle out toward me. "Coming?"

He'd found me and, apparently, was set on following me. Why not take advantage of it? Stepping forward with lingering reservations, I grabbed the bag and nodded. If he wasn't here to help, I'd find out soon enough. At least sleep wouldn't tempt me so much if the wind battered me as we traveled.

I put the strap across my body and climbed on behind him. As I wrapped my arms around his middle, I noticed his flinch.

"And stay away from my neck," he said as he lifted his feet from the road and eased forward.

I ducked behind him within seconds. The wind bit into me with ferocious insistence, driving me closer to him. He twitched occasionally and told me to hold still several times. I didn't have his ability to stay warm though. Finally, red cheeked, I laid my face against his back. Through his thin shirt, he warmed me. Sighing, I closed my watering eyes.

She stood before me in her taupe gown looking sad and serene at the same time. Nothing surrounded us but the tiny glow of thousands of multi-colored life sparks.

"This was the beginning," she said lifting a pale hand to indicate the sparks. Most had a blue center with a grey halo. Almost as many had a blue center with a green halo. Only a few had a yellow center with a green halo. Among those, I saw six unique colors and knew whom they represented.

"The Judgements must maintain balance," she said. "Only they can decide what that balance may be. Every one thousand years you all return, though only one will remember." She

reached forward and touched me softly on top my head. "Choose wisely, or there may not be a world to return to in another one thousand years."

"What the hell was that?" Luke shouted in my face.

I blinked my eyes open, trying to pull myself from my dream. Dream? No, it hadn't felt like the past. What the heck was that? Every one thousand years I returned? How many lives would I need to relive? Those dots...I'd seen them before. One of us had the ability to see the sparks of people around us.

"Well?" Luke continued to look down at me with a furious expression.

Understanding dawned. "Crap! Did I fall asleep?"

"While I was flying down the road on a two-wheeled death trap? Yes!"

He held me cradled in his lap while he still straddled the idling bike. The heat from his thighs warmed my backside. How he'd managed the switch, I had no idea.

"Put me down. Please." The last word came out a bit clipped. My stomach was going crazy being so close to him, and it annoyed me.

"Gladly." He surprised me by setting me down gently.

On my own feet, I rubbed my hands over my face. "I'm sorry. I'm tired." When I glanced back at him, I caught a fleeting look of pity in his eyes. "Save your pity. I don't need it," I said. I didn't need pity. I needed decent sleep and an assurance those things wouldn't catch me in this lifetime.

He held up his hands in surrender and took a deep, calming breath. "Are you going to fall asleep again? Because we won't get far this way."

"Yes, I'll most likely fall asleep again. No matter what I've tried, I can't seem to avoid it."

"Maybe you should stop avoiding it," he suggested with an edge of exasperation in his tone.

I didn't bother answering. He wouldn't understand.

He saw something in my face because he sighed and said, "Loosen the strap of your bag as far as it will go, then get on."

He motioned for me to hurry up when I didn't immediately do it. Stifling an eye roll, I did as he asked. Once I sat behind him, he grabbed the strap and lifted it over his head—while it was still around me. Then, he went one step further and tightened the strap so I pressed against his back. He grumbled the whole time, and that was the only silver lining in the whole situation.

"Take both arms out so it's around your waist," he said.

Understanding he meant to strap me to his back so I wouldn't fall, I complied. But I didn't like it.

As soon as he lifted his feet, the dreams pulled me under.

The Taupe Lady once again stood over a new mother. This woman didn't put the babe to her breast. She set the quiet infant aside and hurried to bury the afterbirth not yet noticing the Taupe Lady. Lying on a coarse blanket shivering in the light warm breeze, I watched her with new eyes.

"The men tracking you have crossed the river," the Taupe Lady said.

Fear clouded my mother's eyes, and she spun to face the lady. "Thank you!" My mother scooped me into her arms.

"I did not tell you so you could leave," the lady explained. "You need them. They are her only protection."

"I am her protection," my mother whispered forcefully as she hugged me to her chest to quiet me.

"You protect her from her father, but he will protect her from those who are much worse. For the love you feel for your child, return to him so her life may be spared."

"Who are you?" my mother asked noticing for the first time that the lady's feet didn't quite touch the ground.

"I am a friend. Save your child and return."

"If I return, he will kill me."

The Taupe Lady's eyes filled with sadness. "Yes, he will," she agreed.

"Then, I cannot." My mother ran with me.

* * * *

I woke lying limply against Luke's back as he braked hard and turned into the parking lot of a small motel.

Instantly alert, I lifted my head. "What are you doing?"

"You keep twitching. You can't ride sleeping. It's not safe," he said over his shoulder as he parked in front of the office.

Not safe? My whole life was not safe. Riding anywhere with one of them was probably not safe. Adding my narcoleptic tendency didn't really decrease my life expectancy that much more.

He loosened the strap as I argued. "Sleeping strapped to you is better than sleeping here. We need to keep moving."

"Believe me, I'm all for hurrying, but I'm not going to risk you falling off." He lifted the strap over his head so we were no longer pressed against each other.

I scrambled to dismount. "I'm not tired anymore." I saw in his eyes he didn't buy it for a second. "I don't want to stay here," I said as I started to panic.

Taking a ride from him was different from locking myself in a room with him. I didn't trust him—us—in a room. There was too much pull going on. My stomach went wild at the idea of a room with a bed and him in it. And my eyes dipped to his snug fitting shirt. Given his reaction when I got close to his neck, I didn't see how this would end well for me.

"Too bad. Inside. Now," he practically growled at me as he pointed to the door marked "Office."

I met his eyes for another moment and then pivoted on my heel intent on walking if I needed to. I took one step toward the road. He stood in front of me before I took the second step. He didn't look happy that I hadn't immediately complied. We scowled at each other. A yawn ruined any hope I had of him taking me seriously. His expression changed to one of concern.

In my crazy, sleep deprived state, all I wanted to do was lean into him. If he happens to kiss me, I thought vaguely, I'll just have to endure. Wait. What? No! No kissing. It led to other things, which led to a life of misery. I shook my head to clear it.

He sighed and tilted his head at me.

"You are so tired, luv. Please. Sleep a few hours," he said.

My stomach went crazy with the pull. Disgusted with myself that a caring tone and a few nice words could cause such a reaction, I snapped at him. "As if sleep is what you really have in mind."

His eyes widened, and he held up his hands. "Sleep. That is all. I can't drive fast with you sleeping. Too many things could happen. I might not be able to catch you in time. If we keep going as we are, snow will cover the roads before we reach the Compound."

"Compound?" I asked, wondering why I was even listening to him.

"It's where Gabby said to bring you. She promised she

would be there."

The way he worded it gave me pause. "No one is holding her there?"

"Holding her there? No. She...visits. Honestly, she doesn't seem to like it very much."

I looked down at the faded blacktop. If they didn't hold Gabby as a prisoner and she remained free to wander as she pleased, it probably meant Luke truly wanted to help me get to her. Though, it could all be a lie. Calling the number he had given me wouldn't prove anything. Any woman could answer, and I wouldn't know the difference.

"I don't trust you. But..." I looked at the motel. Sleep tugged at me. I was doing what I thought the dreams wanted me to do. Maybe they would leave me alone, and I would actually get some real sleep. "I'll stay. Just not with you in the same room."

"Fine."

His easy agreement didn't help settle my nerves, but I still followed him into the office. He paid cash for the room and led the way back outside. A sidewalk, protected by the eaves, ran along the building. We didn't follow it far. He stopped at the door marked with a two. Too close to the office for my comfort.

"I got kicked out of one hotel already. He's going to hear me for sure."

"Maybe you won't have bad dreams," Luke said as he unlocked the door and stepped aside so I could enter.

I snorted but didn't bother disagreeing with him. I entered the room, then turned to look at him with an arched brow. He still stood there with his hand on the doorknob.

"I'll sit on the bench outside and wake you in a few hours."

He started to close the door.

"The key?" Seriously. Did he really think I would be okay with him keeping it?

He smiled. "I'll hold onto it. Better I wake you when you start getting too loud than the owner."

I scowled and opened my mouth to argue, but he closed the door too fast. I stared at it for a moment. Could I do this? Could I fall asleep with one of them close by? What could he do to me while I was sleeping that he couldn't do while awake? Nothing, really. It just made me feel so vulnerable.

Behind me, the mattress sang its siren song luring me enough to turn toward it. It didn't matter that Luke had a key. He could easily break through the door without it. After all, he'd snuck into one hotel room already.

Kicking off my shoes, I did my usual belly dive into the quilt and closed my eyes with my feet still hanging off the end of the bed. This wouldn't last more than a few...

The dream that claimed me had a new twist. It split into four views of the same thing. I was my current-self, yet at the same time, I was all three of the other girls in the dream. Disoriented by all four viewpoints, I struggled, trying to focus on just one.

I crouched in my pen with three other girls. Branches, thicker than any of our arms, jabbed into the ground to make the walls of our pen. Trees towered around us. Sunlight occasionally speckled the ground as the canopy above shifted.

The stench of our feces and unwashed bodies clogged my nose. We'd been kept in the pen for seven days. The youngest girl, with the strawberry blonde hair, had been first. She paced the earthen floor as she glared at our captors who lounged languidly beyond our pen wall. Her tiny stature and youth didn't make her very menacing, yet. But when she hit puberty, she would be a force to reckon with.

The most recent captive sobbed softly. Still in her teens but older than all of us, she'd been made to Claim then mate with someone. She kept her eyes fixed on the ground. I sat next to her with an arm around her shoulders. And, like the youngest, I watched our captors.

The fourth member of the party slept and twitched as she did so.

I felt the pain and anguish of the one crying, the rage of the one pacing, the determination of the one holding her sister, and the pure terror of the one dreaming. We were all the same yet different. Sisters of the same womb. Daughters of the Taupe Lady. Pieces in a game we never wanted to play.

The branch door of our pen drifted open in the breeze. None of us moved to run, but it still caught the attention of the men watching us.

"If she is old enough to look at us with hate, she is old enough to mate," one said as he stood. He towered over all of us. A scrap of leather covered his loins. The rest of him remained dusty and bare.

The sister who paced stopped moving and stared at him, her chin tucked close to her chest so she watched him from under her brow. He strode purposefully toward her.

The dream narrowed so I no longer felt the other three. Just her. Just her anger. Her fear. She knew what he wanted. What he intended to do. She would die.

He gripped my arm tightly and pulled me from the pen. The sobbing one flew forward like a wildcat and tried fighting him. It did no good. She sailed back and hit the branches with a hollow thump. The girl next to her tried pulling my arm back. It didn't matter; he swatted her away, too. His big hand reached for me. I bit him hard and felt my teeth hit bone. He hit me; the flat of his palm connected with a crack. I saw stars. My heart beat wildly. I struggled as he lifted me.

The dream faded and restful oblivion cocooned me. I barely registered the gentle kiss pressed against my forehead. I slept.

* * * *

Stretching my arms wide, my hand lightly smacked into a face. I stilled and opened my eyes. The white ceiling above greeted me. Cautiously turning my head, I met Luke's amused gaze peeking through the fingers of the hand that still covered his face.

"What do you think you're doing?" I sat up with a scowl. We both lay on top the covers; a line of pillows separated us. I felt rested, but waking with him next to me unsettled me.

"You were having a bad dream. I came in to wake you, but you quieted. So I decided to use my time wisely and sleep, too." I narrowed my eyes at him and he quickly added, "I kept it proper. See?" He gestured to the pillows.

"I don't care if you put a —"

"I'm starving. Let's eat." He rose from the bed with a stretch and moved toward the door. I continued to glare at him.

"Don't think I don't know what you're trying to do. I won't let my guard down. A few moments of kindness will not make me fall into your arms."

He stopped by the door and turned to look at me, his face carefully blank. "I don't want you in my arms."

"Liar." I swung my legs off the bed and stood. Did he think

me stupid? I yanked my bag up off the nearby chair.

Luke scratched his jawline as he hesitated by the door. "I don't understand why you're so angry." Frustration laced his words despite his relaxed pose.

I barely understood myself. I didn't really think he wanted to wear me down, but getting angry seemed a better way to keep some distance between us. The idea of someone watching over me just to watch over me...well, that swayed me more than it should have. It also made me miss my mom. She used to do that before my world broke. Before I discovered there were some things she couldn't protect me from. My teeth clenched against my resentment. I hated knowing. I hated the dreams, and at the moment, I hated him, too.

"What's to understand?" I practically screamed at him, angry that he was making me say it. "I'm not safe. I'll never be safe again. I'm so tired, I have no idea how to help myself, and I don't know if I can trust you."

His eyes softened, and he lifted a hand as if he wanted to move toward me. But, he stopped himself, dropped his hand, and sighed softly.

"We can stay here longer so you can rest," he said.

I threw my arms up in the air. "It won't do any good." At his blank look, I said, "I'm reliving all our past lives, mine and my sisters. I've been cut, beaten, starved, raped, drowned, and even blinded."

His eyes hardened at each method of torture I listed, but I barely paid his reaction any attention. Listing the things that I had experienced brought the memories too close to the surface, and there were so many more ways his kind had hurt me that I'd left unsaid.

"Every time I close my eyes, I see more, and there's no rest when that's what I see. When I wake I'm just as tired as I was when I went to sleep. And I don't just see the past, I feel it. Every injury. Every forced intimate moment. If I let myself dwell on it, I won't ever feel whole again." I gave a pained snort. "I'm not really sure I do now. If I've ever had a happy past life, I don't remember it. Instead, I remember the pain, and death. Always death..." I said, starting to cry in anger and in fear. "I don't want to die again," I whispered brokenly. "But if you're here to try to get me to choose you, you can't have me." I said the words to help remind me, too. He was so...nice. It made the Taupe Lady's warning hard to remember. "Even if it means I have to die again."

He growled, and I saw how what I said had affected him. Jaw clenched, he fought the skin-rippling change trying to consume him. He turned and forcefully yanked open the door. The trim splintered near the latch. When he slammed it shut behind him, a piece fell to the floor.

Stunned, I flopped back down on the bed with a slow sigh. I'd baited him—what? Twice now? Three times?—and I was still unharmed, breathing. A crazy half-sob, half-laugh bubbled from my chest.

The roar of his motorcycle reached me. I hopped off the bed and raced to the door, opening it just in time to see him speed away.

Stupefied, I stood in the doorway for several long moments before my brain kicked in. What an idiot for clarifying who I was when I knew I couldn't trust him. Who knew what he was up to? They always appeared in packs. Maybe he was getting the rest of his pack. Then, I thought of Baen. He'd been alone the first time; but he'd made me bite him before he ran off. So, this was different. And I wasn't a clueless, stupid kid this time. Yet, I still made tired mistakes. I needed to move.

Closing the door, I quickly circled the bed looking for my shoes. They weren't there. I checked the bathroom, using it quickly in the process, and didn't see anything there either. My chest started to tighten. I didn't have time to waste but couldn't just leave without them. My feet were tough, but the temperature was dropping. I wouldn't make it far.

Growling in frustration, I grabbed my bag and dug for as many pairs of socks as I could find. Two. I sat on the bed to pull them on over the ones I wore, but didn't get the chance.

I fell into a dream. Hard.

*　*　*　*

A sprinkling of water on my face woke me before I died. Still caught up in the dream, I looked up at Luke and blinked in confusion at his disgruntled expression.

"You already slept ten hours. How can you still be this tired?"

"I'm not," I said sitting up quickly.

He stood before me with a white paper bag and a large thick paper cup in one hand. The other hand shone wetly.

"The dreams take me over sometimes, no matter how rested I am," I mumbled feeling the need to explain. He held out the cup to me. I didn't move to take it as I remembered how he'd taken off. "I thought you left to get the rest of your men."

He huffed a martyr style sigh and sat beside me on the bed. Too close in my opinion.

"What men?"

Instead of answering, I looked down at my hands while

trying to ignore the quick erratic heartbeat his close proximity caused. He misunderstood my move and made a small noise of annoyance.

"Never mind," I mumbled.

"Bethi, I really am here to help you. No strings. I just don't know how," he said softly.

He thought I just didn't trust him. He was right. I didn't. But that wasn't the reason for my hesitancy. I didn't like feeling so dependent on him. Especially since my insides kept going crazy when he was close or when I looked at him or when I smelled him. It was getting ridiculous.

"You are helping me," I said trying for brusque detachment. "If not for you, I'd be walking."

He studied my profile for a moment before handing me the cup. "I thought coffee might help."

My throat dried at the quiet concern laced in with his words, so I accepted the cup and took a hasty swig. It scalded my tongue, and I almost spit it back into the cup. Instead, I swallowed, burning a layer from my throat. Ignoring his concerned frown, I suggested we hit the road. I was uncomfortable just sitting there.

"I brought you something to eat, too," he said opening the bag and pulling out a plastic carton.

He sat there patiently holding out the food, waiting for me to decide.

My mouth watered as a hint of bacony goodness drifted my way. He quirked a slight smile at me as I reached for it, but he willingly handed it over. A stacked breakfast sandwich lay inside. My stomach rumbled as I looked at it. I sat next to him and devoured the offering. He smiled as he watched me. I ignored him.

When I threw the carton in the garbage, he stood, picked up my bag, reached inside his jacket, and pulled out my shoes.

"Gee, thanks," I drawled, reclaiming my missing shoes.

Luke grinned in response and handed me the jacket as well before he shouldered my bag and walked out the door to check us out of the room. I set my almost empty coffee to the side, sat, and peeled off the extra socks.

He'd done it again, helped me without demanding anything in return. Was he just waiting for a moment of weakness before he pounced, or had my dream about Baen pointed me toward help? I wanted to believe Luke was the help I was meant to find. Yet he also did things to make sure I didn't run from him. I mean, come on! He stole my shoes. And did he think I didn't notice him leaving with my bag? I wondered why he did any of it. Was it because he thought I wouldn't be safe if I struck out on my own again or something else? I really wanted the answer to be because he was worried about me. Yet, at the same time, I knew I was being irrational. How many lifetimes had the werewolves shown me that they couldn't be trusted. It far outnumbered the two lifetimes—so far, anyway—that they had tried to keep me safe. Still...I wanted to believe. The thought that he was keeping me captive...well, I needed to believe my life wasn't hopeless.

I beat him to the motorcycle and waited, watching him cross the parking lot. My heart gave a quick stutter as he got closer. He moved with purpose, and his eyes swept over me. I tried to squash any signs of my physical attraction, but I couldn't help watching his long legs clear the seat with ease. To distract myself, I wondered what he'd look like as a dog. Would he have those same menacingly eerie eyes? Would he threaten me with his teeth?

After settling behind him, he motioned to the strap on his shoulder. I grudgingly lifted the bag around my torso. Falling from the back of the bike didn't sound fun.

We pulled away in a hurry. Even with all of the sleep, I felt the tug of the next dream. I tried everything from sticking my face in the wind—versus staying crouched behind Luke—to biting my lip as hard as I could. Eventually, the dream won.

Six

A hand tapping my face pulled me out.

"We need help. A car. This isn't working," he said gently.

"No, this is fine," I mumbled, peeling my eyes open. It really wasn't fine. We were pulled over again. Trees lined the sides of the road in both directions. For a second time, I sat in his lap with the bag and strap twisted around us. The bike still idled.

"Can you make it twenty minutes without sleeping?" he asked.

"I don't know," I admitted. "It seems worse with you."

He looked at me in surprise. "When I'm near you, you don't cry out. I thought your dreams calmed when I..." He didn't finish his sentence, but I filled in the missing parts.

He was right. My dreams did calm when I was near him. I dreamed of helpful things like glimpses of explanations from the Taupe Lady, instead of my constant pointless death. In fact, I'd learned so much more after Luke had found me than in the prior months.

My eyes widened as I considered the implications. Was Luke really the key? In my past lives, after claiming a werewolf, the dreams had come less frequently. And when they did appear, their purpose was more focused. So, if I Claimed Luke...

"I changed my mind," I said quickly. "I will Claim you."

"No!" He flinched as if I'd slapped him, but his gaze drifted to my mouth.

He remained motionless, studying me, his eyes filled with barely checked wanting. It wasn't desire as much as it was the ability to call me his own. I'd seen that look before in other lives. They'd coveted me for the power of my knowledge. Why did he want me? I decided it didn't really matter and held myself still, hoping he was reconsidering his answer. So far, he had kept me safe and treated me well. If Claiming him would end my dreams—or at least slow them—did I need any more proof from him that he would take care of me? He had already shown he was infinitely better than the werewolves I'd Claimed in past lives—except maybe Baen. And it didn't hurt that my heart was beating out *yes* like an SOS.

The look in his eyes grew tender as he brushed a stand of hair from my face. His fingers left a trail of warmth where they brushed my skin. I wanted him to do it again. *Touch me.* His breath hitched when I tilted my head slightly. His fingers trembled as he touched my hair. Encouraged, my hand drifted to his bicep.

The contact broke the spell, and he hastily set me on my feet next to the bike. Like cold water splashed in my face, it brought me back to reality. I needed to Claim him for the right reasons—to get rid of the dreams where I died, and not the wrong reason—because he made my insides quiver.

Being connected by the strap didn't give us much room. It pinned us together and brought my face close to his neck. I blinked at the opportunity, and I didn't wait for permission. I darted in with the intent to end the bad dreams, but my teeth didn't reach my intended target.

Luke had shoved his hand between my face and his neck at the first sign of my move. I should have anticipated his speed, I thought. With my face humiliatingly mashed into the palm of his hand, I grew angry.

"What's your problem? I know you feel the pull. This *is* what's supposed to happen." I resisted stomping my foot as he slipped out of the strap. Standing tall and out of his personal space, I glared at him. He looked angry, too.

"No, it is not. Why did you change your mind?"

"I'm tired of dying!" I cried. "It hurts! What don't you understand? Every time I close my damn eyes, I feel every anguished moment of one of our past lives. Claiming you will make the dreams better." I tried to keep the begging tone from my voice, but by the end, that's what I did. Beg. "Please, Luke."

Some of the tension eased out of him, and he looked at the trees, taking a moment before answering.

"I promised I only wanted to help you. And I will. The dreams are better when I sleep near you. We will keep doing that," he said without meeting my eyes. "Climb on."

I felt like throwing a fit, but then I realized the position I would be in if I climbed back on—right by his neck. Keeping the triumphant grin from my face, I slipped behind him.

For the next twenty minutes, he face-palmed me at least fifty times. When I gave up in frustration and leaned my forehead against his back, his heat started lulling me.

"I'm going under," I managed to mumble before my eyes closed.

"Try to hold on. I called for help. There should be a car

ahead," he called over his shoulder. He sped up instead of slowing down.

A fear-induced adrenaline spike pushed the dream back, and my eyes popped open. "What do you mean you called for help?"

I barely got the words out when an object flew from the woods beside us. Big, black, and furry, it just missed our back tire. In stunned disbelief, I clung to him as we raced on. He'd really done it. He'd called for the rest of his pack.

Luke twitched before me, and I peeked over his shoulder. In one of the mirrors, I saw the reason. My heart leapt into my throat as I twisted to look behind us.

It ran on all fours. Its paws pounded the pavement as it gained on us. With a sleek head and a vicious snarl, it looked just like the werewolves in my dreams. Seeing it all affirmed, I started shaking.

"Hold on," Luke warned me.

Relief flooded me. Not one of his.

"Faster!" I shouted and hit Luke on the back.

He had already twisted the throttle when another shape flew into our path. Luke leaned far to the left and made a swift deep swerve around the second one. I clung to his back panting in fear. We were both going to die. He'd barely recovered from the swerve when something snagged the bag on my back—the same bag strapping me to Luke—and pulled. My breath left me in a whoosh.

With my arms wrapped around his waist, my shoulders screamed in pain as I struggled to hold on. Then suddenly, the pressure eased. The bike flew forward, riderless, as we stayed in place, hanging in the air. The strap still connected us. Luke whipped an arm back to keep me pressed against him while he severed the strap. We landed with a thud just seconds after being unseated. The bike glided for a distance and then fell onto its side on the gravel shoulder.

Despite my bruised and aching butt, I scrambled to my feet. Luke already stood in a semi-crouch near me, facing off with the two dogs that circled us.

"Go," he said nudging me.

"No, thanks," I whispered. Running through the woods away from the only person who might be willing to protect me didn't seem like a good idea. Besides, I'd been chased through the woods before, and it hadn't ended well.

Luke's skin rippled as he partially changed. My heart thumped painfully seeing the truth of what he was. His nails elongated, and his back hunched a bit. He leapt at the wolf to the right with his upper body, and then he swung his legs to kick the one on the left. He scored a solid hit on both seconds before he fully burst into his fur. I backed up two steps staring at the copper-coated wolf.

The wolf on the right shook his head as if to clear it and spun to attack Luke. The other wolf scrambled to its feet, snarling.

Spinning to meet their attack, Luke savagely ripped into the lead attacker's face with his teeth. Blood colored Luke's muzzle as the wolf tried to shake him off. The second wolf circled the pair watching for an opening. Luke's eyes trailed that wolf's progress as he maintained his gruesome hold. If the second one attacked, he would have to let go to protect himself and would lose the upper hand.

I picked up a heavy rock from the shoulder of the road and chucked it at the stalking wolf. Had it been paying attention to me in the slightest, it would have seen it coming. As it was, the rock hit it square on the right side of its head with a sickening sound, eliciting a yelp of pain.

Luke twisted his hold on the first wolf's muzzle as he dropped his hind legs and rolled. He heaved the wolf into the stunned second wolf, then went for the throat. The first wolf couldn't even manage a yelp. There was just a gurgling wheeze. The second wolf, pinned under the first, struggled for a moment before Luke finished it, too. He turned to me, blinking. I couldn't say anything as I continued to stare wide-eyed at the aftermath of the fighting.

Within seconds, both forms shifted back into their skin. Two dead men on the side of the road with ripped out throats. I didn't flinch at the sight. It was depressingly familiar.

Luke took a few steps toward me, claiming my full attention. The same hazel eyes, but a little bigger, stared back at me. Though he didn't bare his teeth at me, he looked far from friendly with the blood around his mouth. My chest tightened to the point that it hurt to breathe. Still, I managed.

He shook out his fur and trotted over to my bag. With his back to me, he shifted to his skin. Honey-kissed skin exposed to the world did what the fighting hadn't. I felt a little faint. Blood and gore? Not a problem. Luke naked, showing me a perfect backside? I lost my composure, what little I had, and a tiny sound escaped me.

"Turn around," he said not looking at me.

"Ha! No way." A slightly hysterical sigh escaped me.

He scowled over his shoulder at me and reached into my bag for his hoodie and a pair of my pajama pants. It gave me a lovely profile view, just barely hiding the naughty bits. A giggle escaped me as he stepped into what he'd grabbed. His scowl twitched, and I knew he wanted to smile, too.

Covered, he picked up the bag, marched over to me wearing tight, high-water Tinker Bell pajama pants, and handed me the bag.

"We'll need to stop for new clothes," he commented with a wry grin.

I stood frozen, fully seeing his face after his change back, and couldn't make myself answer with either a smile or a nod. Instead, I reached into the bag, grabbed a shirt at random, and used it to wipe the blood from around his mouth. My hand shook. Okay, so maybe the blood did affect me.

He saw the blood and gently took the shirt from my hand. He tucked it back into the bag, then went to pick up the bike.

He waved me over as soon as he had it started again.

I numbly walked past the bodies and put my hand on his shoulder to take my place behind him.

"No falling asleep," he warned, setting the bag in front of him. He used his legs and the broken straps to keep it in place.

I wrapped my hands around him and held on as he took off. Though I felt the dreams calling and the occasional tug of sleep, I didn't close my eyes. I was still wound too tightly from what had just happened.

Apparently, my previous thoughts about using an adrenaline rush were right. It would have been a better method than cutting.

SEVEN

After several turns, we made our way into a town where we both used a public restroom to wash. We then picked up some desperately needed clean clothes.

"Who did you call about a car?" I asked after walking out of the bathroom a second time—for changing.

"An Elder. I told him about the attack. He's changed plans with his contacts and suggested we come to a more populated area."

I struggled to remember what an Elder meant, but couldn't. I realized I knew how their kind typically behaved, some of the reasons behind their actions, but nothing about their culture.

"What's an Elder?"

With my Tinker Bell pajamas safely tucked into a new duffle bag, we walked side by side as we slowly made our way to the bike. I noted several long scratches on the once shiny tank and wondered if he cared. He had called the thing a death trap on two wheels after all...

"They are the keepers of our kind. Everything they do, they do in our best interest, unlike pack leaders."

"What do you mean?"

"Pack leaders want to control their members. Elders want to guide them."

"Why have pack leaders, then?"

"Exactly. That's why I don't follow one. The Elders aren't so bad though." He smiled as he mounted the bike.

I climbed on the back and passed him the strap. Once again wearing his jacket, I ducked behind him as he pulled away, but I tried not to lay my head against him. Every time I did, I felt the pull to sleep even more. However, each time I slept against him, the dreams weren't of death.

"Why don't you want to be Claimed?" I asked knowing he'd hear me over the wind.

He turned his head and half-shouted his answer knowing I couldn't hear as well. "I *do* want to be Claimed. Just not now."

That hurt. "I don't get it. Why not? And don't bother denying the pull you feel for me. I know you do."

He shook his head and didn't answer, frustrating me further.

I didn't want to dream about dying anymore and didn't want to spend the rest of this life pressed up against him. Or did I? It wouldn't be the worst fate. But, I truly believed Claiming him would be the key not just to the type of dream I had, but the frequency, too. I could actually go somewhere without worrying about dropping off. Besides, if he felt the pull, he shouldn't have any complaint about me Claiming him. I should be the only one with an issue with Claiming since it gave him a way to keep tabs on me through the link it would establish between us.

I watched the buildings as we snaked our way through town and wondered if there were other men out there waiting for us. When we cleared town, the fields and trees didn't provide any more of a comfort.

(Un)wise

The funeral pyre lit the night sky. My friend's mother stood beside me sobbing. The somber faces of neighbors and family, illuminated by the flickering flames, seemed to float in the darkness. One woman stood out. She looked at my friend's mother with compassion as she made her way around the circle of people. A chord of familiarity struck me, but I couldn't place her since my family had recently moved here.

Using the lights in my mind, I searched for my little brother and father. They had remained in our home while my mother accompanied me. Their life sparks comforted me. Grief over the loss of my friend swamped me. She had fallen ill with a sickness that had also taken several others in neighboring homes. I couldn't understand why anyone needed to die in such a way.

"Death always serves a purpose," the woman, who I'd forgotten for a moment, said from just behind us.

My friend's mother and I turned to look at her.

She reached up and touched the mother's face gently. "Often, others die so more may live. Even the most seemingly random death can have the most profound meaning. Your daughter's illness may spark a need in someone's heart to create a cure for the illness, changing the direction of our society for future generations. Try not to mourn. Her death is not meaningless. Celebrate her life. Celebrate your life. To make her memory count, do not squander opportunities."

The woman turned to me. "She felt like a sister to you but did not share your blood. Do not forget her. Do not forget this feeling of loss. You can be the one to change the future, to make the lives of those around you better. Do not squander your chances."

I glanced at my friend's mother, confused. She met my gaze

*with a stunned tear-filled expression. When we both looked back,
the woman had vanished.*

"Come on, Bethi!" Luke said, his voice sounding distant and
tinny.

I blinked my eyes open to the familiar sight of him looking
down at me. We were once again pulled over to the shoulder of
the road on an idling bike.

"We're never going to get there at this rate."

"I'm not doing this on purpose!" I said irritably as I struggled
to get off his lap.

He sighed. "I know."

I felt his lips brush my hair and stilled. I knew it! He did feel
the pull.

Tilting my head back, I met his gaze again. He looked
guarded. "Why?" I asked, unable to keep the desperation from
my voice. "Why won't you let me Claim you?"

"Because you're afraid and think it's the only way to help
yourself."

"And?"

"And nothing. It's not the way to make that kind of
decision."

"What *is* the way, then?"

A slight flush crept into his cheeks. "With affection, not
fear."

My mouth popped open, and he gently hoisted me off his
lap. Woodenly, I took my seat again. He wanted me to like him?
How in the hell did I end up finding the only damn werewolf who
wanted to take it slow and get to know each other?

"You've been without decent sleep for too long," he said
changing the subject. "We need to hole up somewhere so you

can get some rest. Then, maybe, driving won't be such a challenge."

I doubted it. The ten hours at the last place hadn't seemed to help much, but I didn't argue. I was busy trying to figure out a way to get him to believe I had feelings for him. I found him physically attractive but knew that wasn't what he meant. Actual feelings for one of them? It would be a stretch.

* * * *

We managed to put several miles of traveling time in that day before calling it quits and stopping at another motel. Using some of the money he'd given me, he got a room for us for two nights so I knew he meant business about me catching up on sleep.

As soon as we walked into the room, I claimed the bathroom and got ready for bed not caring about the time of day. Luke didn't comment when I crawled under the covers other than to assure me he would be there keeping an eye on me. Not really what I needed, but I'd take it.

Pain radiated from my legs. My muscles spasmed. Chained to a wall, I couldn't move much to relieve any of the aches. Tears streamed down my face. A tongue licked them away and a low rumble of laughter followed.

I blinked my eyes. Faint shadows danced around me.

"She's nearly useless," a man commented quietly from very close by. The soft sound echoed off the walls.

Damp cool air had me shivering occasionally.

A hand stroked my face.

"Nearly, but not completely," another stated from further away. "Do not touch her. Let her walk once an hour. Whatever ill befalls her, befalls you."

The sound of fading footsteps let me know I was alone with the man who'd touched me. I caught sight of a shadow moving. It was the outline of a person. I turned toward it, trying to focus.

"Stop moving your eyes like you can see. Close them if you want to keep them," he warned with a growl. I closed my eyes while still turned toward the shadow. I knew the threat wasn't idle. However, closing my eyes didn't change what I saw. Even with the lids closed, I watched the shadow approach.

The feeling of a hand on my nonexistent breast distracted me. "You've never lived long enough to Claim," the man whispered.

My stomach flipped in an unpleasant way, and I started to sweat.

His fingers pinched my tender skin, and new tears fell. "This is going to be pleasant."

I sobbed knowing what he intended.

The dream lifted slightly as I was jostled to the side.

"Enough of that," Luke whispered before settling beside me and kissing my forehead.

I wanted to open my eyes, but another dream pulled me under.

The funeral pyre lit the night sky. My friend's mother stood beside me sobbing.

My dream-self looked around at the somber faces of neighbors and family, illuminated by the flickering flames, while my real-self grew angry as one woman's face stood out.

Why would this dream repeat?

The Taupe Lady looked at my friend's mother with compassion as she made her way around the circle of people. A chord of familiarity struck my dream-self.

I wanted to yell at her from across the fire. I willed myself to move but stayed locked in place by my dream-self.

Luke shifted next to me. His movement pulled me from the dream a bit, but not enough that I opened my eyes. I felt him move away for a moment as the dream continued to play out. Then he pulled me back to his side. As soon as my head rested on his warm bare shoulder, the dream faded; and I sank into real sleep.

* * * *

The pressing need to use the bathroom woke me. Warm and relaxed, I didn't immediately move. I wished the urge would go away because I hadn't slept so well in longer than I could remember.

Snuggling in, I realized why. My head lay cushioned on Luke's chest. Bare chest. My left arm lay slung over his waist. Yep, that was bare too. And my leg...I cringed not wanting to think about it. Wait. If I was draped all over him, it meant his neck was only inches away. My insides somersaulted. I opened my eyes and darted forward.

His palm blocked me, slightly mashing my nose, and I groaned in frustration.

"Fine," I grumbled before scooting off the bed and closing myself in the bathroom. His laughter drifted through the door.

After taking care of business and washing up, I stared at the mirror and tried to see myself through his eyes. I looked a little less waifish but not very healthy. I'd lost a bunch of weight and still had circles under my eyes. Definitely not attractive. I splashed water on my face, trying to wash away my insecurities.

He wanted to stay here for two days. I felt as if I'd slept a long time, but I doubted I'd used all of the time he'd dedicated for me to get the rest he felt I needed. I had time to try to wear him down and convince him of my affection. I dried my face, and I gave my reflection a stern get-to-it look.

Opening the bathroom door, I found the bed made and Luke sitting in the room's one chair.

"Get dressed. We'll grab something to eat and walk around a bit if you're up for it."

Nodding, I moved aside to let him use the bathroom, relieved that I didn't have to try right away. I dug out some clothes and ducked back into the bathroom when he had finished.

How had I let boys know I liked them before the dreams exposed the hot mess that was my life? Long looks, cute clothes, smiling conversation. I didn't think any of that would work with Luke. Trying to trick him was pointless, and I didn't want his hand in my face anymore, either. What did that leave me? Being nice and giving it time? Actually letting myself grow feelings for him? I wanted to throw something. Instead, I opened the door and gave him a halfhearted smile.

A few minutes later, we strolled side by side down the sidewalk in the direction the motel manager had pointed. A small gas station offered premade sandwiches and bags of junk food. My stomach rumbled as I eyed the displays, and his echoed it as if they were having a conversation. He grinned and reached for a bag of chips. I grabbed the sandwiches.

With a bag loaded up with goodies, we headed back. He opened the door for me and stood aside to let me in. After kicking off my shoes, I sat on the bed folding my legs under me. He set the bag next to me, grabbed a sandwich from it, and sat on the chair.

"Thank you for the food," I said reaching for my own sandwich. "And for helping me sleep. And the walk. It was good to get outside and not feel like I needed to run."

He stopped chewing and looked at me suspiciously but nodded his welcome. Crap, was I being that obvious? I took a large bite and chewed slowly. Maybe I shouldn't have mentioned the walk. I was just trying to be nice. And thankful. How else could I ease him into the idea that I cared?

I glanced at him and saw he'd already polished off two sandwiches. I forgot to eat and just stared as he consumed another triangle in two bites. Silently, I popped open a bag of chips and offered it to him. He demolished those and looked at my sandwich which I willingly—and perhaps a little fearfully—surrendered.

"How long was I out?"

"Sixteen hours," he mumbled around a dessert cake.

"Sorry. Maybe we should go back and stockpile some more food in case I crash hard again." And so I had something to eat, I thought as I opened the last bag of chips.

He looked up at me with mixed emotions on his face. First, he appeared happy about my suggestion, then a little disheartened. He finished the cake in another bite and took a drink of water from one of the bottles he'd purchased.

"Do you think you'll sleep that long again?"

"I honestly don't know. I don't feel tired yet, but I can feel another dream calling me."

He leaned back and studied me for a moment. "What do you dream about? And I don't mean you dying. Sometimes, the dreams don't seem to disturb you so much."

"If it's not of death, it's about a lady. I think of her as the

Taupe Lady because of the color of the gown she always wears."

"Who is she?"

"I don't know, but from how the people dress in the dreams, I get the feeling she's always been here. Even in my really old dreams, she shows up. She seems like she cares but never really does anything to help me. I mean, she says things that sound like cryptic advice; but if she can show up whenever she wants, why doesn't she show up when I really need her? Why doesn't she step in and stop some of the bad stuff from happening?"

"Maybe she can't," he suggested quietly.

"What do you mean?"

"My kind has rules to follow and laws to obey. Our laws can't be broken even if we wanted to break them. What if she has rules and laws too?"

I thought about it for a moment. "What do you mean you can't break them?"

He sighed and shook his head at me. "Sometimes you seem to know so much about what I am. How did you learn about my kind?"

"My dreams," I answered honestly.

"That's not possible," he said.

"Okay, then how do I know?" He looked at me with a suitably shocked expression, and I continued. "This is what I've figured out. There are dog-men out there that can shift between their dog form and man form."

"I prefer to think of myself as more of a wolf. It's more dignified."

Rolling my eyes, I continued. "They want me and the few women like me for some reason that I haven't yet figured out. We are reborn every one thousand years. There seems to be a period of time within each cycle that we can be reborn several times. Almost every time I'm found, they end up killing me after making me Claim and mate with one of their own." I didn't mention the dreams where I killed myself.

"Almost every time?" he asked tilting his head as his focus intensified.

"Twice I've dreamt of one of your kind trying to *help* me. I still died both times in the end, but someone did try." I thought about those dreams. I'd willingly gone along with their plans to help me and still died. I refused to die again or to go along with someone else's plans in this life. I needed to try something different. But what? Maybe that's what the Taupe Lady meant by every death has a purpose. They all gave me a chance to learn.

He quietly threw away the empty wrappers. I could see his mind turning over what I'd shared.

"Let's get some more food," I said. Seriously, he'd eaten just about everything on his own.

He nodded and walked beside me on our second trip to the gas station.

* * * *

When we got back, I went into the bathroom to change. We'd both been quiet on the walk. I'd mostly debated with myself. Now that he knew I wanted to Claim him in order to avoid a forced Claiming, perhaps he would be reasonable. But seeing his troubled expression after I'd acknowledged I had still died when someone tried to help me had me reconsidering. He truly did seem to want to help me; and if he thought Claiming him would end up getting me killed, I didn't think he'd go for it. Fine. I just needed to convince him that I cared about him and get him to let me Claim him that way. He would eventually forgive me for the deception. I was sure of it.

I stepped out of the bathroom and saw him sitting in the chair, still deep in thought. I wanted to roll my eyes but managed to suppress the urge. I did that a lot I realized. I suppressed urges and feelings because I knew he was too aware of me. It was a habit already. But maybe my reactions to him were the key to all of this. I'd witnessed his reaction to me, but did he really know my reaction to him? In past lives, they'd used it as a means to control me. But I knew better now. I could let the physical reactions show without letting the emotional attraction grow.

Focusing on the flutter I felt every time I looked at him, I let the feeling fill me. The rightness of him, which I usually stomped on with imaginary steel-toed boots, lifted its well-trodden head. My heart somersaulted and stuttered heavily.

Luke's head jerked up in surprise. As he looked at me, a blush spread across my cheeks.

"Would you mind lying down with me? I think you're right. I do seem to sleep better with you."

I didn't miss his quick glance at the door. Frowning, I watched him slowly get to his feet. He looked reluctant.

"Is something wrong?" I asked, truly confused. Was I acting too nice again? Maybe letting him hear my heart stutter hadn't been a good move.

"I, uh, think you should try to sleep on your own for a bit," he muttered.

"I just told you that I—" I rubbed my face and cut off my sharp words. Affection. Show him you care, not that he annoys the crap out of you, I reminded myself. "Okay, fine," I agreed with barely suppressed agitation.

He walked out the door, closing it softly behind him.

Annoyed, I marched to the bed. I wasn't tired, but a dream called. Better to give into it on a bed than try to keep it at bay.

As soon as the blankets covered me, my eyes closed and another past pulled me down.

Perhaps it was still my emotions from before succumbing to the dream, but I felt angry. Rage-filled really. I wanted to rip someone's head off with my own two hands and shove it up their...

"She's awake," a man sighed.

"Thank the skies," someone said contentedly. *"I thought that last cut might have gone too deep."*

I looked down at myself. I lay naked on a pile of blood-covered straw. A cut ran along one of my lower ribs. The glistening blood indicated its newness. I felt the pain, but the rage overshadowed it. I focused on the men crouched over me who eyed me with peaceful detachment, and I drew more emotion from them. Every bit of anger, resentment, prejudice, fear...anything and everything other than an unresisting peace. My wrath grew. Blood started seeping from my various wounds as if my emotion filled me so much that I had no room to spare for the precious liquid. Soon their eyes began to close. Blood poured from me. Rage consumed me as my last breath drifted from my body in a furious cry.

I woke sitting up wide-eyed and panting. Anger shook my body. A growl started growing until it was a shout of rage. When I realized it came from me, I clamped my mouth shut.

"I'm sorry, Bethi," Luke whispered as he stood up from the chair. He peeled off his shirt and slid under the covers with me.

I barely noticed. I wanted to hurt someone. My hands shook with the need.

"Lay down," he coaxed, leaning on an elbow.

Turning to look down at him, I struggled with my urge to punch him in the face. He'd watched me suffer through that dream just as those men had watched one of my sisters bleed out.

"Let go of the dream," he said. His hazel eyes met mine steadily. "I'm here. I won't leave you. Ever." He reached up, wrapped an arm around me, and gently tugged me toward him. "I'm sorry." His lips pressed against my forehead.

The swell of anger began to recede slightly. The leftover emotions from that dream frightened me. Shaking, I laid my head on his chest.

His fingers ran over my hair, soothing me until the shaking stopped and my eyes drifted closed. I didn't want to sleep ever again. I wanted to stay awake and live forever.

Eight

The room was dark when I woke and for a few seconds I thought a dream still held me. Then Luke's fingers shifted in my hair. I sighed against his skin.

"Had enough?" he whispered.

"I guess so," I said lifting my head. He had a nice chest. Warm. Firm. Warm. I started smiling stupidly and reminded myself to cut it out. I needed to convince him of my affection, not me. "Thanks," I mumbled turning away from his perceptive gaze. Even in the dark, I knew he'd probably caught my grin.

Flipping back the covers, I escaped to the bathroom. When I emerged dressed, everything was already packed and waiting.

"Think you can manage to stay awake for a while?"

I nodded. The only pull I felt was my attraction to him. I walked with him to the office to check out. When we stood beside the bike, I remembered his comment about arranging for a car.

"No car yet?" I asked settling behind him.

"I told my contact we stopped along the way. We're still set to meet." He twisted in his seat to look at me. "Are you trying to tell me you're tired already?"

I shook my head with a smile. He'd sounded almost panicked. I wrapped my arms around him after he tightened the strap on the bag. He wasn't taking any chances.

* * * *

We rode through the remainder of the night and watched the sun rise. We stopped for a quick bite then continued, taking breaks often to stretch and walk so I didn't get tired. Before the sun started hugging the horizon, I could feel the tug of dreams again.

"I think we need to stop for the night," I said, tapping his shoulder.

He nodded and sped up. "We're almost there."

We passed a sketchy looking roadside motel in the middle of nowhere to stop at a nicer small place in the next town. By then, the dreams clung to me like water, coating me with a lethargy that gave me the head bobbles.

"Come on, luv," Luke said lifting the strap and wrapping an arm around me so I wouldn't fall off. "Let's get you to bed."

His phrase made me giggle, and he scowled in response.

All the rooms started to look the same to me. I closed myself into the bathroom no longer caring. When I emerged, I didn't look for Luke. The bed called to me. I fell face-first into the mattress and a nightmare of one of our pasts.

A man knelt unflinchingly before another. The long grey hair hanging over his strong shoulders gave him a regal look. Two sets of hands kept him on his knees. He paid them little attention as his eyes held mine. I stood to the side, held captive by someone I couldn't see. The tip of something sharp pressed into the pulse in my neck.

"Tell the Elders," a man wearing a rough tunic and coarsely

woven trousers demanded. He towered before the kneeling man.
The ones holding the prisoner sank their nails into the man's flesh
at their leader's words. "Tell your leaders we have them all."

I knew the leader lied. He did not have all of my sisters. But
he did have me and four others, and I could see where the last
one waited; her spark wasn't far away.

"If you have them all, why do I need to tell the Elders?" the
kneeling man questioned calmly.

"Do as I say or she dies." The leader waved his hand in my
direction.

The captive threw his head back and laughed. A growl rose
from the man behind me. No one else made a sound.

"You laugh?" Instead of looking angry, the leader appeared
curious.

"You are still trying so hard," the captive said with a pitying
smile. "The fight you started is coming. I have told my people
you have her, but we know you will not kill her. Not until the
balance is turned toward your favor." The man met my eyes, and
I caught a glint of deep sorrow reflected back at me. "But they
won't give you what you want. They've discovered their purpose
and will die protecting us."

I didn't understand everything the captive said. What
purpose? But I did understand the rest of his message. Help
would not come in time. I needed to choose. With a sob, I
pressed into the sharp object resting on my neck. It pierced my
skin with very little pain. My captor grunted in surprise. I quickly
twisted around causing irreparable damage. As I collapsed to my
knees, the severed head of the man who'd warned me tumbled
past. A horrible cry went up through the gathered men, but it
didn't drown out their leaders words.

Melissa Haag

"She will be reborn. There is still time in this cycle. If we fail again, we will kill their Elders so they won't remember in time for the next cycle!" He kicked the head as he spoke.

My heartbeat slowed, and a chill crept along my skin.

The bed dipped as Luke lay next to me. He pulled me into his arms, and I rested my head on his bare chest registering his comfort before sinking into normal dreams. Dreams where I went to school, forgot my locker combination and my pants.

* * * *

A low growl pulled me from my sleep. But, it was Luke shoving my head onto a pillow that really woke me.

The mattress bounced as he flew from the bed. I opened my eyes to the sound of splintering wood and bolted upright, blinking stupidly. A large shape filled the demolished doorway. Luke had already almost completely phased into his wolf form and rushed toward the beast coming through the door.

They met with a heavy thud and grappled for each other's throats just inside our room. Vicious snarls and growls filled the air as they both went back on their hind legs. I sat there frozen and gap-jawed watching the fight play out while my chest felt too small for my hammering heart.

The larger one used its weight to push Luke back, unbalancing him. As he fell, he darted in with his sharp teeth. I didn't see if he made contact. A rustle of noise and a shadow of movement from the corner of my eye had me turning in time to watch two shapes fly through the room's wide window.

Still shaking from the first one's arrival, I didn't think, just acted. I rolled from the bed toward the fighting pair and closer to Luke. The newcomers landed crouched on the floor at the foot of the bed while I landed hard on my hip beside the bed.

102

(Un)wise

Luke pivoted to face the two newcomers. The original wolf who had struggled with Luke saw me and reached for me. I scrambled away, barely managed to avoid his searching fingers, and bumped into the nightstand as Luke yanked him back.

A yip-howl rent the air. Luke had sunk his teeth into his opponent's right eye. I gagged by reflex and quickly looked away. No time for that!

Snagging the lamp from the table, I held it by the cord and threw it like a mace. Luke lunged at the third attacker while the second batted away my attempt at a weapon. The lamp shattered, and I grabbed a shard of jagged ceramic before wedging myself under the bed. There wasn't much room; the weight of the bed pressed down on me. I inched to the head of the bed where the nightstands created an additional barrier, giving me more protection.

Above me, the snarls increased, and I tried to curl into a ball—as much as the space would allow—to make my legs and arms harder to grab. *Please don't let him die.* Huddled there, I stared at the fake wood grain of the nightstand trying to quiet my harsh breathing so I could hear. My hand tightened around the shard. I didn't want to use it. A grunt of pain preceded several more yips. I didn't want to do this again. Then, silence fell. I stifled the urge to cry as I waited. One heartbeat. Two. No one tried to pull me from under the bed.

I stayed curled up but lifted my head for just a peek. A pair of eyes stared back at me. I jumped hard enough to hit my head on the bed frame and almost curled back up. The eyes didn't blink... Trembling, I struggled to pull in a breath. The man's cheek lay pressed against the carpet, his body relaxed. Dead. It wasn't Luke. I needed to know. Quietly, I uncurled myself. I didn't completely stretch out. Rather, I extended my arms and legs just enough to shift my weight without emerging from under the bed. Three half-formed wolf bodies littered the floor. Whispers of sound invaded the room as their bodies shifted on the carpet, their dog forms slowly receding to show the men beneath. I didn't recognize any of them.

Relief washed over me, and I rested my head on the floor, closing my eyes. Luke hadn't died.

Small noises continued to sound around me while I struggled to regain control of my breathing and my limbs. It took several minutes after the last rustle of movement to register the complete silence. Where was Luke? Was he hurt? Like an idiot, I'd stayed cowering under the bed instead of checking right away.

I lifted my head and frowned at the vacant spot before me. The lifeless eyes were gone. So was the body attached to them.

Creeping from beneath the bed, I surveyed the room. No bodies, no lamp pieces, no glass. No blood. How was there no blood?

The sheets were rumpled and twisted from my quick escape. The curtains, fluttering outward, drew my attention. I edged toward the window and looked at all the glass and lamp pieces scattered artfully on the ground.

Frowning, I turned back to the room. Where had Luke gone? We needed to move fast. I looked down at myself. I wore a long sleeved top and sleep pants. The cold penetrating the room finally penetrated my thoughts. I couldn't go outside like this. I grabbed the bag and dashed to the bathroom. If Luke wasn't back when I stepped out of the bathroom, I promised myself that I would leave without him.

I flew through changing, and when I stepped out, Luke sat waiting on the edge of the bed, his expression filled with concern. I wanted to fly at him and throw myself in his arms but held myself back.

That was twice now that they'd found us. A heaviness settled over me. Was there really only one outcome for me? Hopelessness blanketed my desperation to find an answer where I didn't die.

"Are you all right?" he asked softly, standing.

When he walked toward me, I flinched involuntarily. Apparently, I wasn't all right. Seeing, hearing, and knowing he'd killed five men shook me. It wasn't that I didn't appreciate his defense. I did. But knowing that my life had once again started the death cycle broke me down inside. Two wolves finding us I could try to pass off as a fluke, to deny the inevitability of my death, and to tease myself with maybes. Maybe Luke, one of the good guys, could help me. Maybe I would live this time. Five wasn't a fluke. Those maybes were a fool's dream. I just needed to come to grips with my fate. I would die. Horribly.

He stopped advancing and eyed me sadly.

"It will be okay, Bethi. I left money and an explanation with the manager for the broken window. We should go."

I nodded numbly and watched him pick up the duffle bag. He held a hand out toward me, but I ignored it and walked through the door. My hope to stop the dreams didn't matter anymore. The countdown to the end had started.

* * * *

Sitting once again on the back of the bike, the scenery rushed past. I didn't see any of it. I didn't remember getting on the bike. The sight of a gouged eye blinded me to all of it.

Instead, I dwelled on the dead of this life and past lives. The loud sound of the battering wind faded as the ticking of the countdown deafened me. I stayed locked behind Luke, feeling him turning occasionally, but not hearing him, not seeing him until he pulled to the shoulder and cut the engine.

"Bethi?" he said turning to look at me. "I am sorry about this morning. Those were not typical challenges. They did not back down. I had no choice."

Challenge? I blinked at him trying to bring myself back. I remembered the fights from past lives where two wolves fought for the right to their Mate. He thought he was fighting for his right to me? Part of me wanted to cry because he hadn't really believed me, or put together what I'd been telling him. Another part wanted to cry because his interest, or lack thereof, was pointless.

"Don't be sorry," I said flatly. "It wasn't a challenge. There will be more wolves. They will come until I choose, or I die."

Luke opened his mouth to say something more but stopped after searching my hopeless gaze. He turned around, told me to hold on tight, and took off from the shoulder. We flew, and this time the tearing wind reminded me I wasn't dead yet.

*　*　*　*

Woods and a cloud-laden sky brought an early twilight. The wind picked up as I stood in stunned immobility. On the ground, a man lay gasping. The gurgling wet noise of his inhale told me he wouldn't live long. I stumbled backward and tripped over another prone form.

Something ran past me too fast to see clearly. Not far away another member of our party cried out and then fell silent. I didn't run. Turning in a circle, I tried identifying who darted around me within the shadows.

A voice, directly behind me, stilled my movement and sent shivers racing over my skin. "So beautiful." A hand stroked my hair. Fear made my heart race.

"Do you still doubt me?" a familiar voice called.

I turned to watch my group's leader emerge from the shadows completely unharmed.

"You were right," the man behind me agreed.

I stared at the approaching man with dawning horror. "You betrayed your people," I gasped looking again at the bodies lying nearby.

"Not my people," the man I thought I knew growled. "My people do not run from a fight, not even to spare a single life."

The man behind me laughed. "Now that we have her, where was she leading you?"

"She had knowledge of a plant that will bring us wealth. It relieves pain." The betrayer stepped closer. "We will need someone to test it," he said.

I spun and ran, knowing it was useless. They could have outran me, but, instead, made a game of the chase. My sides ached, and my breath came in painful gasps.

"Enough play time," the betrayer called to his companion.

Something bumped into me, knocking me to the ground. Pinned by an unyielding mass, I sobbed as the man licked my neck.

"You will be delicious," he whispered.

NINE

"Bethi," Luke called my name and tapped my face.

I opened my eyes with my heart still pounding.

"Why didn't you lean against me? The dreams aren't as bad then," he scolded with a concerned frown.

I blinked at him as the memory of my sister's death continued to cloud my thoughts.

"Betrayer," I whispered.

Luke looked shocked. "I would never betray you," he whispered. Some obscure emotion flicked into his eyes and for a moment he looked so helplessly lost. "Never," he breathed as if talking to himself. Then, determination replaced it and he slowly leaned toward me.

My breath caught as his gaze snared me. Trapped, I watched his eyes drop to my mouth. My heart skipped a beat, but not in fear. I knew he heard it too when his arms tightened fractionally and his fingers feathered over my hair.

"I *will* protect you," he said softly. His lips brushed my top lip, the barest of touches, before he retreated slightly.

My heart struggled painfully as my stomach twisted in anticipation.

"You are everything I am. Without you..."

In his arms, I believed him. A small burst of hope warmed me. What if, instead of worrying about living or dying, I just...lived?

Dropping my eyes to his lips, a shaky breath escaped me; and I lifted my mouth to his. A spark ignited in my stomach. Our lips touched for less than a second before he pulled back quickly.

I wanted to yell and cry. Instead, I took a deep breath and tried to quell my frustration. The stubborn man wouldn't even look at me.

"Why?"

"Why what?" he asked distractedly, eyeing the road ahead.

"Why protect me? I'm not your Mate."

His eyes met mine, and the intensity of his look robbed me of words.

"Do not mistake my patience for disinterest." He gently threaded his fingers through my hair, and I held my breath. His lips lifted in a half smile at my hopeful look, but he dropped his hand.

"I wasn't sure if you wanted to stop yet," he said with a nod toward a building I hadn't noticed. We sat in the parking lot of a hotel.

"No," I said in panic, struggling to get off his lap. I did *not* want to stay at another hotel. I could still see the dead man's eyes from under the bed. A shudder ripped through me.

"Shh," he whispered wrapping his arms around me and pulling me close. "It will be okay."

"No. It won't. They won't give up."

A flush crept into Luke's face. "Have you died in this life? Not this cycle, but this life? No. Do you know why?" He met my eyes and leaned in close. "Because you have me. Because I won't *let* you die. I've already sent a call asking for someone to meet us. We don't need to—"

My head shot up knocking into his jaw as the last two dreams clicked into place. How could I be so stupid?

His mouth closed with a snap, and he grunted but didn't set me aside.

"What did you say?" I demanded trapping his face between my hands. "What did you tell them?"

Surprise colored his eyes as he answered cautiously. "That we would be here and needed an Elder and a few others to help escort you back to the Compound."

"When?" I insisted.

"A few moments before I woke you," he answered, clearly puzzled.

So just a few minutes ago? I dropped my hands and hopped off the bike, scanning the road in both directions. All clear, but the trees around us could hide anything. I wished I could see those sparks like my sister.

"Go get a room. Hurry!" I motioned him toward the main door. He opened his mouth to ask more, but I started power walking.

As soon as I cleared the door, I pasted on my chipper face, the one I'd used so often to hide the fact I wasn't sleeping, and asked for a room. Luke, just a few steps behind me, paid for the room as I filled out the form using my fake ID. I took a moment to write the hotel's phone number on the palm of my hand, too.

I hurried down the hall to the room and opened the door, making sure to touch the handle and the wood. Luke stood watching me with concern. I didn't step further into the room.

Instead, I closed the door again and retraced my steps, heading back outside. He followed me without comment.

"What are we doing?" he asked when we reached the bike.

"We're leaving, but you need to keep quiet about it." I motioned for him to get on. He didn't hesitate to settle on the seat. "Don't tell anyone. If I'm right, that room will have visitors soon." He glanced toward the hotel, and I saw he finally understood.

I swung my leg over the seat and slung the strap over his head. He started the engine as he removed the slack. Pressed against him, we pulled out of the parking lot heading west. I tapped his shoulder.

"Go south!"

Taking the next turn, we headed south for the next two hours. I had enough rest that I evaded the dreams calling me. When I thought enough time had passed, I tapped his stomach to get his attention.

"I think we can stop," I said as we sped down a main highway.

He signaled for the next exit, and we took the northern route to the next town.

He turned his head and asked, "Are we getting a room?"

"No, not yet. We just need a pay phone."

He pulled into a gas station, and I quickly ducked out of the strap before hopping off. I moved to the phone and dialed the hotel's number. Pretending to be a reporter, I asked if they would offer a comment regarding their recent break in. The guy on the phone started an exciting tale until his manager cut him off. I hung up the phone and turned to look at Luke. He'd moved from the bike to stand close to me.

"Did you hear most of that?"

He nodded. The muscles in his jaw stood out from clenching it so hard.

"Someone is betraying you," I said softly. "I think we need to be more careful with the route we take to the Compound. They know where we're headed and will be waiting. It should be safe to get a room in the next town. No more communicating. With anyone." I rubbed a hand over my face, tired.

He moved forward, slightly widening his arms as if to hug me. Yeah, right. I quickly stepped away and walked toward the bike. Too much disappointment in one day wasn't good for a girl. Anyway, the countdown to the imminent end of my life still ticked away, and we stood in the open taunting it.

"Bethi," he said with slight exasperation.

I didn't turn back to look at him. "We need to keep moving. The dreams are calling again," I said to explain my hurry.

* * * *

We found a room next to a sportsmen outlet before the sun set. I'd managed to stay awake for most of the ride, but exhaustion tugged at me. Once inside the room, I kicked off my shoes and landed on the bed completely ignoring Luke.

The hand hitting my face knocked me off balance. I stumbled but spread my stance to avoid falling.

"Which one are you?" he demanded as he hit me again. Fire lit my face; each strike had created a burning path across my cheek and jaw.

I remained silent. My father and brother stood a short distance away and watched despite their urge to rush forward.

"What is your ability?" he roared, his anger growing.

Smack.

(Un)wise

I struggled to maintain my mental hold on my father as the last hit broke skin and a trickle of blood ran down my cheek. My father's anger crawled into me as he yelled at the man to stop. He curled his fist, and I willed my brother to lift a hand and rest it on Father's shoulder. Fear of the group of men surrounding us overshadowed my brother's anger.

"Do you see lights in your mind?" my tormentor growled through his elongating teeth.

I tried again to assert my will over his. Most people's wills felt like a thick sturdy rope, easy to grab and to hold. Once I held someone's will, I easily implanted thoughts into their minds as if the thought were their own. The men around us were different. The slim slick strands of their wills slipped from my grasp. In the half of a second I touched their wills, nothing ever happened.

Smack. I'd waited too long to answer.

"Have you seen things that helped your family become prosperous?"

Several of the men looked at my father's wealthy clothes, a gift from my mother's father and nothing to do with my ability.

"Do you calm those around you?"

My eyes flared slightly before I could stop the reaction. The man hesitated.

"No," he murmured to himself, watching me. "You cannot be her. Her presence is felt by everyone. Her purpose is to calm and prevent fighting." He reached forward and lightly touched the open wound on my cheek. His fingertip came away bloody. "I would not feel so angry right now if you were her," he added with a slight narrowing of his eyes. "Why then did you react to the question? Do you know where she is?"

I kept my gaze locked on his, afraid to give anything further *away. I had no idea who he spoke of.*

He licked the blood off his finger with an evil smile and glanced at my father and brother. "You are not their Hope or their Prosperity. If you were Wisdom, you would have run when we first appeared. You are not Peace, and Courage always dies young." He turned to me with a bark of laughter. "I smell your loving father's anger and your brother's fear. Yet, they remain here neither running nor fighting. Do you find that odd, my dear?"

I kept my face carefully relaxed as I turned to look at my family.

The man stepped closer to me, his features rippling and contorting. "Asking you questions will result in nothing answered, will it not? Perhaps we need to ask someone else."

Keeping my eyes locked with my father, I said, "I love you. I am sorry." Tears gathered in my father's eyes, and his panic flared within me a moment before I calmed it and pushed the urge to sleep at him and my brother.

The men behind them howled in outrage as my father and brother collapsed to the ground. The man before me laughed. "You will need your Strength," he said a moment before he bent forward and viciously clamped his teeth into my shoulder.

I howled in pain and fought harder to grab his will. As slippery as before, the thread of his will escaped my grasp. He straightened and pulled me up by his teeth. Another scream ripped through me. Giving up on my attempt to hold his will, I imagined my will as a stiff unbreakable rod of metal and jammed it toward him. Fighting for breath and control, I hammered at his thin string of will. The pain in my shoulder grew—

"Bethi! Wake up!" Luke's hand patted my cheek gently.

(Un)wise

Pulled out of the dream, I bolted upright and flinched away from Luke's touch. Wide-eyed and panting, I reached for my shoulder where the echo of the bite still throbbed. My gaze darted around the room as the dream continued to haunt me.

Luke held up his hands, looking worried. "It's okay. It's me, Luke."

I swallowed hard and wiped the sweat from my face. "I know it's you," I mumbled as he sat beside me. "Where were you?" His promise never to leave me had only lasted, what? Two days?

He set something on top of the blanket between us. The long wicked blade of a hunting knife caught the light. It had a sturdy handle for a sure grip. It made me nervous. Why was there a knife on the bed?

"It's yours," he said. His gaze trapped mine. For once, he looked unsure. He rubbed a hand on the side of his neck in agitation. "I thought it might help you feel safer. I'll show you how to use it." When I didn't say anything he added, "I want you to feel safe. I want to see the fear fade."

I struggled with my emotions, angry that he'd left me. I was vulnerable not just to my dreams but to anyone looking for me. It annoyed me that he still didn't get it.

"It's not just fear. Imagine discovering you're not who you thought you were, that you belong to a dangerous hidden world. Imagine closing your eyes and seeing yourself and your loved ones die again and again. The fear in your eyes would be eclipsed by your desperation to stop it all." Tearing my gaze from his, I looked at the gleaming steel. "They are coming. They always do." I reached out and touched the knife before standing.

He watched me with sad eyes.

"Thank you for the knife. I already know how to use it," I didn't add that the knowledge wasn't from this life.

A memory tickled my mind but refused to come forward. I had the vague impression of standing in the middle of a large battle, bathed in blood that was not my own, as I tried to defend those who tried to defend me. The moves, agile and sure, filled my mind without the details of who I fought or why. I had no doubt I'd eventually recall all the details, but the vague impression was enough to make me hope that day wouldn't come any time soon.

"The knife might help," I said as I walked to the bathroom forcing my hand from my shoulder. Glancing at the clock, I saw it was just after nine.

In the shower, I let myself cry. I was beyond done with the dreams and feeling so desperate and crazy all the time. Why was I fighting so hard to hold on to a life I hated so much? The answer helped firm my determination. I didn't want to be born again into the same crappy cycle facing the same hopeless situation. With this life, I needed to make a difference. I rinsed away my self-pity and finished washing.

When I stepped back into the main room, Luke waited with my bag at his feet. The knife was still on the bed but now with a sheath. His eyes roved my face as I strode to the bed and picked up the knife. I didn't want to see his concern. Instead, I studied his gift to me. I could strap the knife to my bag so it would be easily accessible, but no one would know I had a weapon because I needed to face crazed man-dogs. Well, people didn't know yet anyway. So having it on the outside of the bag would make me look like a troublemaker or worse. Moving closer to Luke, I bent and tucked the knife into the bag. Right along the side so I could find it quickly if needed. Convenient, yet out of sight.

"You all right?"

"Honestly?" I wondered if he really wanted to know. Sometimes people asked, but didn't care. Meeting my eyes, he nodded. "The answer hasn't changed. No, I'm not all right. But the knife gives me—" I took a slow deep breath as I struggled with how to explain what it meant. "A tiny bit of power over my fate." What Luke didn't realize was that if I couldn't use it against my attacker...well, at least I might escape rape and torture this time around.

A glimmer of helplessness shone in his eyes before he looked away. "Are you ready to leave?"

"I think I've slept enough, if that's what you're asking." Shouldering the bag, I followed him out the door.

We stopped at a gas station after several hours to pick up maps so we could plan our route. I wanted to groan when he gave me a general idea of the Compound's location. West wasn't exactly right. Try north. Why Canada? I thought with a shiver. I decided then to start wearing layers of clothing.

Studying the map, I saw the problem right away. We had plenty of options until we neared the Compound. Then our routes narrowed down to three. I had no illusions. They would be waiting for us.

The dreams called to me while we rode that day, but I successfully avoided succumbing to them as we wove an erratic pattern northwest.

Taking a break, we found a restaurant for a real meal. I felt exposed walking into such an open, normal space. I wanted food, but I wanted safety more. Luke held the door for me, and I felt his troubled gaze as I passed him, but he didn't say anything. Picking a booth, I slid in, and he surprised me by sitting next to me.

"Relax," he breathed a moment before the waitress came. She gave us menus and asked for our drink order, barely looking at us in her hurry. When she walked away, Luke turned slightly toward me draping his arm over the back of the bench seat. I met his gaze. He smiled and spoke his next words softly so only I heard them. "Maybe I should have bought you a gun."

The absurdity of his comment struck me, and I laughed as he'd intended. "I don't think it would have made a difference." I hesitated playfully, then said, "Well, maybe it would have."

His grin fell, and he grew serious. "I'd buy you an arsenal if it would help you feel safe." The gruff words and the affection behind them tugged my heart making my stomach twist crazily. His hand moved slightly, so close to the side of my face.

The waitress came with our drinks, and he straightened in his seat leaving me in confused frustration. He ran so hot and cold. He wanted me. I knew he did. But yet, he didn't. Why was he fighting it?

Our waitress asked if we were ready to order. Without looking at the menu, I ordered a burger and fries. She took note of it and looked at Luke. Her smile grew just a bit brighter, and she shifted her stance, cocking her hip in a flirty way. I rolled my eyes.

"He'll have two burgers and an order of fries," I told her before he could speak. She gave me a fake smile, wrote the order on her stupid little pad, collected our menus, and walked away.

"Twat," I mumbled.

He gave me a look.

"What? There aren't any kids around, and I was quiet."

His lips twitched, and he turned toward me once again.

I mimicked his pose careful not to touch him. I didn't want to freak out my stomach or fall asleep. I watched his eyes for a moment, liking the amusement that still danced in them, but decided we needed to address some real issues.

"You know they will be waiting for us, right?"

"Let's talk about something else," he said softly. "I like it better when you have fire or laughter in your eyes instead of what I see now."

"What do you see?"

"Fear."

I narrowed my eyes.

"Pardon. Despair." He spoke softly, his unwavering regard making me feel vulnerable.

I couldn't help the despair. It lived and breathed in me. Sometimes, he helped me forget though. Distracted me. Like when I tried to bite him. A blush crept into my cheeks as I remembered my failed attempts.

His gaze changed. A glimpse of coveting sparked in the depths of it as he lifted his hand from the back of the bench. I dropped my own arm out of the way. He reached forward just a bit and lightly ran the back of his forefinger along my cheek.

I barely felt his slow, soft touch, but my heart stuttered anyway.

He closed his eyes for a moment. "I see your despair and it makes me..." He exhaled slowly before opening his eyes. His intensity pinned me. "I want to hurt whoever put that emotion in your eyes."

"I don't get you. If you feel that strongly about me, why can't I Claim you?"

He abruptly shook his head. "Let's talk about something—"

"Else," I finished for him, annoyed. I paused for a moment, seeing the waitress approach again. "You're a twat, too."

He threw his head back with a laugh just as she stopped by our table. Her eyes glazed over a bit as her eyes swept his face and throat. I briefly considered clawing her eyes out before reining myself in. Whoa, where did that come from? Biting my lip, I quelled my immediate need to freak out over the strong surge of possessiveness that had just rushed me. Nature had set him up as a possibility for me so of course I'd feel that way. It didn't mean anything. I wasn't actually stupid enough to fall for him. But, until we reached his friends at the Compound, if I couldn't bite him, no one else would be allowed to nibble. Because...well, just because.

"Can I get you a refill?" she asked him softly.

"He's fine," I answered, staring her down.

He kept his eyes on me, and they danced with silent laughter. Yeah, I wanted to smack him again.

She walked away to check on her other tables.

"If we can't talk about *them* or *us*, what should we talk about?"

"You. What do you like doing? What are your interests?"

My mouth popped open. "Are you serious?" We were running toward what I considered our impending deaths, and he wanted to get to know me?

He nodded, and I rolled my eyes. "I like breathing and am interested in staying alive."

"Bethi," he practically growled.

Maybe this would help convince him. "Okay, okay. So, interests. Well, before I started losing my mind I—" What had I done? I went to school, hung out with friends, sighed over boys, worried about clothes. "I was self-centered and immature. My interests don't really matter beyond that, do they? Not after everything I've seen."

"I think you're being a little hard on yourself."

"That's just it. I don't think I am. I think the human society lets me be too easy on myself. I have more responsibility to be a better person than what I've been in the past. Sure, I wasn't horrible, but I wasn't great either. Shouldn't we all strive for great?" I thought of the dream with the Taupe Lady and my friend's funeral. "Shouldn't we all strive to make a difference? To impact the lives around us in a positive way? To make our experiences count?"

He watched me with a growing seriousness. "That is a lot of responsibility for someone so young."

"See. That's what I mean. No, it's not. If we held each other to a higher level of accountability, if we raised our children with those expectations and guided them with our own examples of higher achievement, it wouldn't be too much. We would be a better people because of it. Instead, we took a wrong turn somewhere and ended up on Excuses-Are-Like-Assholes Boulevard."

He opened his mouth to comment, but I shifted my attention from him to the waitress carrying our plates. He turned, saw her, and sighed. I read the promise in his eyes to continue our conversation later; and inwardly, I cringed. I went from trying to convince him I cared to stepping up on a soapbox I didn't know I had. And I still felt like I had more to vent. I blamed it on sleep deprivation, bad dreams, and his completely gorgeous hazel eyes.

The waitress set our food on the table and left after our assurances we didn't need anything else. I kept busy with dousing my fries in ketchup, letting the silence build for a moment. "Can I ask why we can't talk about *us*?"

He held out his hand for the ketchup. "It makes me uncomfortable."

I surrendered the bottle and watched him neatly add it to his burger. "Not getting into details, but what part makes you uncomfortable?"

"All of it."

That didn't make any sense. He took a huge bite of his burger while I struggled with my frustration. Stubborn man.

He reached past me for the salt as I leaned forward for the pepper. His hand brushed the curve of my breast, and he jerked back as if scorched. His gaze locked on his hand, and he sat there frozen.

He hadn't bumped into me hard. No damage done. It'd been an accident. So what was his deal? He continued to...just sit there. I ducked my head trying to make eye contact, but he avoided it.

His reaction to the incident was starting to offend me. "It's a boob," I bit out, annoyed. "I have two of them. They don't do much. They just sit there. They definitely don't bite, so stop acting like they're going to come after you. Grow up."

"Please stop talking about them," he said in a stiff strangled voice.

I didn't let up. "You know, sometimes it helps to name the things you fear. Let's call the right one Everest and the left one

Fuji. Two mountainous ranges waiting to be...." I never finished. He had cleared the restaurant's door in a few furious strides, leaving me sitting alone.

It felt good to get under his skin, to see him react in a way that wasn't calm and confident. It bothered me that it was at my expense. What was so wrong with me that he freaked out at the slightest touch? Other than the fact that some other werewolves wanted to kill me and I had dreams that made me scream loud enough to shake the nearest window...I mean really, who didn't have some kind of baggage?

He didn't go far. My eyes tracked him as he paced back and forth before the restaurant's front windows. His scowl didn't let up, and I didn't feel so frustrated anymore. Smirking, I shook my head and continued eating my fries. He cast an occasional glance in my direction but didn't appear to calm down.

When I finished my fries and burger, I waited until he glanced at me to take a fry from his plate. His steps hesitated and his scowl changed to a frown as, with a challenging smirk, I ate the fry. I reached for his second burger. He stopped pacing and watched me through the window. His focused stare and complete stillness seemed a little spooky. The other patrons cast nervous glances at him.

Slowly, I lifted the burger to my mouth unable to stop my teasing grin. His eyes narrowed, and he reached for the door. I took a huge bite and hastily set the burger back on his plate.

In just a few steps, he stood by the table looking down at me, his expression carefully blank.

"Well? Did you lose your appetite or not?" I asked.

He slid into the opposite seat and pulled his plate toward him, not saying a word. His avoidance hurt a little. He didn't want to talk about us, he didn't want to talk about the trouble that was out there waiting for us, and he didn't want to talk about my boobs—which was pretty much the same as talking about us. As I watched him eat, I had an idea.

"Tell you what. I'll let you have two closed subjects between us. Two topics we'll keep completely off limits. Three is ridiculous." My tone carried a bit of hostility, but I didn't really care.

He closed his eyes, finished swallowing, and sighed.

"So which one are we going to talk about...our plan to reach the Compound, the reason you won't let me Claim you, or my boobs? You choose."

He set his burger on his plate and took a drink. "They will be waiting for us on all three roads. We could try to leave the bike and take to the woods, but I think they will have scouts ready for that as well. And we'd be slower on foot. Our best bet is to anticipate them and break through before they know when to expect us."

"So the longer we take to get there..."

"The more likely they are to be ready for us," he agreed.

After my stunt at the last hotel room, they'd probably caught onto the fact that we knew they were after us.

"Any word from that Elder?" I asked.

"He asked for an update, but I kept it vague. He's not pushing for anything more. He offered his assistance if we needed anything further."

That sounded non-threatening. Perhaps we were wrong about him. Still, I'd rather not take the chance.

"Okay then, wolf-man, let's get going." I waved the waitress over for the bill as he finished in one huge bite. I waited impatiently as he paid and she flirted. Now that he'd admitted what I already knew—they would be waiting for us—I wanted to get going. With relief, I walked out the restaurant door.

"Tired?" he asked before we reached the bike.

"No," I lied. After a day on the bike, I was ready for bed even without the pull of waiting dreams, but I didn't want to delay getting to the Compound.

He turned to glance at me and only shook his head, not believing me. "We can't go far with you tired."

"And if we take too long to get there, it will only be worse." I'd had enough creatures flying out of the trees at me. I didn't want to give them extra time to gather.

"I could call Gabby and let her know."

"No, we don't know who is betraying us."

"You think she would?" he settled on the bike and fully turned toward me tilting his head to study my expression.

"No, she wouldn't. At least, not purposely. But, who does she believe she can trust? She could say something to the wrong person. If we stayed on our own, we might actually make it to the gates of the Compound." I swung my leg over the back and settled behind him offering the strap. "I'll do my best to stay awake," I promised.

TEN

Birdsong and sunlight drifted along the spring breeze that teased my hair. My hair, not someone else's or a past me. I recognized where I stood. It was the meadow of my other dreams. Only, the great stone monoliths had aged and weathered to stunted broken pillars. Was this then a real dream, pointless and meant to be forgotten as soon as I woke? Unsure, I waited for the Taupe Lady to appear.

Nothing moved in the open field surrounding the stones. I turned in a slow circle. The dream felt empty, a shadow of what it should be if it were a memory. Yet, real dreams, the pointless kind, were so rare now. I couldn't believe this was one of them.

"We need to talk," I called out. I wanted to shout my questions and make threats, mostly just to vent, but I held it all in hoping she would come to me if I was nice.

The wind carried her answer to me. "My daughter. Your path is your own to choose. I can influence it no more than I have already done. Remember," she whispered. "Dream."

The dream shifted.

I sat on a bed covered with a light pink quilt and squeezed the teddy bear in my arms as I listened to the footsteps pause outside my door. Using my sight, I checked everyone's location in the house.

Justin had come home for winter break just tonight. I hadn't met him before but had talked to him on the phone. He'd been so nice to me. His mom usually fostered two kids at a time. They had the room, she'd said, in their hearts and in their house. I'd hoped it would be different here. The other foster girl with me didn't really like me, but the other girls usually didn't. Justin, though, had seemed so nice. I'd hoped he would just stay away at school.

When he'd given me a hug in greeting, it had been just a little too tight. When he'd pulled back and looked me in the eye, I knew.

I gently lifted the phone from the receiver with a heavy heart. I'd already disabled the sound so he wouldn't hear me dial from in the hallway. The knob on the door turned, and I quickly set the phone to the side.

"What are you doing, Justin?" I asked calmly as he opened the door.

"I just wanted to check on you," he said with a smile. He stepped in and closed the door behind him.

I clutched the bear tighter. "I'm fine. I think you should leave."

"Don't be like that," he begged softly as he sat on the edge of the bed. "I see you got the bear I sent," he nodded toward the bear I clutched. I'd hoped it would remind him of my age.

"How old are you?" I asked.

"Twenty-one. Why are you asking?" He smiled and reached a hand to smooth over my hair.

"Because I'm twelve, and you shouldn't be touching me. Not

even my hair."

He sighed and dropped his hand, his eyes growing puzzled. Then he nodded slowly. "You're right. I'm sorry. Good night, Gabby." He leaned forward with the intent of kissing me. I dodged out of the way, bumping the table that held the phone.

"Don't," I warned. "Justin, I like your mom, but with you here, I can't stay."

The door to my room opened, and Justin's mom looked from me to her son. Her face was white with shock, and she loosely held a phone in her hand. Justin looked at her phone, then the phone on the table by my bed.

"What are you doing in here?"

He scowled. "Nothing."

His mom's eyes shifted to me.

"It's time I leave," I said softly. She nodded and dialed the phone.

The dream shifted.

My foster dad leaned over my chair, his arm brushing against my breast as he served me mashed potatoes. I met the eyes of my foster mom at the end of the table. Her eyes filled with tears, and she looked away. After dinner, I rushed to the phone and dialed a number I knew by heart.

The dream shifted.

Alixe and I had gotten on well for three months before services called asking if she could take on another teen. She assured them I was an angel and that she would have no trouble adding another. When she hung up, she told me that Brandon would be joining our happy home. I tried not to show my disappointment. I asked his age. Fourteen, same as me. Maybe that would make a difference.

We worked together to make the single bed in the third room. She told me to let her know if there was any trouble. Brandon came to the door an hour later. He stood with his head down trying to hide his face. His swollen eye and nose told his story better than his slumped shoulders and dirty clothes.

Alixe coaxed him in and spoke with the officer dropping him off. The boy's abuse was clear. Still, when he risked a look up and met my eyes, I saw a change in him. A small one. He glanced back down quickly, but the slump in his shoulders was gone.

The next morning, I woke with him standing beside my bed, staring at me.

"Why do I feel like this?" he whispered to me, close to tears. His hands shook. I wanted to cry, too. I wished I knew why the men around me acted as they did...why they couldn't just leave me alone.

"If you ignore me, it will help," I whispered back. He nodded but didn't move.

Finally, he sighed, wiped at his tears, and winced when he touched the swollen skin. Then he left.

I sat with Alixe at the breakfast table after he'd eaten and left the room.

"He needs help," I said softly. She nodded, looking sad. "I don't think me being here will help him. He needs you more than I do. Please. Call services. Let them know we talked, and I need a new home so you can focus on Brandon."

The dream shifted.

I sat at the dinner table across from an older man, warily keeping an eye on him as he ate with gusto. It was my third night in his house and so far everything had gone great. I didn't let myself get too hopeful, though. My faith in men hadn't held up well after my experiences with foster care and school.

He forked in the last bite of spaghetti and meat sauce—more sauce than meat—from his plate and sat back with a sigh. He frowned at my plate. "I know it's not much," he said.

I shook my head. "Sam, it's fine. I'm just not that hungry." I eyed the huge mound of noodles on my plate.

He glanced at my plate, too, and grinned. "I'll remember to cut the serving back next time," he promised. I agreed and rose to put the rest into a container and wash my dishes. He stood and waited for his turn at the sink. He kept a respectful distance between us.

When I was about to leave the room with my school bag, he called my name. I glanced back at him. He looked a little lost as he met my gaze. "You'll tell me if you need something, right? Lunch money or a ride to the mall?"

I nodded wondering what he really meant with this unusual line of questioning. He must have sensed my confusion because he sighed and gave a self-deprecating smile. "Cubs are easy. Feed them, give them your time, and they are happy. You don't need much food, and you prefer to be alone. I don't know how to raise a human. A human girl is even more," he waved his hand at me, "confusing."

A tiny smile crept onto my face seeing him so flustered. Living with a werewolf already beat living with any foster family, except maybe the last one. My smile faded, and I felt a tad lonely for Barb.

"If I need anything, I'll let you know." I turned and left the kitchen.

The dreams stopped. Darkness claimed me for a moment

before *her* voice floated in.

"Every moment you live offers you a chance to learn. Your experiences and your reactions to them make you who you are. Who are you, daughter? And what have you learned?

The dreams started again. I didn't struggle against them, wanting to know more about what I faced.

My stepfather, Richard, looked pale as Blake suggested I take the children outside to play. At just over a year, my brother couldn't really play outside yet, and the baby shouldn't be in the sun. I knew that from my mom. My eyes watered thinking of her. We'd just had her funeral a few days ago.

Regardless, Richard told me to take them both outside. One of Blake's friends followed us out. Either Blake or one of his associates had been with us since Mom died. I didn't really like any of them. Mostly because Mom hadn't. Aden fussed, and I gently set him against my shoulder, rocking him side to side.

"Shut that kid up," the man with us growled.

I frowned at him but started whispering to the baby, trying anyway.

"Bring the older one back," Blake called from inside.

The man strode over and for a moment, I thought he would grab me. Then he reached down and plucked Liam up by his tiny little arm. Liam screamed and just dangled there not understanding.

"Stop!" I yelled, trying to reach for Liam while still holding Aden. The man held him away and went inside. I raced after him, holding Aden tight.

Richard sat at the table crying, his face in his hands, not even looking at his son.

"Set him down," Blake ordered. His eyes remained on me. I

*thought he meant Aden, and I clutched him tighter. But his friend
set Liam down. "That's not how you carry a child," Blake said to
the man. His voice held little censor. He squatted before Liam,
who sat in a sobbing heap on the floor.*

*"You do love your brothers, don't you, Michelle." He patted
Liam on the head and stood again. "I'll be helping your father for
a while, until he's on his feet again."*

*I briefly glanced at Richard, not correcting Blake. He wasn't
my father, but he'd loved my mom very much. If he felt half the
pain I did, I understood how he felt.*

*"I'm sorry for your loss," Blake said evenly before turning
toward Richard. "The contractors will start work this afternoon.
We need to keep you all safe."*

The dream shifted.

*I sat in the boys' room playing quietly with them. The stifling
sterile room echoed back even their quietest whispers, but this
was the only place in the house that they were allowed to play.
The easiest place to monitor us—me.*

Richard strode through the door with purpose.

*"The last tip did marginally well. Blake would like to thank
you and asked me to find out what you would like as a reward."*

*This was Blake's game. Every time one of my premonitions
did well—they all did well—Blake offered a reward. In the
beginning, I had used these opportunities to ask for new toys for
my brothers or new clothes for us or even to be allowed a few
minutes outside. But I'd caught on to what I was doing. Each
time I asked for something, I let them know what mattered to
me. Last night, Blake had proven my theory correct by
threatening to take all outside time away from the boys if I didn't
sit down and eat with him and his associates.*

"Please tell him I am happy with whatever reward he chooses," I murmured without looking up from our puzzle.

"Michelle, he will insist that you choose," Richard said with worry in his voice. It was the first time in a long time he'd acted human. I glanced up in time to see his fear-filled eyes rest on Liam.

He feared for their safety. So did I. I needed to find a way to escape. Until then, I would pretend to play Blake's game. "A ribbon. For my hair, please."

The dream shifted.

A gag covered my mouth as tears streamed down my cheeks. The gag didn't hurt. The cord tying my hands didn't even hurt. My head though, it throbbed and ached, the pain dull and sharp at the same time, snaking its way through every cell in my brain as the premonition repeated itself.

Blake stood over me smirking.

"I told you, you would be punished if you tried to run." He bent down to where I'd fallen to my side on the floor. The premonition had been running through my mind for almost two days. They'd let me eat and drink in the beginning, unbinding my hands and removing the gag, while they wore earplugs and earmuffs with music. They'd tried getting me to eat and drink a while ago, but I refused. The pain was too much.

I sniffled as my nose started to run. My eyes had been watering for hours now. Blake reached forward and touched the wetness just under my nose. He pulled back and showed me his fingers. It wasn't just a runny nose. Blood smeared his fingertips.

"Do you understand, yet? You need me, Michelle. Who else can you tell this information to?"

I closed my eyes with a sob, wishing the pain would end.

Behind the gag, I moved my lips weakly, mumbling the information because I couldn't help myself.

The cord holding my wrists together loosened. Without thought, my shaking hand flew to my mouth to tear away the gag. I sobbed out the information, and the pain immediately stopped. I didn't stop sobbing for a long time.

Luke called my name, and I struggled to wake as I felt the dream try to shift. I didn't want to remember any more. I wanted my own reality back. As crappy as it was. Someone pounded on a door, helping to pull me out of sleep's hold.

I blinked my eyes open, cringing at the cold water hitting my face as I looked up into the spray of the showerhead. It took me a moment to remember what had happened. Tired after a few more hours of riding, we'd found yet another hotel. He said he'd run and get food. I said I would take a shower. I'd kept it cold thinking I'd stay awake. Instead, I'd set myself up for hypothermia.

I shivered uncontrollably and wiped water from my face. My numb legs didn't want to move and my tailbone throbbed painfully.

"She's trying to kill me," I muttered as I struggled to lift myself from the bottom of the tub.

The door flew open with a crack, disturbing the air and making the shower curtain flutter. It stuck to my skin, and I curled my lip. Gross. Hotel shower curtain. Touching me. I frantically batted it away thinking of all the nasty things on it—and once my mind was on the subject, all the nasty things at the bottom of the hotel tub—when the curtain was suddenly torn aside.

Luke stared down at me. Rage and panic filled his eyes.

(Un)wise

"What the hell?" I sputtered trying to grab the curtain and cover myself, no longer so picky about it touching me. Red crept up his neck as I watched.

Flustered, he let the curtain go, but he still had the sense to reach around to turn off the water. His eyes raked my face. "You fell asleep again, didn't you?" he asked with soft reproach.

"Of course I did! I *always* fall asleep. Now, get out!" Embarrassment and anger warred for dominance. It was one thing to joke about us, to try to Claim him, and to kid about my boobs. But, to have him actually *see* me? All of me? I wanted to curl up in a ball of shame. I didn't eat right and looked like hell. The scars on my arms still stood out vividly which was why I wore clothes to cover them. And he'd seen *everything*. I'd noted the shock in his eyes before he surrendered the curtain.

"Be out in two minutes, or I'm coming back in," he warned, closing the door behind him.

"If you come back in, you better be naked too," I shouted at the closed door, anger finally winning.

With shaking limbs, I pulled myself from the tub and wrapped myself in a towel. I used the other towel—the one meant for Luke—to dry my hair. Those dreams shook me. The first three had been the same girl. Gabby. No doubt the same Gabby Luke kept talking about. The second set of dreams also involved a single star. Michelle. Their lives sucked just like mine. It didn't make me feel any better.

Taking my time, I brushed my teeth and gradually warmed enough that the blue tint faded from my lips. More than two minutes had passed, and I gave myself a weak smirk in the mirror.

Pulling my bag close, I dug for clean clothes. Not finding

any, I settled for the cleanest. I took my time getting dressed.

Finally, I stepped out of the bathroom. I ran my fingers through my damp tangled hair and gave him the barest glance before I moved to the hotel's TV guide, pretending to read it.

"Either we get where we're going tomorrow, or we need to find a laundromat. Everything's dirty," I commented.

Silence greeted me. Stifling the urge to scrunch up my face in annoyance, I took a calming breath and turned to face him.

Luke reclined on the bed, his hands behind his head, as he watched me move around the room. His shirt stretched tight over his chest. I struggled to pull my gaze away. His exposed arms flexed as he moved one out from behind his head. On the inside, I sighed.

"Come on," he said, waving me over. "Get some sleep."

He knew sleeping in a cold shower didn't qualify as rest, but I hadn't expected him to be on the bed waiting for me after my smart remark. I shuffled to the bed in my stocking feet and lay beside him, not too eager to sleep just yet.

He pulled me to his side, slid an arm under my head, and tucked me under his chin. His heat melted away the lingering chill of the shower. His willingness to get so close while I was still awake puzzled me—he usually waited until I was already slipping into a dream. He lightly ran a hand down my covered arm. Right over the cuts I'd once made in desperation. I closed my eyes in shame.

"Don't," he whispered. "Not with me. I'm not here to judge you. I'm here to keep you safe. Always. Even from yourself."

His arm tightened around me. This time I dove for the dream tugging at my consciousness. Anything to escape the little tug at my heart his words caused.

(Un)wise

We left the room several hours later. I didn't think he'd slept at all, but I had five hours of sweet nothing—well, not nothing. I'd woken to my face plastered to his bare chest. Best five hours of sleep ever.

"We should reach the Compound by nightfall."

When we stepped into the parking lot, Luke's stride paused. He tilted his head back, scented the light breeze, grabbed my hand, and pulled me toward the bike. I didn't stop to wonder why. He'd smelled something. I quickly slipped the bag across my body and climbed on behind him as my eyes searched for the cause. Luke started the bike with a roar.

Just then, two men stepped from the office. My heart leapt, and my arms involuntarily tightened around Luke. He took off with a squeal of the back tire. The bike slipped under us a bit, but I risked a look back. Where the men had stood, two large dogs stared after us. They didn't give chase. Instead, they turned and ran into the woods.

"They're not following," I called to Luke.

He nodded and opened the throttle. My stomach rolled at the surge in speed. Thankfully, I hadn't eaten anything.

We merged with an interstate that took us south, not north. I wanted to moan in frustration, but understood his decision. Since we were so close to our goal, they would know our intended direction. Hopping on the interstate would throw them off. Heck, it threw me off. I had no idea which way we intended to come in from.

How had they found us though? We'd been careful, zigzagging all over the place in a non-pattern. I'd been watching the map. Maybe Luke was right. They had sentinels waiting for us. But we were still so many miles away. Could they have so many in their pack as that? I doubted it. Maybe it'd just been luck. Or maybe, he'd told someone again. I rested my head against his back, emotionally drained. I'd fluctuated between "just let me die" and "I don't want to die" too many times to count. I didn't know what I wanted anymore except to be left alone. I had never asked to be in the middle of a werewolf tug of war.

We drove for hours the wrong way and then got off at an exit heading east so we could circle back around. Despite his efforts, I knew it would be pointless. Like he'd said, they would be waiting—because somehow, they always seemed to know where to expect us. I knew what I needed to do.

When he offered to stop, I pointed to a laundromat. He nodded and pulled in. He loosened the bag, and I slid off, taking the bag with me. His troubled gaze never wavered from me as he followed me into the light airy building.

He used the change machine as I shoved everything in a washer. After adding quarters and dumping in the powder detergent from the packet I'd bought at the vending machine, I finally faced him. He eyed me warily. Apparently his wolfie senses knew something was up. I let out a long, slow breath, calmed myself, and let the beginning of a dream wrap its arms around me—not enough to sleep, just enough to slow my pulse. I had to mask a lie.

"I saw a fast food place a few blocks away. I'll get us something."

He frowned at me. "I'll go with."

"No way. We'll lose our stuff. It's two blocks away and we're in the middle of town," I arched a brow at him and patted the bag I still had slung over my shoulder. "I have protection and can carry everything with this. Two burgers?"

"Three," he grumped reaching into his wallet and giving me a twenty. We'd used all the money he'd given me for rooms along the way.

I plucked it from his fingers with a smile. "Probably a good idea," I agreed. "You may not have fries by the time I walk back."

He smiled at me as he sat down to watch the machine.

I strode out the door, turned right, and didn't look back. Not far away, I flagged down a ride and asked them if they could take me north. Staring out the window, trying to ignore the ache growing in my chest, I watched the mile markers go by.

* * * *

My jaw popped on my third yawn. The couple had taken me over an hour north. They dropped me off and wished me luck. I smiled and waved as they pulled away. My stomach grumbled, and I thought of the twenty in my pocket. I still had a long way to go; and with no Luke, I needed to save the cash for when I really needed it.

Going into the gas station, I used the restroom and drank from the water fountain. The clerk watched me in the convenience mirror. Apparently my days of looking like a runaway weren't over. I ignored him and headed out the door to begin my long trek—the gas station hadn't had anyone who'd looked willing enough to give me a ride. Plus, the clerk would have probably called it in.

I trudged north for an hour, lost in my thoughts of this life and past lives. Why had the Taupe Lady directed my dreams to Gabby and Michelle's pasts? Why in order? And why couldn't I recall all the details like I could with other past lives? Because they weren't dead yet? It made sense. How could I remember everything when everything hadn't yet occurred? Why direct my dreams at all, though? She claimed she couldn't interfere, but then did just that, hadn't she?

Something had me lifting my head instead of watching my feet. The trees around me had lost their leaves, and I could once again see my breath in the air. I huddled in Luke's jacket and wondered if he'd figured it out yet.

A twig snapped, and a group of three men stepped from the woods onto the shoulder in front of me. Steam rose from their skin. Shorts provided their only covering. Their smiles froze my insides. My feet stopped moving, but my mind whirred with possibilities. Distract and run!

"He went that way," I called pointing to my left. They all turned, and I sprinted to the right, crashing into the trees and ignoring the bite of the branches as they whipped my face.

Eleven

I ran. They toyed with me. With their speed, I knew they could catch me at any moment. But what fun would that be, I thought bitterly. The echoes of past lives hit me. Same game, same chase. My anger grew, fueling my legs. I pushed past the pain and kept moving. Just like my dreams, I sought something. A place to jump. A way to die cleanly. They couldn't have me. The price for the world was too high.

A coughing laugh from behind me signaled their full transformation. I dodged around trees gasping for air, not slowing. Was it too much to ask for a random cliff in the woods every now and again?

Fear pooled in my stomach as my leg failed with a cramp. I fell hard but didn't lay in a pathetic heap for more than a heartbeat. I got my knees under me and as I sprang up, I thrust my hand into my bag, which was still slung across my body. My quick moves didn't matter. They were already upon me, their panting louder than my own as they laughed.

Pulling my hand from the bag, I surprised them with my knife. My gift from Luke. I felt a pang thinking of him. Leaving hadn't kept me any safer.

One of the men shifted back enough to speak, but his mouth was still too long for the words to come out clearly. "What do you think to do with that?"

Around us the trees remained quiet. Only the distant chirping of birds reminded me I wasn't alone.

"What did you hope to accomplish by chasing me?" I countered.

"Blake told us you would know. You're the dreamer," he said further shifting into a man.

"Your new leader?" I asked while willing myself to breathe deeply and trying to quell my fear.

They didn't answer but it didn't matter. Their leader changed each cycle, but their goals did not.

"If I'm the dreamer, then we all know the outcome," I said. "Walk away and maybe I'll live for another day."

"I don't think so, little girl," he said as he eyed my knife.

"I'd hoped history wouldn't repeat itself this time. I'm tired of dying." The fear left me. Only sorrow remained as I spun the knife deftly and plunged it toward my soft middle.

The man roared and moved before the tip did more than pierce the surface. I'd underestimated their speed. But, when he batted it out of my hands, he didn't realize he furthered my cause. A thin trail of fire blazed across my middle, superficial at best, but his nostrils flared as he scented my blood. I shifted my stance, bracing myself.

He growled but didn't touch me further. We stood facing each other with me slightly bent holding an arm against the sting on my stomach. The other two stood several paces behind their spokesperson.

"Come with us on your own and spare yourself some pain."

Spare myself pain? He had just acknowledged I remembered my—our—past lives. "Stupid dog," I laughed.

He cuffed me upside the head, knocking me to my side. I staggered but did not fall. It hurt my cut but brought me closer to my knife. I didn't look at the shining blade resting on the decaying leaves. Instead, I straightened and faced him again.

"Your brain mustn't have expanded again with that last shift."

This time he slapped me. It was hard enough to justify a stumble a few more steps to my right.

"See?" I managed on a pain-filled exhale. "Pain is all you know how to give. There won't be any sparing of anything but kindness and mercy."

He snorted. "Mercy is for the weak."

"No. Mercy is for anyone with a big enough vocabulary to —"

I didn't get to finish the insult. He knocked me hard. The side of my face exploded in agony as I went down. This time, right on the knife. I laughed like a madwoman as I lay there. No one moved to touch me again. Were they trying to figure out what was so funny? It didn't matter. I'd reached my goal. They wouldn't have me this time.

Putting my arms under myself, I palmed the handle and stood, hiding my weapon behind my back, trying to angle the blade for my next fall.

"Stupid," I taunted.

Before he could move, something big and dark flew toward one of the beasts, knocking it into a tree. I didn't take my eyes from the man in front of me, but it looked like another one of them, half transformed.

The attention of the one in front of me didn't waver, either. As soon as one of his own hit the tree, he immediately grabbed for me. I slashed out with the knife, taking him by surprise. The wild swing relieved him of a not quite human digit. He screamed as behind him another member of his pack flew at the new attacker.

The wolf before me ignored the blood dripping from his hand and crouched slightly, watching me closely. His injury had wiped his patronizingly amused expression from his face. Tense, he hesitated, unsure how to come at me.

I grinned at him. "Stupid and slow. A bad combination in a fight."

His lip curled back in a silent snarl a moment before he lunged toward me. I swung the knife up and over in a diagonal slash that caught his chest and part of his face when he pulled back. My arm ached from the force I'd used. I knew I wouldn't take him by surprise again. Or could I?

He lunged once more, but this time I did not swing for him. I brought the knife up to my own neck. Seeing the edge poised at my throat, he suddenly flew backwards, away from me. The move gave me a clear view of who'd joined the fight.

Luke, shifted to a mix of more wolf than man, held my tormentor by the throat. The man's flesh bulged between Luke's fingers. The man flailed but didn't make a sound. He couldn't. Luke spun, putting his back to me at the same time his arm twitched. A loud popping crack sounded. The man stilled.

In the silence, I caught a distant sound of drumming feet hitting the ground. My shoulders slumped and the unfurling hope within me quickly withered. Too many this time.

Luke tossed the dead man aside and pivoted toward the

sound. His strong back shielded me from the horde racing toward us. For just a moment, I rested my forehead against the solid wall of him. I breathed deeply smelling his sweat and soap. He didn't move. His focus remained on the oncoming pack. He would die for me. My chest tightened, and I struggled with my next inhale. I didn't want that. But I knew he wouldn't leave.

The drumming grew louder. Branches snapped as the wolves forced their way toward us. A howl rent the air.

How had I been so stubbornly stupid? In a way, I still was. Too afraid to admit, even to myself, how much I cared for the man standing in front of me. I'd squandered any chance for happiness—no matter how brief—in this life. I hoped the memory of Luke and how I felt for him would give me more courage in the next one. Courage to trust. Courage to see the truth. He wasn't one of them.

"I will hold the memory of you in my heart forever," I managed to say before a single tear rolled down my cheek. That's all I had time for. I hoped he knew what he meant to me. Straightening, I flipped the knife so the handle was clasped in my hand, but the blade along my forearm angled outward. I hoped it would be harder to knock out of my hand that way.

As the first of them erupted from the underbrush, Luke spun out with his claws, slashing through the wolf's soft underbelly. Its sharp cry pierced the air and signaled the start of madness.

I braced myself, ready for anything, but nothing broke through Luke's guard with the first wave. He knocked body after body back, eviscerating those he could. Blood soaked the ground, but he held firm.

A movement away from the main attack caught my attention. I looked away from the carnage to see several sneaking around us. Turning, I stood with my back to Luke.

I stood in a bloodied field. Bodies littered the ground around me, but still more came. I moved like water, bending and flowing over the mass that would kill me, anger fueling me. I had no claws, but the knives struck them just as well.

The vision slammed into me, then left me as I blinked at the dogs who'd come several steps closer. The echo of that epic battle burrowed into my mind and wouldn't let go. I could *fight*. Loosening my stance, I slightly bent my knees, ready on the balls of my feet. I could do better than a lucky swing that might claim a finger. I could *kill*. Adrenaline surged through me. I looked at the numbers around us and doubted it would be enough.

The first one crept toward me, and I felt Luke shift behind me.

"Focus on your side," I said as I moved like water once again, but for the first time in this life. Wide stance...lean to the side and sweep the arm out as you move, I thought. The blade slid through flesh and bumped bone. I pulled the blade back and shifted my weight to the other side to kick out, knocking the shocked beast to the side.

I grinned. *I got this!* Using my muscles in ways they had never been used in this lifetime, I continued sweeping and slashing my blade. The sharp edge bit into the fur covered flesh of three of them before they partially shifted. They didn't want to kill me so their fangs and claws had less use than opposable thumbs. Still, I had an advantage for a while. Then, I noticed some of the cuts I'd made starting to knit together. I needed to do more than wound. My mind knew the moves, but my untrained body often fell short on delivery.

Soon their anger over my continued slices had them striking

harder. Aches formed where they'd managed to sneak through my guard and hit me. Those punishing blows were meant to wear me down. It worked.

An attacker caught my arm and pulled me forward as something bumped into me from behind, off balancing me so I fell toward my attacker's chest. I face planted into the disgustingly wet furred chest then felt a blow vibrate through his body. He jerked oddly. His grip loosened. I pulled back and looked up at his face as he let go. Bile rose to my throat at the sight of the bloody stump of his neck. He fell to the side. I swallowed heavily and looked for the next attacker.

Fewer stood before me than there'd been a moment ago. And those still around me had shifted their attention from me to Luke. Risking a quick glance, I saw why.

Several jumped on him at once, weighing him down as they grappled with his swinging arms. The remaining men joined in, knowing as I did, that if they brought Luke down, they would have me. None of them paid me any attention, now.

Luke's tendons stood out with strain as he continued to struggle. An attacker bit into Luke's neck and held on. Luke didn't have time to shake the man before another attacker flew at him. No one noticed that I had shifted my focus to the wolf still attached to him. I flipped the blade in my hand and threw it. It sank into the biter's side. The man grunted but didn't loosen his hold. Luke gripped another man's head, twisted the man's neck savagely, then turned to the next attacker before the body fell. But Luke's movements were slow and sluggish because of the man whose teeth still pierced him.

I stepped forward and pulled the handle of my knife, now stuck in the man's middle, up until the blade resisted. The man, screaming in pain, let go. Luke continued to fight. I stepped back, flowing into my ready stance, waiting. The sounds of Luke's struggles faded to the background as I maintained my focus. Rage and retribution filled the man's gaze. His claws elongated, his fingers receding to make room for their full length. With a snarl, he reached for me. But he didn't move far. Luke sent his last attacker flying, then twisted to address the man I faced. He raked the man, gutting him in a spray of blood, from groin to throat.

Looking away, I scanned the area around us, the trees, the undergrowth, searching for more. The thud of the man's body falling to the ground heralded a harsh kind of silence.

Luke's ragged breaths blended with mine, the only noise filling the air. Nothing moved. The animals around us remained silent. Then, a single bird chirped. My eyes flew to Luke's. He too remained partially crouched. But nothing happened.

We'd done it.

I slowly straightened, wincing at the various little pains that tingled into my awareness. My wounds didn't concern me as much as Luke's did. Blood painted his clothes and dotted his half-transformed face. I bent and grabbed a shirt from the bag. With each breath, his features settled back into the man I knew. Except his eyes. They stayed dilated, overly large and completely focused on me. I started shaking from too much adrenaline and nothing to use it on. Or maybe shock. Who knew?

He took two steps forward, plucked the knife from my hand, and dropped it to the ground. Anger remained in his eyes. His jaw muscles twitched rhythmically. His neck bled from the bite, but he didn't seem to notice.

I shrugged out of his jacket and stripped out of the hoodie

so I could use it to press against the wound. He jerked slightly at my touch and placed a hand on my waist.

In an unexpected move, he snagged the hem of my shirt with a finger and lifted it high enough to see the slice across my stomach. I'd forgotten about that. His attention brought the pain back into focus. It hurt. He glanced at the cut and then dropped the hem, his eyes devouring me again. His hand stayed on my side, warm and comforting. He stepped close.

He still looked mad, and the lingering signs of his shift unnerved me. Yet, I kept pressure on the bite. I couldn't afford a passed out werewolf. My hand continued to tremble, and he reached up to close his hand around mine. I wondered how much his bite hurt. Still staring at his neck, he surprised me when he leaned forward to rest his forehead against mine. My gaze flew to his, but he had closed his eyes. He breathed deeply, then released my hand. Gently, he wrapped his arms around me and pulled me to him. His mouth brushed my hair. The hug started out light but grew tighter until I squeaked involuntarily in pain.

His arms loosened, and he pulled back enough that I could see his face. His anguish. His frustration.

"Don't," he started saying, but his voice broke and he had to stop. He swallowed hard and briefly closed his eyes. When he opened them again, his look made my heart turnover. Need. Desperate need flooded the hazel beauty of the eyes I'd come to know so well.

He leaned in, lifted a hand, and slid his fingers through my hair. His gaze followed the movement which started at my temple and ended with his fingers cupping the back of my head. Despite the pains, my stomach went crazy and my settling pulse leapt. Then, he did the same with his other hand. He held me gently, studying every inch of my face. He leaned in further, moving closer until his lips hovered over mine. My heartbeat tripled its already exhaustive efforts.

"Don't ever try to tell me goodbye again," he warned in a thick voice. "We're not done yet."

He closed the minute gap separating us, crushing his lips against mine. He set fire to my thoughts and burned away all my pain with his touch. I forgot to breathe. His fingers held me still as he tilted his head and demanded more, needing the affirmation that we were both still alive. The teasing patient man was gone. With his mouth, he claimed me in a way I'd thought he hadn't wanted, a way he'd hidden from me. I lifted my hands to his shoulders holding him in return, not wanting this to stop. I kissed him back, finally sure fate knew what the heck it was doing.

The desperation began to fade, and I felt faint when he tore his lips from mine. He didn't relinquish his hold though. As I gasped for air, he kept my senses spinning wildly with soft kisses to my cheek. My jaw. My neck. Tingles raced over me at the first touch of his lips on my neck. His lips softened and returned to skim my own with small little kisses that started a yearning in me. A yearning I well understood from previous lives.

Too soon he pulled back, leaving me shaking, and my breaths coming out in hot little clouds. Without his attention, the cold wrapped around me, and the pain crept back in. I wrapped an arm protectively over my middle. His pupils shrank while I watched, and a twinge of regret crept in with the change.

"I'm sorry," he apologized gruffly, looking away. I reached out a hand to comfort him and whatever he felt sorry about.

None of this was his fault. The burden of guilt laid solely on me. I shouldn't have tried walking away.

"That won't happen again," he spoke slowly, his jaw muscles clenching. Then he looked at me with promise burning in his eyes. "Until you're eighteen."

My mouth popped open, and I made a choking sound while my brain tried to come up with the words to articulate my feelings.

"And don't ever try hurting yourself again," he growled.

"Are you kidding me?" I half-yelled, half-gasped, completely ignoring his reprimand as the shock of finally understanding his standoffish attitude toward me wore off, and my brain started functioning again. "That's the problem? We almost just *died*. We almost lost a chance for an us," I flailed a hand back and forth between us, "and you're worried about how old I am?"

"Bethi."

"Don't Bethi me," I hissed. "First stop, I'm molesting your butt, and you're going to like it!" We both felt the pull, we both had feelings for each other, and I suffered dream after dream because the timing wasn't right for him? What did he think a few months would do for us?

I picked my blade up from the ground before the literal meaning of what I'd just said sank in. Luke's smirk didn't help cool my temper. I stomped off—as much as I could with a gigantic cut decorating my stomach and aches in places I hadn't known I possessed—in the direction I hoped led toward his bike. I slayed small saplings and maimed trees in my wrath. He trailed behind me, wisely remaining quiet.

"How did you find me?" I asked after I cooled down.

"Your scent." After a moment of silence, he asked, "Why

did you leave?"

I let out a slow breath. "That's not important anymore. I won't leave again." Not even when he frustrated the heck out of me. Now that I knew his reasons, I'd stick to him like glue. "How long until we reach the Compound? This is only going to get worse."

"Tomorrow."

I glanced at him and met his troubled gaze. I reached out and clasped his hand. He let me, twining his fingers through mine.

*   *   *   *

When we reached the bike, we both stared at each other. The gore on him was too much to possibly be real. Ugh! I'd kissed that.

He studied me just as intently. Untangling his fingers from mine, he reached up to brush a hand gently along my cheek. "You're pale," he commented. "And you're still bleeding. We need to get that looked at."

I didn't move. "Or you could just take us to a hotel, I could clean up and you could help me with some gauze and tape." He looked like he was about to argue so I added, "We can't afford the questions a hospital would ask."

He reluctantly nodded and moved toward the bike.

"We can't ride around with you looking like that," I said, stopping him.

"What do you suggest?"

I pointed to the nearby marsh, which had a thin layer of ice over the water it offered.

His lips twitched. "You're liking this, aren't you?"

"I'll get Tinker Bell ready. And you better hurry. Who knows what's still headed in this direction."

He snorted, but got back off the bike and pulled his shirt over his head. The muscles in his back rippled as he tossed the shirt aside. I fought not to sigh. I was liking this. Far too much.

Twelve

Fortunately, the Tinker Bell pajamas were unnecessary. He had most of our clean laundry—including a pair of pants for himself—in his saddlebags.

He washed while I stood shivering on the gravel shoulder. I pretended the shivers were a reaction to his muscled back flexing each time he bent to rinse away more blood. In reality, exhaustion had claimed its due. The sprint through the trees, the fight, and the blood loss took their toll. Dreams whispered to me, and the insistency of them depressed me. What more could I possibly learn other than more pain and death? And sadly, I didn't have the strength to wrestle Luke down and Claim him, like I'd threatened to, to stop them.

Standing in the cold facing the inevitable, I just wanted to get on the bike, wrap my arms around his waist, and let them have me. I knew he wouldn't like me sleeping while we drove, but I didn't want to delay getting to the Compound by stopping at one more hotel and falling asleep there. It just increased the chances of another run-in with the others.

He doused his hair one more time and turned toward me as he shook the water from it. Sunlight glinted off the droplets that flew. Rivulets ran down his chest. Steam rolled off him. When he turned still dripping water, his eyes roamed over my face for a moment. Concern crept into his eyes as his gaze flicked to the arm I held to my middle. I didn't try to straighten or pull it away. The cut hurt. I couldn't hide that. But it wouldn't stop my determination to push on.

"If we drive straight through, how long 'til we get there?"

"If nothing happens? Ten to twelve hours depending on the roads we take."

"We need to push through. I can't take another run in," I said. He opened his mouth to argue. "No, Luke," I sighed before he spoke. "I can't. I'm done. Do you get it? Just, *done*." I hurt too much physically, and I had the depressing knowledge that I would hurt more in the near future due to the dreams. I lacked the optimism to fool myself into believing we'd make it through what waited.

He strode over to me with an intense light in his eyes. Both hands gripped my arms lightly. He gave them a gentle squeeze and then pulled me to his chest, hugging me close despite the arm still wrapped protectively around my stomach. His lips grazed my hair, and he laid his cheek on top my head.

"Don't give up," he whispered. "Not now."

He held me for a moment. I soaked up the comfort and the heat he radiated. I really wanted everything to be okay. I just knew we were in too deep for it to be that way.

"We need to get moving," I said. "Every minute we stay in one place, the more likely they are to find us again."

He pulled back and lifted my chin so my eyes met his. We studied each other for several minutes. His eyes expressed more than his words because his worry and fear shone there. "We'll get there," he promised.

He wanted my acknowledgement, but I wouldn't lie. Instead, my gaze drifted down to his lips. The memory of his kiss started my heart thumping in a heavy rhythm. I didn't want to think about the Compound, the journey there, or the men who'd be waiting to attack us. I wanted to lose myself in the way he made me feel just one more time.

My other arm took on a life of its own and drifted from my side to his back. The heat of his skin warmed my cold fingers as I traced the ridges on his muscles.

"Bethi," he begged. "Don't."

His stupid, misguided moral compass was a pain in my butt. "Don't what? Don't think of how that kiss felt? Don't wish that you'd let your guard down enough to let it happen again so I can forget everything else and imagine a world where just you and I exist? A safe place where I can sleep without haunting dreams? A place where men don't chase me down and cut me? Yeah, I better not. Reality and morals are way better, anyway."

I pulled away from him and walked toward the bike. He hesitated a moment and then followed. He didn't leave me waiting long or remind me that I'd technically cut myself. I dug through the bag and handed him a clean shirt without looking at him. I couldn't. I'd start drooling and become more bitter. It didn't matter. The memory of his pecs and his muscled shoulders...I sighed and eased my leg over the bike settling behind him.

I flung the strap of my bag over his head and wrapped my arms around his waist. No air existed between us. My cheek pressed against his back. I closed my eyes even as he warned me not to fall asleep.

"Just get us there before I bleed out. And don't stop because I fall asleep. Just nudge me or something."

He pulled off the gravel shoulder with ease. A chill wind whipped my hair around my face. Even with the layers I wore, I'd freeze by the time we got to our destination. Only a werewolf would bring a motorcycle for a human in November.

We drove north pushing straight toward our destination, forgoing the erratic back road routes. We met up with a group of five other riders on motorcycles. I smiled at one before lying my head back down on Luke's back. We would draw less attention with others.

Penny grabbed the toy from my hand and hit me.

"It's mine," she yelled, her face turning red.

It wasn't her toy. It had been lying on the ground when we'd both arrived at the park. Her mother tried reasoning with Penny, but Penny swung out a hand and hit her mother's face. Her mother, shocked by her daughter's sudden tantrum, didn't move to stop the second swing.

I liked Mrs. Hught and didn't want to see Penny hit her anymore. "Stop." I said it softly, but clearly, pushing the thought and the inaction toward Penny. Penny's arms dropped to her side. Her face grew even redder, and she turned to glare at me.

She knew what I could do and had made me promise never to do it to her. It was a promise I had to break.

"You can't hit your mommy," I tried to explain.

"I can do anything I want," she screeched at me. But we both knew that wasn't true. The hatred in her eyes burned me, and I released her will.

She turned away from me, threw her arms around her mother's neck, and cried. "I want to go home," she sobbed. "I don't want Charlene to have a sleepover anymore."

I emerged from the dream slightly when Luke reached around to push me toward the center of his back. I'd slid to the side, dangerously unbalancing us. Shivering, I sank right back into the next waiting dream.

Sitting at the long black counter in biology class, I tried to ignore Penny's quiet mutterings from the table behind me. We hadn't been friends since first grade, which suited me fine. Middle school had killed any lingering traces of friendship. For two and a half years, she'd tormented me, spread rumors, and caused me nothing but trouble.

I'd been pulled into the counselor's office at least twice a week for the last three months to discuss the malicious relationship we had. The school was just trying to cover themselves in a bullying case, but I had sat there and listened to Penny's pathetic explanations for the rumors she'd started.

Something hit the back of my head. I turned as I reached back to feel my hair. Gum. Penny didn't meet my eyes but looked straight at the teacher as if she'd been paying attention the whole time.

"Ms. Farech. Is there a problem?" Mr. Melski asked from the front of the room.

"Yes." I struggled to keep all the emotion from my voice. "Someone just threw gum in my hair." I stood and picked up my books. "I'll see if someone in the office can help."

His eyes flicked to Penny. The faculty knew. So why in the heck did they let her sit behind me? It was a small school. Because we were in the same grade, we had most of our classes together. Not all, though, because I'd managed to squeak into a few of the advanced ones. Hard classes, but I loved them because she wasn't there.

I kept my pace even as I walked out the door.

The secretary, an older woman who yelled at most kids, made a sympathetic noise when I walked in and showed her the gum. I hadn't touched it much and had walked carefully so it wasn't too embedded.

"Why on earth does Penny dislike you so much?" she asked as she worked.

"Because when we were kids, I told her not to hit her mom." The truth, yet not all of it. Penny was the only one who knew my secret. Never once did I give the rumors she had started any credence. But, she and I both knew I could do what she claimed. I just didn't let her push me to do it openly.

The secretary extracted the gum wad within minutes, only taking a few strands with it.

"Make sure you don't sit near her at the assembly," she warned just before I left.

As if I would purposely do so.

I went to the bathroom to check my hair before heading back to class. Hopefully Penny wasn't chewing more gum in anticipation of my return. The door opened behind me. Penny's eyes met mine in the mirror.

"Why?" I asked, turning. "What do you get from doing this? You were never mean when we were little." She continued to eye me hatefully. I tried again. "We were friends once."

"Ha!" she barked bitterly. "You were never my friend. You never listened to me."

I knew exactly what she meant. She'd wanted me to use my ability to make her mom look away so we could sneak candy when we went to her house. She didn't understand as I did that

*my ability wasn't meant for that. Somehow I'd always known I
shouldn't misuse my power.*

"You always asked too much," I said sadly. "Just let this go."

*"No. At some point you'll make a mistake, and I want to be
there so everyone knows I was right about you." She reached out
and slapped the books from my arms. They tumbled to the floor.*

*"All you're going to prove is how mean you can be," I said
glancing down at the books. She didn't answer.*

*When I bent to pick them up, she pushed me over. I snapped
and grabbed hold of her will.*

*"Stop." She froze poised in a half-crouch ready to come after
me. I held her still with my will, but I forced nothing else on her. I
felt bad enough for holding her like that. "I'm really sorry, Penny,
but this has gone on long enough. Forget your hate. Remember
the friendship we once had." I picked up my books and stood.
"Don't try to hurt me again."*

*I walked out the door intending to get a good head start
before I released her. From behind, I heard her yell through the
door, "I still can't move!"*

The dream shifted, but not far. I still wore the same clothes.

*Sitting on the gym bleachers surrounded by the entire
student body, I looked around warily for Penny. She would hate
me even more, now. I should have made her forget. I just
couldn't bring myself to mess with someone's head like that. It
wasn't like anyone really believed her. Other than the bullying,
she wasn't a threat to me. I had no justification for taking the
extreme measure of robbing her of her memories.*

*"As some of you know, there have been cases of bullying.
This is a serious matter that this school will not take lightly. We
have a short film to help educate you on what steps should be*

taken if you are bullied, or witness bullying."

The overhead lights dimmed and a beam of light from the AV room near the top of the gym pierced the gloom. The AV room, a recent addition accessed by a set of stairs outside of the gym, was prized by the faculty as a means to broadcast school news.

A shot of the girl's bathroom burst onto the white gym wall we used for projection. My mouth popped open as I saw myself walk into the bathroom and go to the mirror. Some students near me started laughing quietly. The faculty, standing on the gym floor, started conferring in whispers as on screen, Penny walked in and we started talking.

One of the teachers left the gym presumably to reach the AV room and stop the movie. The lights in the gym turned on as Penny knocked the books out of my hand. No one moved. Everyone stayed focused on the projection. My stomach filled with piercing shards of ice.

"The assembly is over. Return to your last hour class. Those with Physical Education should go to the locker rooms and wait there," the principal shouted, unable to use his microphone as the PA had been taken over by my voice, "All you're going to prove is how mean you can be."

No one moved. All eyes remained riveted on Penny as she stared at me, and I moved to retrieve the books. I could taste my panic, the flavor disgustingly reminiscent of vomit. Penny had finally succeeded.

I closed my eyes as the recording of my voice rang out. "Stop." A murmuring rose in the gym, loud enough that others started shushing their neighbors as I gave Penny my little speech and then left the bathroom.

Opening my eyes, I caught the angle of the video change as the cameraman climbed off the toilet and opened the stall door to zoom in on Penny's outraged face. Penny's words, "I still can't move," echoed through the eerily quiet gym. The last image on the wall was of Penny suddenly falling to the floor. The projection shut off.

My face heated unnaturally. Someone next to me whispered to her neighbor, "Holy crap! Penny wasn't lying."

I sat up in the bleachers, surrounded by my peers. All eyes turned to me. A side door opened, and a teacher escorted a beaming Penny into the gym. As I stood, I grabbed everyone's will but hers and planted a seed. My voice rang out. "You just witnessed proof of Penny's dogged determination to expose something extraordinary. Instead, all she did was paint herself as a bully and show she has an amazing ability to act."

Releasing their wills, I nudged my way through my stunned classmates. As I moved, I heard things like, "I can't believe she was so mean," and, "I would have slapped her face instead of walking out."

Penny's smug expression faltered as she noticed the change in everyone. Her mouth popped open as she stared at me. I walked up to Penny while holding the faculty back with simple wait-and-see thoughts. I stopped just in front of her.

"Whoever you had filming did a wonderful job," I said. "If you're this good over a no name nothing like me, I can only imagine how good you'll be when you're reporting on something real. Good luck."

The sudden silence penetrated my dream. I emerged with my heart racing wondering why we'd stopped. I lifted my cheek from the warm spot on Luke's back and, in the gloom around us, took in the shape of an old barn on a slight hill in the distance.

"Why did we stop?" I asked when he loosened the strap.

"I'd rather approach the Compound in daylight," he said quietly.

My determination to push through bowed to his practical reasoning. I didn't really want to face a horde in the dark either. I didn't have their enhanced eyesight.

"How is the cut?"

I pulled the strap from over his head and climbed off the back. My legs ached from sitting so long, but I didn't try stretching them out. The back of his shirt was stained with my blood, but it looked dark and dry. I shrugged in response to his question and asked, "Why here?"

He walked over to me, unzipped the jacket, and once again gently tugged at the hem of my shirt. Only this time, it didn't lift. The blood had dried to the shirt. He frowned as he answered, "They are too used to looking at hotels. I thought this would be safer."

"This" meant sleeping in the barn. He continued to look worriedly at my stomach as if he could see through the fabric. "Some real sleep sounds good," I murmured, trying to reassure him.

He sighed and gently touched my cheek. "You'll tell me if it starts hurting," he ordered softly.

I snorted. "It hasn't stopped hurting."

He smiled at me and dropped his hand. "I imagine not," he commented as he shifted the bike into neutral and began pushing it toward the building. I zipped back up and slowly followed. Patches of snow coated the ground between tufts of long grass. Shivers trembled through me.

The barn leaned heavily to one side. Many of its old boards had rotted at the base. Still, Luke pushed the bike into the gaping door. Any hint of the dusk's fading light disappeared after two steps. Disturbing the layer of dust covering the floor with my steps caused the smell of old, musty hay to fill my nose, and I sneezed once. It killed my stomach.

"I'll look around," he said a moment before he disappeared into the dark. I looked back at the door, just barely outlined now, and stayed where I stood.

"It's empty and untouched. We'll stay here for a few hours."

He took me by the hand and led me further into the black. He flicked on a tiny LED flashlight attached to the bike keys and pointed to an empty stall partitioned by a half wall. I blushed as I understood and quickly grabbed the flashlight and shooed him away. I'd lived many lifetimes without the convenience of a toilet, but that was in the past. I liked flushing and washing.

After I finished, I moved into the hay-filled aisle, clicked off the flashlight, and shuffled toward the front of the building.

"Here," Luke murmured after I'd walked half the length. I paused and felt a tug on the bag. He led me off to the side and gently nudged me down onto some old hay.

"If I wake up to bugs crawling on me, I will not be happy," I whispered waiting for him to settle next to me.

When he lay still, I used my hands to find him. He lay on his back, and I pressed close to his side. His warmth became a halo around me.

"I promise, I will keep them off of you," his low voice rumbled under my ear as I settled my cheek on his chest. Too bad he kept his shirt on. Skin to skin, I tended not to dream at all. I flattened my hand on his shirt and let my fingers thaw.

"I'm glad you're warm," I mumbled, my eyes already closing. At least I wasn't freezing. My stomach hurt, my legs ached from all the kicking and moving I'd done during the fight, and my arms just felt like they would fall off. Dreaming might not be the worst.

"Though she's a pleasure to be around, we've noticed she's very aggressive with others. I wanted to suggest an outlet for her energy." The daycare administrator handed my father a slip of paper. We sat in her office, just the three of us. My legs dangled from the chair, and I idly swung them back and forth. Moving helped. I didn't feel so mad then. I arched my neck to look at the paper. It had a picture of a man kicking and some words. I didn't care about the words, though. I liked the picture. I liked kicking.

The dream shifted.

The other kids congregated around the playground equipment, laughing and chasing each other. I stood back, watching them play with a smile, but not joining. Whenever I tried, they stopped playing to lie around. Sometimes a few of them even took naps. Meanwhile, something inside me grew, tightening my skin to the point of discomfort, to the point I grew angry. So I stood on the outskirts, never really joining, and they let me be though they threw an occasional friendly wave my way. Everybody liked me. They couldn't help it. I made them feel good.

A new boy walked over to one of my classmates and took the ball from her hands. Her lips quivered, but she didn't cry. Instead she walked away. I felt indignant for her and watched the boy stalk away from the group to play sullenly with the ball. I frowned at him.

With most of my classmates further away, I approached him knowing my skin wouldn't tighten too much.

"Why did you do that?" I demanded.

He looked up at me with narrowed eyes. Anger, hurt, and uncertainty flooded me.

"Why are you so mad?" I asked. Usually the people around me were happy. But even happiness, when I soaked up too much, made me feel tight inside.

His eyes opened a little wider before they narrowed again. He balled his fist and swung at me.

I blocked just as my instructor had taught me. The boy dropped the ball to try another swing. I blocked again. He gave a growl of frustration and started swinging wildly. I continued to block the blows, flowing into the different stances and moves, enjoying the movement. The emotions poured off him, and I unwillingly soaked them up, but what we did helped burn them out of me. Soon I could see him tiring and took two quick steps back. I didn't want to drain him. I liked that he didn't lie down like the other kids did. He was different, and playing with him helped me. I felt deflated in a good way. I bowed to him as I'd been taught.

I smiled at his shocked expression. "Do you want me to show you how to block next recess?"

He nodded his mop of sandy blonde hair. I felt the tears hiding behind his grey eyes and reached for his hand, willing to help him again. I took his hurt away as the teacher walked over to us to scold us for fighting.

"We weren't fighting," I explained. "We're training. He's my partner now." I wouldn't need to stand alone anymore.

The teacher shook her head indulgently and shooed us

inside.

"What's your name?" the boy asked.

"Isabelle. What's yours?"

"Ethan."

*   *   *   *

"We're less than an hour away," Luke called over his shoulder. The move twisted the healing bite on his neck. I hated seeing it, probably as much as he hated the cut on my stomach. His injury, at least, healed faster.

I nodded in response, but otherwise kept scrunched behind Luke. Heavy wet snow blanketed the ground. The wind bit into my skin, chilling it until it stung. I couldn't tell if I felt so cold because of the temperature, which barely hovered above freezing, or because of a fever. My stomach had hurt when I woke, and I worried that the moldy air, or dirty clothes I wore, might have caused an infection.

"Shit," Luke swore and swerved.

I lifted my head from his back, but didn't see anything. Turning, I saw a werewolf running behind us. Before I could panic, Luke opened the throttle, and the bike screamed down the road, distancing us from our pursuer.

"They know," he yelled back at me.

No kidding. I clung to Luke, watching our pursuer. There were only three roads into the pack's territory and ultimately to the Compound. One came in from the north, one from the southwest, and another from the east. We'd abandoned the eastern route when we'd run into them last time. When they'd found me south of here, we'd kept heading north hoping they'd think we'd switch from the obvious. There was no turning around anymore. We were too close. They now knew our direction and would be ready.

The lone wolf stopped running and stood in the middle of the paved lane, no doubt communicating to the rest of the pack. The bike screamed down the road. I didn't dare try peeking around Luke to see how fast we went. If the wind had hurt before, it really tore at me now. We rode for another ten minutes without sighting anything. Then, hell opened its mouth and started spitting at us.

A fully changed werewolf ran in front of us, trying to slow Luke down. Luke didn't let up on the throttle. Somehow, he avoided the beast without dumping the bike. I locked my hands around his waist and carefully looked back. The furry shapes of too many werewolves to count in a glance ran behind us. Determined to gain ground.

Luke used his left hand to dig in his right pocket and pulled out his cell phone. He pressed a few buttons and held it to his ear. Fearing what driving one handed at these speeds could do to us, I wanted to close my eyes but didn't think that was too smart.

"Gabby, I have a problem," he shouted over the roar of the engine.

A problem was a bit of an understatement. We had an army of werewolves following us, a traitor in Luke's band of friends, and he was calling for help while driving at breakneck speeds. I couldn't decide what to freak out over more.

Something flew from the left, hitting the tank with a loud bang and knocking the phone from Luke's hand. As the object had flashed toward us, I'd thought it looked like a chunk of wood but couldn't be sure. The phone hit me in the face and fell between us. A growl erupted uncomfortably close to our right.

Maybe a call for help wasn't out of order.

I shimmied an arm between us, snatched the phone up, and tried to redial the number. The first try didn't go through. The second time, it went through, and I was so excited the phone almost slid from my fingers.

"Luke?" a female voice answered after the first ring.

"No. Bethi. We need help," I shouted into the phone. The wind made it almost impossible to hear if she said anything back. "There are too many. They can't take me. If they do, we *all* die. Please!" I shouted which road we raced down. I closed the phone and kept it scrunched in my fist.

More werewolves started pouring from the trees in front of us.

"Don't let go!" Luke shouted as he began swerving. He tilted us so far once, I thought we were going down for sure. But he righted us and opened the throttle again.

The mass of wolves chasing us had gained too much ground when we slowed slightly because of the swerving. One caught my jacket, but I held tight to Luke and heard a tear. Another ran beside the bike, but I caught it—and me—by surprise by kicking out with my foot and connecting with its face. The blow tripped him up more than hurt him, but it knocked him back into his followers causing several of them to fall back.

Ahead of us, a group of six wolves burst from the woods and raced toward us. Now that they knew our direction, they were probably pulling their numbers from the other routes.

"If you get us out of this alive, I swear I'll stop trying to ambush-Claim you," I yelled to Luke.

I braced myself as the oncoming wolves flew at us...and sailed over our heads into the pack of wolves following us. I twisted around in surprise. Help had arrived.

Two moved incredibly fast, taking a chunk out of the mass following us. The other four raced alongside us, keeping most of the wolves out of our way.

Ahead, a bend in the road obscured our view of what lay beyond. Luke eased up on the throttle, and I wondered if he had the same suspicion as I did about what waited ahead. He skidded to a dangerous sideways stop that made my stomach try to crawl out of my mouth, severed the strap connecting us, and leapt from the bike. Already transforming.

The remaining force chasing us collided with our four escorts. Luke joined them, fighting savagely, tearing into anyone who got too close to me. The other werewolves circled us, outnumbering us six to one. I scrambled from the bike too fast and felt the knitting cut on my stomach reopen. Wetness trailed down my stomach, and I cringed. A wave of dizziness washed over me. All of the wolves around me caught the scent, and the rapid movements slowed. Their gazes flew to me as I stumbled and bumped into the bike. It rocked but steadied under me. I bent toward the ground to catch my breath and shake the murk from my head.

No food, no water, and bleeding. Not a good combination.

When I lifted my head, seven wolves circled around me keeping the others at bay. I fumbled in the bag for my knife, relieved when I clasped the handle. An attacking wolf leapt high trying to clear the circle, but one of my defenders jumped up to meet him. The move knocked them both back into the waiting melee and created an opening in my defense. Another of the enemy ran forward to take advantage of the break, but a sleek grey wolf spun from the circle and used a swipe of his claws to rip away the throat of the attacker.

My eyes scanned the forms as I looked for Luke's coppery coat. I found him in a sea of attackers—Luke had been the wolf who'd blocked the attacker's jump. They bit at Luke, tearing into his skin as he swirled, swiped, and savaged those around him. None of the defenders encircling me moved to help Luke. Without thought, I shuffled toward him. My heart hammered, and my palms grew cold and clammy as another line of blood marred Luke's coat.

"No," I whispered as another attacker sunk his teeth into Luke's neck. Luke still hadn't recovered from the last bite he'd received. Possessiveness swelled along with anger.

"I have run," I croaked with an emotion-tight voice. I straightened and dropped the arm protecting my middle. "I have bled." I moved forward, determined. "I have *remembered*." My voice rose and some of those on the outskirts of the fighting angled their heads to watch me. "I am the Wisdom of the Judgements, and I will not fail again!" I screamed at them, flipping the knife in my hand, and throwing hard through the tangle of bodies. The blade flew true, sinking into the eye socket of the one attached to Luke. "Bite him again and I will rip your tongue from your mouth!" I promised.

Two turned from Luke and moved toward me. I touched the hindquarter of the grey wolf in front of me.

"Pick me up," I demanded, not caring that he fought with several wolves. He slashed wildly, spun toward me, shifting so his arms looked more human and capable of throwing, and lifted me.

"Throw me to him," I said, pointing at the screaming wolf clawing at the knife in his eye. I saw the grey wolf's hesitation to throw me into that mess and touched his face.

"Now!"

Catapulted into the air, I tucked into a ball and closed my eyes as I somersaulted toward Luke. *Remember. Remember.* I'd never done this myself. Never my own body. But another of my sisters had. I opened my eyes as I felt the downward pull of gravity. The wolf was just below me. He wasn't paying attention, but others around him were. They moved to try to catch me. Luke looked up, causing an opening for another injury.

I swore again, untucked myself, and twisted to land on the wolf with the knife in his eye, bringing us both to the ground. The impact killed my stomach, ripping me further. I grunted in pain but still managed to pull the knife from his eye. It caught slightly on the bone of his socket. The wolf screamed. I silenced him with a swipe before I stood. A wall of man-wolf bodies leaned in around me. Luke growled and raged just beyond.

"Time to die," I whispered with a slight smile.

Several pairs of eyes widened in surprise as I swiped out in a spinning turn and sliced open their soft underbellies. Yeah, I knew how bad that hurt. Ignoring the grunts of pain, I dodged their attempts to grab at me. I fell to my knees and swiped again, darting the blade behind their knees. Three dropped to my level. Three more crowded in. The handle started to slip in my grip. I swung out again.

A horn blared long and loud. A few of the wolves around me looked up as a white wolf landed on the three new wolves thinking to have at me. Another wolf with a brown coat landed behind me, his growl sent a shiver down my spine. He didn't attack anyone. He partially transformed to lift me, his big hands gentle. Something in his soft brown eyes stayed my knife.

He jumped and brought me back into the circle of six bodies

that still surrounded the bike. There he set me on my feet with a firm "stay" and leapt back into the dying fray. Despite the odds, we were winning. Four of the wolves fighting with us moved with such incredible speed and agility that they each faced at least four opponents at once.

Bodies started flying through the air as the wolf who'd saved me started throwing the injured and dead away from the immediate area. The attackers' numbers halved. And then, as one, they turned and fled. No one gave chase. As the road cleared of attackers, two cars sped past and turned the curve in the road that I knew led to the Compound. Several of the wolves turned their heads to watch the vehicles pass, but no one made a move to stop or follow them. In the window of one, I saw a little boy's face.

I bent slightly, curving an arm around my stomach again and was surprised my guts weren't leaking out, yet. Then Luke was beside me, pushing me toward the bike. He bled from several lacerations and no longer wore a shirt. Tinker Bell covered his bottom half. I smiled and sobbed at the same time.

Luke sat on the bike, and someone lifted me up behind him. Everyone moved quickly. We all recognized the need to leave before another bout could begin. I draped against him too hurt and tired to do more. Finding a clean spot near his shoulder blade, I turned my head and gave him a kiss.

Somehow, we'd done it again. Survived. Tears trailed down my cheeks to drip onto his skin.

The wolves ran beside us as we sped to the Compound. I shook and clung to Luke. Blood covered his back, again.

Thirteen

Admittedly, I'd expected more from the Compound than what I saw when I lifted my head from Luke's back. A scattering of dilapidated buildings came into view. Someone had put a lot of effort into in an attempt to make them look better. The old wooden structures worried me. I'd watched my family die in flames so many times.

Luke pulled the bike up to the porch, right next to one of the two cars that had sped past us. Wolves surrounded us. Some had helped us during the fight, but a few new ones joined the group. A short brunette woman stepped outside with a robe and tossed it to the white wolf who caught the material with its mouth.

"Come on," Luke said, holding out an arm so I could dismount first.

My stomach cramped with pain as I tried to stand. I hesitated to swing my leg off the bike.

"How badly were you hurt?" a woman asked from behind me.

An older woman with white hair wore the robe the white wolf had caught. The white wolf was gone. I shouldn't have been surprised. Girls could fight, too. I knew that. Yet, I'd foolishly assumed they'd all been male back there.

"Just a nick," I mumbled. I wasn't about to admit any weakness in front of the large group. Who knew which of them might betray me? The woman with the white hair moved to my side and helped me off the bike. She was stronger than she looked.

"Let's get you inside." Still holding my arm, she turned to glance at the brown wolf. "Jim, Emmitt's saying the boys are worried." She herded me toward the door while calling out instructions. "You should go reassure them. Grey and Sam can handle things out here." Everyone did as she said. Since inside was safer than outside, I didn't try to fight her.

A stack of pants waited just inside the door. Made sense.

I shuffled a few more steps before Luke turned and scooped me up in his arms.

"About time," the woman reprimanded.

"Who are you?" I asked, peering over Luke's shoulder at her.

"Winifred Lewis. You can call me Nana Wini," she said with a kind smile. "The woman behind me is Mary, and the man who will be following us shortly, the one who pulled you from that dog pile, is Jim." She looked at me expectantly.

"Oh, I'm Bethi."

"Luke, bring her upstairs. Second door on the right should be open," she said as we neared a set of stairs. "We'll be right up with some bandages."

Luke took the stairs two at a time and had me in a chair in short order.

As soon as he sat me down, he dropped to his knees in front of me and cupped my face between his hands. After everything we'd just gone through, his gentle touch brought tears back to my eyes.

We'd made it. But the place I'd thought would save me was a dump of tinderbox buildings out in the woods. We'd be dead in hours. I already felt dead inside. And tired. All that running. The fighting. Had there been any point to it?

The worry in his eyes tugged at my heart, and I felt a stab of guilt as I thought of everything he'd gone through to get me here.

"Go," I said, reaching up to squeeze one of his hands. "Take a shower and put on your own pants."

He snorted a laugh, then smoothed a thumb over my cheek.

"I'd rather stay with you." His gaze flicked to my very bloodstained shirt.

"There's nothing for you to do right now," I said, crossing an arm over my stomach. I didn't want him to look at it before I could. "They'll fix me up, I'm sure."

Reluctantly, he stood. I arched a brow and shooed him toward the door. Watching him walk away, I couldn't remember Tinker Bell ever looking so good.

When he closed the door behind him, I eased out of the shredded jacket and lifted the shirt. I almost gagged. Pulling it back down, I eyed the blood-soaked fabric. The cut needed stitches. A lot of them, really. I did *not* want to be awake for that. I'd had enough pain for...oh, ever.

The door opened behind me, and an older man with merry grey eyes poked his head in. When he saw me, he smiled and held up my bag. Perfect. I waved him into the room and accepted the bag. He nodded and left without a word, but I caught his worried glance at my stomach.

(Un)wise

I tipped the bag onto the floor and found my bottle of pills. I still had two sleeping pills mixed in with the other ones I'd tried.

I swallowed them dry and leaned back into the chair.

"That bad?" Luke asked, startling me.

"What do you mean?"

"Pain pills?" he asked, coming over to take the bottle from me. His shirt showed dark patches from putting it on wet, and it clung to his skin. His hair was still damp too. He couldn't have been gone for more than a few minutes.

A frown settled on his face when he studied the prescription label and the unknown name on it. "How many did you take?"

"Relax. It's just a bottle. I keep other stuff in there. I took two sleeping pills."

His eyes flicked to my blood-soaked shirt. He squatted down near me, balanced on his heels, and lifted the hem of my shirt. His shocked gaze flew to mine.

"I know. It'll need stiches. No hospital though, okay?" I grabbed his hand and begged with my eyes until he nodded. "The dreams will knock me out, and the pills will keep me under." I did a slow blink without trying. Already they called to me.

"Luke," I whispered. "They're not done trying. Tell the others to soak the buildings. I've died by fire before, and it's not fun."

*   *   *   *

I suffered the same dream duality as I had before, but more. My present-self, my past-self, and the past-selves of four of my sisters. The multiple views disoriented me, and I fought to focus on just one.

Heat flickered over my stomach like tiny flames dancing on my skin. I wanted to look down, but my eyes remained focused on the horde before me.

My fingers gently squeezed the hand wrapped within mine before I looked to my sister.

Through her eyes, I looked back at me. Again, my present-self suffered a wave of vertigo. My stomach twisted with pain, but I couldn't tell from which of us it stemmed.

"All will be well," I promised my sister.

I pushed away the discomfort and tried to focus. My sister squeezed back as her eyes closed.

"What do you see?" I asked.

Concentrating on my sister, I jumped perspectives.

A swarm of glowing lights filled my mind. Blue-green, blue-grey, yellow-green, and then us. The humans were far from us. We'd agreed to leave them out of our fight. The blue-grey almost outnumbered blue-green.

"They will not win. They do not have Courage. Her spark no longer exists," I said on a sob. Knowing they would not win did not soothe the loss of our sister.

"Be strong. They may not win the Judgement, but they may win this fight."

A hand closed over my shoulder and peace flowed through me, taking away fear, hate, worry, even the odd outside feeling of pain in my stomach. I breathed deeply and struggled not to smile. I fought to hold onto my worry.

"Stop, sister. Save yourself for them. We will need you," I begged.

Changing perspectives again, I surged into a mind filled with so much fear, hate, worry, pain, and doubt.

I struggled to breathe. My skin felt too tight as if all the emotion inside of me fought to burst out. Fists clenched, teeth gritted, I growled, "And we need you focused. They will learn to fear me."

"Sisters, join hands," another of us spoke, drawing our attention.

Turning, we clasped hands. Five of us: Strength, Hope, Prosperity, Wisdom, and Peace.

"Courage will always be with us," Strength spoke with confidence as a surge of power flowed through us.

My present-self struggled as what each of the past-selves experienced in that moment flooded me.

The sparks in my mind ignited, glowing brightly...

Emotions surged within me as I had the capacity to drain even more from those around us...

Glimpses of the battle to come floated around in the white infinity of my mind...

Flashes of the past rekindled my purpose.

Our purpose.

"The Urbat have grown too strong. We must reduce their numbers or face a worse fate the next cycle," I, Wisdom, predicted.

"I have no claws, but give me a knife and I will do my part," I, Peace, intoned. Seething rage boiled within me. I itched to pace the field.

"I can only see our fates in this life, not the next. We will stay back and do what we can. Be well and be loved in your next lives," I, Prosperity, said softly, pulling Strength and Hope from the circle.

I looked at my sister, Peace. "I remember how to fight thanks to your past lives, but I don't have the skills you have from this life."

I watched her pull another knife from the leather belt at her waist. She handed it to me hilt first.

"Grip it firmly and don't let go. Swing it around like a wild woman until it feels like your arm will fall off. Then keep swinging. Make them bleed. Make them sorry. Make them see their fate."

An eerie howl rent the air, and it began. The werewolves around us surged forward, meeting the Urbat in the middle of the field. Hand in hand, we ran.

The dream shifted, but not much.

I stood in the center of the red field, the center of the storm, surrounded by a moment of stillness. Bodies lay about me, all reverted to human form. My friends. My adopted family. My protectors. I looked down at the vacant vibrant blue eyes of my sister. She'd fought well with just memories.

A small distance away, the battle continued. Here, I looked around in misery. We'd hoped to decimate their numbers. Instead, they'd succeeded in decimating ours, almost exterminating the Elders, the keepers of knowledge for the werewolves. I glanced around at the Urbat fighters. They didn't believe in Elders. They didn't want any group to hold such power over them. Leaders led. If they were not strong enough to do so, they were challenged and replaced with ones who were stronger.

Their emotions drenched the field. I inhaled slowly and deeply, pulling the stagnant mass toward me. For those closest to me, I siphoned their consuming hate, leaving only traces of fanaticism. Several fell to their opponents during their confusion. I felt bloated and tight. Still I inhaled again, pulling more from them, expanding my reach to pull from every Urbat on the field.

Something trickled from my nose, eyes, and ears. I kept breathing in, impossibly filling my lungs, and myself, with everything I could.

Something inside me popped, and a flaring pain seared through my stomach. I knew I needed to let go. I gathered everything I held, everything that made me boil and shake with rage, and released it all at once, killing the still staggering Urbat where they stood. The few friends who remained staggered as well. Blood ran from their ears as they toppled to the ground. I fell to my knees as they fell. The world surrendered to darkness. The time for Judgement faded.

The dream repeated countless times. I absorbed every sight, thought, and feeling from each perspective before I finally floated to the surface. I now understood the war that had raged, since the beginning of time, between the Urbat and Werewolves.

"Bethi," Luke demanded near my ear. Then, not so loud, he asked, "Why isn't she waking up?"

"Go. Away." My lips didn't want to move. My mouth tasted like I'd kissed a skunk's butt, and my stomach hurt. Bad. Still reeling from the graphic dream of death, hate, and pain, I wanted to be left alone. For a long time.

Someone gently touched my head, smoothing a hand over my hair. The touch disappeared a moment before a door opened and closed.

In the silence, I recapped my current life, compared it to past lives, and didn't like the similarities leading up to the finale. I tried licking my lips and instead moaned.

"Do you need a drink?" a new voice asked.

Opening my eyes, I looked at an unfamiliar face. Wait, no. I blinked at her and remembered. I almost smiled at myself. As if I could forget anything. Winifred. Nana Wini. But I stopped the smile because I didn't want her to think I was smiling at her. More than ever, I didn't know who to trust. I needed Hope. I needed to know which of the wolves around me were Urbat and which were Werewolves. Only Hope could tell me that. Knowing the difference between the two wouldn't determine my trust, but it was a start.

I nodded, and she handed me a glass of water. I drank slowly and grimaced.

"Can you help me up? I need a toothbrush."

She nodded.

Setting the glass aside, I gripped her hand and slowly stood. The gash on my stomach felt hot and tight. It pulled a little. I lifted my shirt and looked at it. Neat little stitches ran along my skin where the cut had been.

"I did the best I could. Luke insisted you did not want to go to the hospital."

"Too dangerous," I agreed, moving to my bag and grabbing my toothbrush. The longer I stood, the more I could straighten up. Still, I brushed my teeth, with a slight bend. She stood near watching me closely.

"You really need to change into something clean."

I spit, rinsed, and turned to face her. Her steady gaze met mine. She seemed kind enough, but I couldn't trust anyone.

"Where'd Luke go?" I doubted he'd actually listened to my muttered "go away."

She stepped back to let me out of the tiny bathroom. "He went to get the others. They've been waiting for you."

Just then, the door to the room flew open. Luke strode in followed closely by another man with short dark hair.

"What happened to my bike?" the newcomer demanded, looking ready to strangle Luke.

Two women followed the man. The first one, olive skinned with dark hair, looked worried and the second one, a short blonde pixie, appeared slightly concerned. A second man followed the group in. I couldn't see much of his face due to the dark hair hanging in his eyes and a full beard. Still, his lips twitched as if he shared the amusement of the woman he followed.

"Emmitt," the first woman said, laying a hand on his back. Emmitt stopped his advance and glared at Luke, who ignored them all since his gaze was locked on me. The worry in his eyes told me enough.

"Michelle, he trashed it. It looks like he dumped it," Emmitt said without turning to look at Michelle. "Jim felt guilty enough that it was stolen. He won't even look at me now. You owe me an explanation," he said, pushing Luke's shoulder.

"Ah, there you are," I mumbled. "We were just talking about you. You must be Peter Gibbons." Luke gave me a puzzled look and everyone else ignored me. Obviously, they didn't get the movie reference and had no idea how much I didn't care about their drama at the moment.

Luke tore his gaze from mine. "I don't owe you anything," he said. "But if you ask nice, maybe I'll tell you what happened so you can go running to daddy."

Emmitt moved incredibly fast and grabbed Luke by the throat with a loose hold that allowed Luke to laugh. Michelle paled. I took a step forward. That man's neck was getting way too much attention lately by everyone but me. Before I took another step, a hand clamped down on my shoulder, stopping me.

Luke reached up and knocked Emmitt's hand aside. Both started growling.

I looked back at Nana Wini and with a cold voice said, "Don't touch me."

Her eyes widened in shock, and she immediately released me. Neither Luke nor Emmitt paid me any attention until I stepped up to them and smacked them both in the chest.

"Stop. Both of you."

Luke immediately grew serious and backed up a step, while Emmitt's jaw twitched. He fought not to follow Luke's retreat.

The shaggy man snorted slightly, and I arched a brow at him. "Something to say?"

The woman standing in front of him flicked a glance back at him. "He'd hoped to see Luke get his butt kicked."

"Do you have any friends here?" I said, glancing at Luke.

He grinned at me. "Probably not."

Sighing, I dropped my hand and looked at Emmitt. "He did dump the bike. Several times. Each time it was because we were being attacked." I slanted my head and eyed them all.

Emmitt turned his attention to me, his eyes sweeping me from head to foot. His nostrils flared, and I knew he smelled the blood still very visible on my shirt.

"I would have been a lot worse off without him," I said, acknowledging the truth. If the Urbat would have found me first... I cringed at the thought.

Emmitt sighed and nodded. "It's always *my* bike." The dark haired woman patted his back with a slight smile on her face.

My eyes locked on her, and a memory triggered. "Michelle," I murmured. One of my sisters. The one who had

the two brothers she'd tried to protect. I wondered if she'd
found a way. She eyed me curiously, obviously wondering how I
knew her name. "We need to talk."

My gaze drifted to the other one, her childlike face brought
a sad pang. "Thank you for sending him, Gabby." I glanced at
Luke sheepishly. "I wasn't very cooperative at first."

She smiled but didn't get a chance to answer.

"Well, Little One, here she is. Now what?" Luke said,
impatiently.

My eyes narrowed at him. Little One? She had a pet name?

I looked back at Emmitt. "I changed my mind. Hit him." I
turned away and went back to stand by Nana Wini who watched
me with a slight tilt to her head. Luke's expression turned
slightly pained as his eyes followed my progress.

"Bethi," he said as the shaggy man laughed.

What did he have against Luke?

"Everybody out," I said, then changed my mind. "Except you
two." I pointed at Michelle and Gabby.

"Why?" Emmitt asked, casting a glare at Luke.

The shaggy man stepped forward enough to rest his hand on
Gabby's back. Good. She was taken. I fought not to scowl at
Luke again. It explained why shaggy man didn't like him.

"Because I need to talk to them. In private."

"This isn't the place to do it, then," Gabby said. "Too many
sharp ears here."

She was right. I looked thoughtfully at the walls of the
room. They would only block so much from werewolf or Urbat
ears. I nodded in agreement. She turned and walked out the
door. The others followed with Emmitt giving Luke one last look
of promised retribution. Luke stayed and eyed me. I wanted to

stand straight but knew it would hurt too much, so I didn't bother.

"Do you want me to carry you?" he asked quietly.

I snorted. "No, you can save your heroics for Little One." Idiot. I shuffled past him and heard Nana Wini follow.

The whole group wandered down a set of stairs, turned several corners, and entered a small room. Luke and Nana Wini followed. Everyone stood in the room, waiting around a table that filled the center of the room. I shook my head before Emmitt could close the door.

"Private means the three of us." Instead of looking at him, I looked at Gabby and Michelle. "There are things we need to talk about. Things no one else would believe," I added. Gabby looked a little wary but turned to meet her man's eyes. Shaggy-man's lips turned down in a slight frown. Emmitt didn't look any happier.

"For Pete's sake! What do you think's going to happen in here?"

"She's right," Michelle said with a small smile at Emmitt. "We'll be fine in here. You should check on the boys."

Emmitt leaned forward and kissed her softly on the lips before turning to leave. Her eyes never left him as he walked out the door. The other woman turned to look at the shaggy man. Neither spoke. They just looked at each other. Finally, he sighed, touched her cheek lightly, and exited.

The three of us turned our eyes on the remaining two.

Nana Wini met Michelle's eyes. "She has new stitches and should try not to pull them."

"She's right here," I mumbled, sitting on one of the chairs.

Nana smiled at me and left.

"I'm not leaving," Luke said softly.

Out in the hall I heard, "If he's not leaving..."

"Just shut the door already," I snapped. Luke closed the door on a growl in the hall, his smirk annoying me. He leaned against it, ensuring our privacy.

"I'm Bethi," I said ignoring him.

"I'm Michelle," Michelle said. "How did you know my name?"

Gabby remained quiet. "You're not curious how I knew your name too?" I asked.

She glanced at Luke. "I assumed he told you."

I shook my head. "No. It would be a nice answer though. A normal answer." Gabby's eyes dropped to the table. She knew what I was working up to. Good. "Are you ready for the truth? The truth about your abilities, and why we are the way we are?" Both of their eyes rounded. Michelle slowly sank into a chair. Gabby still stood. "Well, to be honest, I don't know all the details, but I'm pretty sure I know more than you.

"I remember," I said meeting their eyes. "That's my lovely ability. We've existed before and will exist again...and again." The thought of having to keep enduring this made me want to cry. I settled for taking a slow calming breath. "Each life we've lived before, I will eventually remember. Each death. Each emotion," I had to stop again. Maybe it was the pain of the stitches weighing on me, but everything just seemed so hopeless again.

"I can see what will happen with the stock market. Well, I used to, anyway," Michelle admitted.

I nodded. "I know. I saw you. You were curled up in a ball," I tipped my head back looking up at the ceiling as the memory of her pain washed over me. "It felt like your head had already exploded, exposing every nerve ending within you to even more pain." I met her shocked gaze. "I saw a man pick up your little brother by his arm and carry him into the house. The other one was just a baby."

Gabby's gaze flicked to Michelle. I could still see the distrust there.

"I saw you too, Gabby. All those homes. You could never let your guard down."

Finally, she sank into a chair, and I knew they believed me.

"We're not alone. There are six of us. We need to find the others but can't trust anyone. When we do, we die...or worse."

Michelle looked troubled.

"You said you knew why we had our abilities?" Gabby asked. "Kind of."

"I see lights," she admitted. "I just want to know why."

"Because you're our Hope. But also our biggest weakness. With you, they would be able to find us all."

Her eyes widened in understanding. "Six of us," she whispered.

I gave her a smile. "And you," I said looking at Michelle, "are Prosperity. You always bring fortune to those around you."

"And you know all this because you remember?" Gabby asked.

"It's not simply remembering. I relive our past lives through dreams. Not just my past lives but all of ours. When I wake up, they stay with me—every detail. Our abilities and how we used them in those lives." I tapped my head. "We've died so many times."

"So you know what our abilities are for? Why we are like

this?"

"The dreams are still coming. I'm not naive enough to believe I've learned everything. But I do know we exist because something was needed to keep the balance between humans, werewolves, and the dogs of death," I answered tiredly.

"Excuse me?" Michelle glanced at Gabby as if saying "did you hear that too?"

"Urbat. A cousin to Lycan," I explained. "They're close, but not quite the same. They tried to wipe out the werewolves almost a thousand years ago."

"Oh," Michelle said, looking suddenly enlightened. "I think Nana Wini told me something about that. But she didn't mention any cousins. Just that there was a huge fight—they weren't sure of the reason—and that it decimated their numbers."

"Of both sides," I said before turning to Gabby for confirmation. "Right? You can see the difference in their sparks. Are there more werewolves or Urbat?"

Gabby looked slightly stunned. "I knew it," she murmured. "Two different kinds." Her expression grew vacant and then troubled. "There are more Urbat. At least double." Her worried gaze flicked to the door, and she chewed on her lip for a moment. "So what does it mean that I'm Hope?"

"So far, I just know that you're the key to bringing all of us together. You know where the other three are."

Her attention returned to me. "Two," she corrected. "Charlene is one of us, too."

"Who's Charlene?" The name sounded familiar. "Where is she?"

"Here," Michelle said. "She's Emmitt's mother."

"Mother?" Emmitt had to be at least in his twenties. "How old is she?"

Michelle shrugged. "In her forties. I'm not exactly sure."

"What's her ability?" I asked.

"She admitted she could control people."

Of course! The dream starring Penny the bully. I felt like jumping up and down and cheering. "Strength," I sighed with a happy grin. "We are just missing Peace and Courage."

I looked at Gabby. "Where are they?"

Gabby's gaze grew slightly unfocused, and I was glad she didn't ask what I meant. "Both on the East Coast. One is very far north and the other just a little south."

"One is with Blake," Michelle said in a quiet, deeply troubled tone.

"Who's Blake?" I asked a moment before the memory resurfaced. Her stepfather's business partner.

"He kept me prisoner for my premonitions. I thought he was a werewolf, too. But I've heard that word before. Urbat. One of his men was talking about Urbat ruling the world. We have to tell the others that another kind exists," she said, meeting my eyes. Worry filled her gaze. "The Elders have been trying to find Blake through their connection. But they can't. After I met Emmitt, I had a vision of Blake with a tall, blind girl. She called him Father. She seemed okay with him." She shrugged and explained further. "He definitely didn't strike me as a good person when he kept me locked up, but he seemed to treat her well. Kissed her head and everything."

My stomach flipped in a sickening way. One of *them* had one of *us* and treated her well? A cramp started in my chest, and I struggled to keep my face straight as she continued.

"I'm sure she's one of us. The visions I've had so far have all proved to be of us, people with abilities. I saw you in the mall talking to some other girls," she said to me. "And you, sitting on the floor with Clay in wolf form by your side."

Clay. So that was the Shaggy-man's name, I thought absently as I continued to spiral into a dark, depressed place. With their numbers, if they already had one of us, was there any hope?

"You were both reading," she told Gabby. "There's only been five different girls in my visions. The other is a really angry redhead."

That pulled me out of my thoughts for a moment for a harsh, pained laugh.

"That would be Peace." I recalled the dream of the little girl on the playground. Isabelle. But I kept that to myself. "We need her." I felt the tug of a dream coming on and wanted to groan. I'd found them. We were together. Wasn't that enough? "We need her," I repeated. I needed her. Or Luke. If Luke would just let me Claim him, these dreams would stop.

"Are you okay?" Michelle asked.

"No. I'm not," I snapped, sighed, and then apologized. "The dreams I have are less than pleasant, and they won't let up." I changed the subject back to the issues at hand. "Gabby, you pinpointed me enough to send Luke. We need you to do the same for the other two."

She zoned out for a minute. "We can get to one, but not the other. The one in the north is surrounded by the other ones."

If the redhead was Peace that meant...

"The one in the north, the tall blind one that Blake has, must be Courage." If they didn't know Peace's location, we could still get to her. I tried not to dwell on the impossibility of getting Courage. That just left the threat at hand. "Have there been any attacks here since we arrived?" I asked, recalling my warning to Luke. Both women shook their heads. Why hadn't they attacked? What were they waiting for?

"Are there any Urbat here?" I asked Gabby.

She shook her head at me. "But I've seen them before. A few of them attacked us. And then there's Elder Joshua."

An Elder. I looked up at the ceiling and tried to think. We needed to expose the traitors and remove them before we could even consider making a move toward Peace.

"He was the one I contacted."

Luke's voice surprised me. I'd forgotten he was there.

"Someone betrayed us on the way here," I told them. "That's why there were so many attacks." But why not bigger groups of them? If the werewolves already had three, why would they risk me, the fourth, joining them? "There's a lot more to discuss, but I'm about to pass out," I admitted when the dreams nudged me again. My time was almost up.

"Gabby, keep an eye on the Urbat. If they start grouping and heading this way, we need to give everyone a warning." I sighed and tried not to remember what the Urbat had done in the past. "The children should be evacuated, now."

A sharp knock sounded at the door. A moment later it pushed open.

"Time's up," Clay said.

Gabby grinned at him and waved him in. Emmitt followed closely behind, elbowing Luke on his way past. The dream's tug grew more insistent.

"Please keep quiet about all of this," I said, standing. Then, to impress on them the seriousness of our situation, I repeated what I'd told Luke. "You have no idea what's coming our way, but I do. I've been raped, beaten, cut," I lifted my shirt to show them all the stitched gash, "starved, drowned, blinded, burned...you name it, I've lived it. *We've* lived it. You just don't remember. Don't trust anyone with your safety. When we do, we die. And I'll be the one who has to remember."

Turning, I left the silent room. Nana Wini stood just outside the door. Her expression told me she'd heard what I'd said.

Luke stole my opportunity to say anything to her by scooping me up into his arms. I shot him a disgruntled look still upset with his use of a pet name on another girl. But his angry, clenched jaw kept my mouth shut. I'd been too recently abused to have reminded him of all the other abuses I'd suffered. I rested my head against his shoulder and let him carry me.

"It was just a name," he said after a moment.

I didn't answer, keeping my head on his shoulder. But I felt better knowing he understood his mistake.

He gently set me on my feet just inside the tiny apartment's door, and cupped my face in his hands. "There's no room for anyone else in my heart," he said softly. "Only you."

"Then why?" I pleaded. If I was in his heart, then why did I have to wait to Claim him?

"Because I promised I would protect you," he said. His eyes burned with fierce resolve. "Even from myself."

The dream tugged, and my next blink turned into a three-second nap. A fingertip traced my eyebrow.

"You need rest," he said, wrapping an arm around me and guiding me down the hall.

I did. I promised myself I would argue some more about the

logic behind letting me Claim him now. But after a nap.

Fully dressed, I crawled up on the mattress, eased onto my side, and curled up protectively around my aching stomach. Stupid idea to cut myself. Didn't work and now the pain lingered. Always pain. With that thought, the dream pulled me as Luke's weight depressed the mattress next to me.

Fourteen

I sat up, shaking from the details of the dream. More death! Sweat coated my face, not from a fever, but the memory. Why had I dreamed that? I turned and noted the empty cold spot next to me. He'd left me, that's why. After his sweet comment about holding me in his heart, he'd left me. He knew what I suffered. I weakly swiped at my face, removing the moisture and wishing I could remove the memory. Exhaling slowing, I reflected on what I'd learned. My sister Courage always died young.

Light still shone through the room's window. I glanced at the numbers on the digital clock. Less than an hour had passed. Two pills and a glass of water waited on the small lamp stand next to the bed. Without hesitation, I swallowed them down. I could have cared less what they were at that point. I'd have taken anything from painkillers to cyanide. I definitely hadn't gotten the rest I needed.

My stomach ached from sitting up so quickly. I gingerly rolled off the bed and rose to a crouched stand. I hobbled out of the bedroom to look for Luke. I found Michelle waiting on the couch in the living room, but no Luke. She stood when she saw me. Her concern for me was evident on her face.

"Luke asked me to wait here so you wouldn't be alone. I know you said the dreams were bad, but..."

I looked away from her uncomfortably and wondered how much I'd yelled.

"Luke said he left you some pills."

"Yeah, I already took them. What were they?"

"Something for the pain."

Darn.

"Nana and Sam want to talk to you when you're up."

"I'm not up yet," I said as I shuffled toward the bathroom.

Michelle followed me to the door. "They want to know what's going on. Gabby and I haven't said anything. But after you left, Sam tried talking to Gabby and they ended up yelling at each other. Clay looked all bristly like he wanted to hit Sam."

I rolled my eyes, finished up, and opened the door. "And I care why?"

"Sam's an Elder. Gabby's—" The door opened with a bang stopping Michelle's words.

"Gabby's getting annoyed," Gabby said, striding into the room and closing the door behind her. "They let you go because you're hurt, but as soon as you were gone, we were bombarded with questions. They even sent for Luke to grill him."

I couldn't help the panicked look that crept into my eyes. It was too soon to reveal everything. It explained his absence, though.

"We didn't say anything," Gabby assured me again. "Look, I wasn't sure who to trust before you got here, but after talking to you, I don't think we can do this alone. I think we need to talk to the Elders. At least *some* of them."

Michelle nodded her head in agreement.

(Un)wise

We were all thinking of Elder Joshua. "I'm sorry I left you. I can't control when the dreams come and go anymore."

"It's okay," Michelle said. "Luke explained that to us."

"Us?"

"Me, Gabby, Clay, and Emmitt. They didn't trust Luke alone with us," Michelle said with an apologetic shrug.

"What did he do to deserve all of this hostility?"

"He stole Emmitt's bike."

"And he and some of his friends ganged up on Clay before I Claimed him," Gabby added. "Luke's your Mate, right?"

"He is a possibility," I agreed.

Her frown grew more pronounced. Her eyes flicked around the room. "I'd really like to talk to you alone, again. I have so many questions."

The door opened. "As do I," Nana said softly. "But I think it would be best if you sat while we discussed this. I don't like how pale you are." She motioned me toward the couch.

"This would be better in the soundproofed room," Gabby said quickly.

"Of course," Nana agreed.

As we walked to the room—at a very slow pace because of me—I contemplated where I wanted to start and what exactly to explain. I couldn't completely trust the Elders with everything I knew. Not yet. I didn't have the right answers to explain our purpose fully. Sure, we were here to maintain balance between the three groups, but how? I wasn't sure I was ready to share the who. At least, not until we weeded out the Urbat hiding in the pack. I believed wholly that the Taupe Lady's warning was serious. The world would burn if we failed. Though I trusted that knowledge, I doubted that anyone else would.

The door to the room stood open. Two other men sat inside. I recognized one. He'd brought up my bag.

Nana made official introductions as we sat. "Bethi, this is Sam and Grey, Elders. People you can trust. Elder Joshua is on his way here. We are missing two others, who are currently assisting in Europe, but we will communicate with them through our link."

I didn't say anything about her trust comment.

"Hello, Sam." So, that was the man who Gabby had argued with. He looked nice enough. Grey hair, neatly dressed. The memory of him eating spaghetti surfaced. He reminded me of my grandpa. I smiled and looked at the other one Nana had indicated. "Grey," I added as an acknowledgement as he shut the door. "Thank you all for your help. I didn't think Luke and I would make it here when they all came on us like that."

Sam cleared his throat, his troubled gaze meeting mine. "We'd never seen anything like that. Our kind...we're peaceful."

I nodded. He seemed so sincere. Could the betrayal go deeper than Joshua?

"We've had instances where we couldn't communicate with a few of our kind in the past, but never so many. Can you tell us why they were attacking you?" Sam asked.

Michelle glanced at me, but I didn't meet her gaze.

"The simple answer is that they were trying to take me back to their leader. There are so many things I don't know. Who their leader is and what they want to do with me when they get me." I rested my hands on the table, took a calming breath, and began my careful tiptoe around explanations that would trip me up and darted to the ones that would get me the result I needed.

"But I think it has to do with what's happening to me. I'm

reliving past lives through my dreams. This has been going on for several months. Somehow, those guys learned that I had these dreams and started chasing me. When Luke showed up, I thought he was one. As you know, we were pretty much chased the whole way. Luke kept me safe." I could feel Gabby's eyes on me and struggled not to meet her gaze. "Anyway, he brought me here, thinking you might be able to help me." I couldn't come up with anything better without spilling that there was a definitive difference between the people at the table and the people who'd chased me.

"Why do they care if you are having these dreams?" Nana asked.

"I'm not sure. The dreams seem like pieces to a puzzle. Some of them are fitting together, but I haven't fit enough of them together to figure out the big picture."

"Tell us more about the dreams."

I regretted that Nana had overheard what I'd suffered in them and hoped she'd let me get away with a vague answer. "Mostly they are the same thing. Something is chasing me or comes to my home. Usually it looks like a really large dog. Then it changes into the shape of a man. Those dreams always end with me dying."

"You've dreamt of us killing you?"

No, it was the Urbat. But I couldn't say that.

"Not just me," I said looking at Michelle and Gabby. "I've seen their past lives, too. We all die."

The room was eerily quiet for a moment.

"Why?" Nana asked looking deeply troubled.

I took an easy breath feeling as if I'd just cleared the minefield. "That's why I was willing to come with Luke. Like I said, some things I pieced together, but there are a lot of 'whys' I haven't figured out. I was hoping I'd find help here, that you'd have more answers."

Nana, Grey, and Sam shared a look. "We need some time to speak," Sam said slowly. "Is there anything more you know that could help us?"

He saved me from a complete lie by adding that last bit. There was plenty more that I knew but nothing that would help them. Not until Joshua arrived. Michelle and Gabby watched me shake my head. Neither of them spoke.

"After all of those dreams, I doubted everything I thought I knew," I said with a shrug.

Sam glanced at Nana. The significant pause told me they were communicating silently.

"Michelle, Gabby, help Bethi to the commons for something to eat, please. Your men are waiting there for you," Nana said.

"Sure," Gabby said quickly exiting her chair and moving to open the door. Michelle offered a hand to help me stand. Neither said anything as we left, and I felt relieved. I'd given the Elders enough information to get them off our backs, for now. I just needed to figure out what to do about Joshua. If he had an unusual spark, we couldn't trust him. But what to do about it?

When we entered a huge room filled with tables and chairs, I only caught a glimpse of it before Clay strode toward us. He stopped just in front of Gabby, preventing all of us from moving any further. The heavenly smells of turkey and stuffing drifted to me as his eyes swept over Gabby's face. My stomach cramped. This time from hunger.

"She's fine, big guy, but my stomach's really hurting. Would you mind—" I didn't get to finish the sentence before Clay was jostled aside with a growl from behind.

"Move already," Luke snapped at Clay, scooping me up.

Clay's eyes narrowed as they settled on Luke. Gabby curled her fingers in his hand. He stopped his glaring and gave her his full attention. "I'm fine. Bethi's not. We're supposed to get her something to eat."

I caught Clay's nod before Luke turned, almost bumping us into Emmitt. Two little boys circled around him like satellites. Luke huffed, and I reached up to smack the back of his head lightly. "The decisions you make and the words you speak influence the people around you. Be aware of your influence," I quoted.

His lips twitched, and he looked down at the boys. "Excuse me, please," he said politely.

They scampered out of his way, and Emmitt stepped aside, his eyes on Michelle.

"Didn't you take the pills?" Luke asked softly, carrying me to a cushioned chair.

"I took them." My stomach cramped, and I tried to remember when I'd last eaten. "Nana mentioned something about food." Instead of setting me in the chair, he sat and settled me on his lap.

"I'll get it for you," Michelle called moving toward the kitchen. Emmitt followed closely behind.

Clay moved to the chair across from us and sat, his eyes never leaving Gabby. Gabby perched on one of his knees and smiled slightly when he set a hand on her waist.

"How long have you two been together?" I asked. I really just wanted to know how safe she was. Claimed was good, but Mated was better.

"Clay has been living with me since the end of August." Her smile widened. "But I just recently Claimed him."

"Not Mated?" I wondered.

She shook her head. Well, crap.

Michelle returned just then with a sandwich. "Here you go."

I accepted the plate with a smile of thanks. "How long have you and Emmitt been together?" Taking a bite of the sandwich, I listened to Michelle say they'd been Claimed for several months and were planning a wedding. Another one not Mated. Dangerous business. I glanced at Emmitt who was watching me closely. We were still all ripe for Urbat picking. I wished again that Luke would just give in and at least let me Claim him.

"What about you two?" Emmitt asked.

I shrugged and took another bite. Everyone continued to wait patiently for my answer. Even Luke, the jerk, was quiet. Fine.

"He has a problem with my boobs." I took another bite of my sandwich.

Luke made a choking noise, and I grinned. "Secretly, I think he's hoping if he waits until I'm eighteen they might grow a bit more."

Emmitt's face betrayed nothing as his gaze flicked between me and Luke. Clay's whiskers split to show two rows of perfect white teeth. His eyes were on Luke. I didn't want to turn around to see why. Michelle looked slightly shocked and worried. Gabby was frowning at Luke.

"They're kinda like the elephant in the room. We're not allowed to talk about them."

Luke stood with me in his arms, turned, dumped me—gently—in the chair, and strode away. I grinned at the group.

"That's usually how he reacts if I do talk about them."

"So you haven't Claimed him yet?" Gabby asked.

I snorted. "Nope. He won't let me. He's pretty quick to protect his precious neck. I got smacked in the face, like, at least fifty times on the trip here." I polished off the sandwich with a sigh. That had to have been the best sandwich ever.

"That makes no sense," Gabby stated. "I was so sure." She looked in the direction that Luke had walked off and moved to stand. The content, happy feeling left my stomach.

Clay wrapped his hand around her wrist to stop her. I took a slow breath and tried to let go of the anxiety filling me. She was my sister. I would need to depend on her. So why was I so jealous of her and her relationship with Luke?

She turned and met Clay's eyes. "It's okay. I'll be right back. I have to know," she said quietly.

Michelle shifted uncomfortably in her seat. See, the restless part of me yelled. Even she sensed that Gabby shouldn't want to go chasing after Luke. I shushed myself.

Clay sighed and let go, but surprised me by following her. She didn't seem to mind.

"Do you want something to drink?" Michelle asked quietly, pulling my attention back to the remaining two.

"Sure." I stood to go with her since I didn't want to sit and dwell on what had just happened.

"The Elders don't have much to go off of," she said quietly.

I smiled at her evasive wording. "No. They don't," I slowly agreed. "Maybe Elder Joshua's arrival will help?" I still wasn't sure what to do about him or how to expose him so he wouldn't tell the other Urbat that I'd figured them out.

She glanced at me with a slight frown, and I could see her

making the connections. "I hope so," she murmured.

In the kitchen, I had to pause for a moment to gape in amazement. The heavenly smells that dotted the commons intensified as I stepped through the door. Several ovens lined the walls. The counters and stovetops were spread with numerous ingredients and dishes in various stages of preparation. So much food...

An older woman with long blonde hair came over to us. She smiled at Michelle. "Another sandwich?"

Michelle looked at me.

I watched another woman pull a turkey from the oven. The crisp brown skin called to me. "Turkey," I mumbled in a zombie-like fashion.

The woman laughed and turned to watch the other woman baste the bird. "It'll be another three hours until they're done. Eighteen birds in all," she confided.

Tearing my eyes from the food, I really looked at her for the first time. "Charlene," I whispered recalling the memory of the girl at school. She didn't look much different. Sure, a little older, but the face was unmistakable.

"Do I know you?"

"Charlene, this is Bethi," Michelle introduced us.

Charlene held out her hand. I looked down at it briefly before meeting her eyes again. "I think it's better if we don't," I said softly. She dropped her hand and eyed me curiously. "You have a lot of food to cook, and I don't want to be responsible for knocking you on your butt. But I'm glad to have met you." Charlene's eyes flared in surprise.

"Same here," she said. "I'll get you something more to snack on. You look like you need it."

(Un)wise

"You know how it is when you're on the run. You're so busy moving your feet you forget to shove something in your mouth."

She nodded again—the look in her eyes told me she really did understand what it felt like to be on the run—before turning away to get a plate. She loaded it with two pieces of pumpkin pie covered with a mountain of whipped cream, a large scoop of fluffy stuff hiding mini marshmallows, and an enormous square of bread pudding with cranberries.

"This should help," she said handing over the heavy plate.

Saliva pooled in my mouth. I could only nod as I turned away. My stomach pulled a little as I carried the plate.

"Can I carry that for you?" Emmitt offered. I looked up. Apprehension spread through me. His eyes saw too much.

"Sure," I said with false ease as I surrendered the plate.

The others had returned and sat in our recently abandoned seats. Seeing Luke sitting there calmly, his eyes meeting Gabby's in some sort of silent communication hurt me even as those stupid crazy butterflies took flight in my stomach.

"If you're feeling tired," Emmitt said softly, "you could take this back to your room."

I stopped walking and turned to him, meeting his eyes. "I'm not really tired as much as I just want to be alone for a while," I said honestly, knowing that Luke could hear me. "So going back to my room sounds great. Would you come get me when something interesting happens?"

He nodded and turned to lead the way back.

* * * *

After Emmitt and Michelle left me in my apartment, I sat on the couch and shoved in a forkful of pumpkin pie. Still warm. I sighed and took another bite. I missed my mom. She made great pumpkin pie when we got together with her side of the family. Cousins, aunts, uncles, my grandpa. I wondered if she was with them. I hoped she was. So many times I had lost the ones I loved. In a way, it helped me now. I still hurt for my mother in this life but also had a numb sort of protection from the hurt. Like scar tissue.

"So you want to be alone, huh?" Luke said as he let himself in and softly closed the door. "A bit rude, don't you think?"

"No more rude than you running off in a drama queen fit so 'Little One' follows you," I said.

He walked around the couch so he stood before me. His expression was slightly amused. "You're jealous."

I wanted to throw my fork at him. "No kidding. Look, either want me or don't, but stop playing the middle ground. I'm tired of waiting for you." That wiped the humor from his expression.

"What do you mean?"

"I mean, I had to suffer through a dream where I was drowned as a baby. If you would have let me Claim you, I'd have more control over the dreams. If you would have stayed by me, I wouldn't have dreamed that at all." Well, maybe not, but he didn't need to know that.

"Bethi, I'm sorry about leaving you. The Elders had questions and wouldn't be ignored."

"I won't be ignored, Luke. Decide."

"There's no decision. We are meant to be together. We just need to be patient for a little while longer. When you turn eighteen—"

"Just stop," I yelled. "Do you hear yourself? Do you even know what you're saying?" I lowered my voice in an imitation of him. "'Bethi, I want to be with you, but first I need you to suffer for three more months. Being killed another ninety times—minimum—isn't asking too much so I can feel virtuous when I allow you to Claim me."

He bent down in front of me and plucked the plate from my hands. "Bethi, I swear. I will not leave you again. I won't allow you to suffer another death," he said softly, brushing the loose hair back from my face.

"I already suffered one too many," I said, standing. "If you add up all the years I've lived across all my lives, I celebrated my one thousandth birthday a couple decades ago. You're not cradle robbing, you're grave robbing. Think on that."

He sighed and stood, too. We stayed like that for a moment. Me glaring and him skimming my face with an increasingly tender look. He stepped close and brushed his finger over my skin, tracing my right eyebrow and then feathering into my hair.

"You have the most amazing eyes," he whispered.

"I've heard that before," I said, struggling against the hope building in my chest.

He leaned in and my heart started to hammer. The last time he'd kissed me he'd said it wouldn't happen again. Did it mean he'd actually heard me? Had he changed his mind? My breath caught as I waited for him to close the last inch between us.

"I will do anything for you," he continued. "Even wait." He turned his head and kissed my cheek—my flippin cheek.

I started shaking. "Get out. Before I hurt myself trying to hit you."

He sighed and backed away. "Bethi—"

"No. No more. Go." I turned my head away unable to look at him.

Stupid idiot.

He left the room. I slumped back into my seat, picked up the plate of dessert he'd taken from me, and gorged myself. Pie, good. Luke, bad.

After the last bite, I settled back with a groan. It felt horrible, in a good way, to be so full again; and it put me in a thoughtful mood.

Once Joshua was here, and we eliminated the threat of further information leaking to the Urbat, we could plan our next steps. Until then, I knew Gabby was watching for a sneak attack. I wished I could talk to her about it but couldn't risk raising the suspicion of the Elders by sneaking into the padded room for a private conversation. That meant being patient and waiting. Just like Luke had asked me to.

Screw waiting and screw Luke. I went to my room and strapped on the sheath and knife. I hated waiting, and I hated feeling so defenseless physically and mentally. I knew Claiming wasn't necessarily permanent. I wanted Luke despite his pigheaded hesitation. But maybe I could find someone willing to let me Claim him until Luke was ready. I could care less who I bit. I just wanted the dreaming to stop. At least, the death dreams. And, those would once I Claimed someone. They had in the past. The other dreams were fine, and I could still learn from them.

I left the room and made my way to the commons. On the way there, I heard a lot of laughing and noise coming from another apartment. The door stood open. Inside, Michelle watched as two young boys wrestled with teens just a bit older than me.

"Paul, cheated," one cried.

"Did not," the other little boy shouted back.

(Un)wise

"Liam. Aden. If you two are going to fight about this, then play time with Paul and Henry is done," Michelle said.

There was a bunch of whining as the teens stood. I stepped back and waited for them to leave. They noticed me after they closed the door. I smiled. Either would do nicely.

* * * *

Paul sat across from me looking nervous, his gaze darting around the room. Henry had fled as soon as I'd explained the favor I needed.

"He'll kill me just to have you back."

"It won't come to that," I promised.

"Yes, it will. You don't know our ways. He'll challenge me to the death. I really want to help you, but I won't have a chance."

"Please," I begged. As a Judgement, I knew I held a certain level of attraction for all of them. Why was this so hard then? Technically, I'd been rejected three times now, counting Luke as a single rejection. Maybe I needed to stand up on one of the tables and start shouting it out. Take me! I'm yours!

A dream started tugging at me.

"If there wasn't anyone else interested in you, I would agree," he promised me. "But if he doesn't kill me, my mom will."

"Yeah, yeah," I waved away his concern. "If he were really interested, why am I still unClaimed?"

Paul looked unsure. "I'm really sorry, Bethi." His words held a note of finality.

"Whatever," I mumbled and stood. When I turned, I caught Luke watching me from a few seats over. My eyes narrowed. He ignored me and looked at Paul, giving him a quick wink.

209

The dream hit me upside the head with a frying pan, and I staggered as I took a step toward the kitchen. The dizzy wave passed over me quickly, barely interrupting my slow progress. Still, Luke stood and moved to my side.

"Are you all right?" he asked with concern.

"Peachy," I answered, tugging my arm from his grasp. Whatever dream waited, it waited impatiently. I could only imagine what horrors it wanted to share with me. I met Luke's gaze. He had the power to change the message it bore just with his presence. Why did he continue to hurt me by keeping himself from me?

"I just need something to drink."

He gave me a gentle smile that twisted my stomach with wishful thinking. "I'll get it for you."

He moved off to the kitchen. I moved off toward the doors.

* * * *

I meant to go outside to find someone else to beg to be my valentine. Instead, I collapsed in the hall with a dream tripping my feet.

A thin, bare shell of darkness covered my eyes. I could easily see shapes through it. Swirls of grey floated in and out of my frame of vision. Voices whispered. Some sounded like grating, unintelligible noise. Others spoke in clear tones.

Regardless of the sounds of the voices, the message was clear. "Free us."

Unable to move, blinking but seeing nothing more than shadow, I lay trapped in a hellish unfeeling world.

Then she came. She stood out in vibrant clarity, her taupe grown robbing the surrounding shades of grey of their unique beauty. Her pale face held a kindness I'd never before witnessed.

(Un)wise

"Child," she whispered. "You can see me as the others cannot. Stand strong though you lack Strength. Be calm though you lack Peace. Wait for Wisdom. She will find you."

Pain burst in the back of my head. "Move!" someone yelled. I forced my small legs to move, taking steps into the unknown with hands outstretched, hoping I wouldn't fall. Hoping that if I did, someone would catch me.

The dream shifted, pulling me deeper.

I ran through the tall grass, the fronds whipping my face, making tiny cuts as I passed. The dry rustle of the grass behind me marked my pursuers.

I struggled to pull myself from the dream. Why was I always running? Once again, I'd merged with my past-self.

"Come on, little one. Tell us what you saw," a voice laughed.

A claw raked my back, parting flesh. I screamed in pain and terror.

"Bethi, wake up!"

I woke swinging. The flat of my palm connected with Luke's face. He looked surprised and quickly captured my hand in his gentle fingers.

Tears leaked from the corners of my eyes as the residual pain lingered on my back. "Get away from me."

"Bethi, I'm sorry—"

"I'm sorry. I'm sorry... Try being something else for a change. Like on time," I snapped picking myself up off the floor.

Hurt reflected in his eyes as he picked up a glass from the floor and handed it to me. "Here's the drink you asked for."

I took the glass and watched him walk away. He was always doing that. Walking away. But then again, so was I. We were hopeless.

FIFTEEN

I sipped the water and slowly walked the halls. After the pain had faded from my back, I regretted my words. I roamed, slightly lost, and hoped to find Luke, but I didn't see him anywhere.

We were at a stalemate. He wanted to wait, and I desperately needed to Claim him now. Neither of us wanted to bend. Well, I'd been willing to bend by selecting someone else, *temporarily*. But he didn't like that idea either. I needed a way to convince him to help me before it was too late. He didn't seem to understand the risks. The attack on the way here showed the desperation of the Urbat. What would they do next? I needed to Claim Luke to calm the dreams so I could focus on their real message. It would also make it easier for him to find me if they took me. If I were completely honest with myself, I just wanted to Claim him because he was mine. Done. Forget the Urbat. Forget the whole the-world-will-burn crap. I just wanted Luke. I sighed. But I couldn't just forget everything. Elder Joshua concerned me. Having the pack of Urbat pull back concerned me. Why hadn't they attacked? There had to be something more, something bigger going on that I hadn't yet

(Un)wise

figured out. And I needed to, fast.

A few more steps, and I recognized where I was. The door to the padded room stood before me. Closed, but I didn't care. I needed help. Maybe the Elders could help me force Luke's hand. I opened it, surprising Nana, Grey, Sam, and a new guy.

"Oh," I mumbled. "Sorry." I moved to close the door but Nana stopped me.

"It's all right, Bethi. Come in. This is Elder Joshua. We were just discussing you."

The Urbat Elder. He watched me closely, and I made sure to keep my face a blank mask. Having him here was better. We could keep an eye on him. I again wished there was a way to control him.

Inspiration struck. Finally! Luck was on my side.

Closing the door, I smiled pathetically at the group. "Sorry for interrupting. Nana, what's your policy on killing potential Mates?"

Nana looked concerned, Grey amused, and Sam curious. Joshua's reaction was just as I'd hoped. Cautious. Trying to figure me out.

"It's Luke," I said to Nana. "He's being completely stubborn about my age, and I think I'm going to hurt him pretty soon."

Grey actually laughed. Nana smiled in understanding.

"Do you have time to take a break and help me talk some sense into him?" I asked her. I knew there was no talking sense into him. He'd already explained he didn't have a pack leader because he didn't want to be forced to follow rules. Elders only enforced laws. I just needed to talk to her in private, away from the other Elders.

"Certainly," she agreed standing. "I'll return promptly," she

213

assured the rest.

Anticipation made my head spin. I wrapped my arm through Nana's and leaned on her for support as we walked the halls. I'd found a way to stop my dreams, a way to forestall the next Urbat attack, a way to keep tabs on Joshua, and maybe a way to force Luke to hold still so I could Claim him.

I planned to Claim Joshua *temporarily*. Sure there would be risks. Luke would be both furious and hurt with my solution. Joshua would have the ability to find me wherever I went as long as we were Claimed. But the benefits outweighed the risks. Joshua would be driven to protect me. Even from his own kind.

The real problem was getting Joshua to let me bite him. I needed to get him alone, play it carefully, and hope Luke would forgive me afterward.

"Can you tell Luke to meet us in our room?"

"Already done," she assured me.

The door opened before we reached it. Luke stood there waiting.

Nana preceded me. His eyes tracked my progress as I shuffled through the door. My heart beat heavily, and I suffered a moment of doubt. His declaration of what I meant to him, all the times he'd come after me...If I did this, it would do more than hurt him. I wanted to go to him, wrap my arms around his waist, and hold him tight. But I knew he wouldn't let me. His resistance to us as a couple was the whole problem. I'd lived too many short lives. I wasn't about to let any opportunity pass by in this one. I would solve our problem for us. I just hoped he wouldn't hate me afterwards.

"'Bout time you're where you should be," I grumbled struggling with the guilt that filled me. As I passed him, he reached out, his fingers tracing the shell of my ear and tucking back a loose strand of hair. I forced my feet to keep moving.

"Now," Nana started, sitting on the couch and waiting for Luke to close the door and join us. "What is the problem here?"

Luke stood beside my chair, his hands tucked casually in his pockets. He glanced at me with a clear question in his eyes. Oh, the games I played.

"Before we start is it possible for you not to share this with the rest of the Elders? I know you have a special connection with them and everything," I glanced at Luke quickly, playing into my hesitation, "but I really don't want anyone else knowing this. I mean you can tell if someone is close enough to hear, too, right?"

"Of course. For the moment, we have privacy. And I won't share the details of private conversations unless I ask first."

"Do you swear?"

"I do."

"Fine. Nothing is shared from this point forward unless you ask me." I sat across from her. "I lied," I said flatly. "Oh, Luke really is annoying me with his whole Puritan attitude," I assured her when she glanced at him. "I lied about something else. Rather, I didn't tell you everything. But for a very good reason. Now, I need you to trust me." I smiled. "Funny asking for trust after admitting to a lie," I said with a shrug. I took a deep breath, reached for Nana's hand and stared into her eyes so she would see and feel the truth of what I had to say. "Joshua is not one of you. He's an Urbat." Her eyebrows rose in question, but I hurried to explain. "I couldn't say anything before because I hadn't figured out what to do about it, but I have a plan now."

"What's an Urbat?"

"The Urbat are a cousin to the werewolf. Not quite the same, but very close. There's more, but we don't have the time or the privacy to get into it."

She sat quiet for a moment. I knew she had many questions for me, but hoped she wouldn't push for more.

"What do you plan to do?" she asked finally.

I sat back with a slight smile. "That's where I need your trust. I can't tell you yet because it depends on Joshua believing me and you. I'm a great liar to your kind. I know the tricks. Scent. Heart rate. All that stuff. If you can't lie, I need you to stay here. If you can lie, I need you to back me up."

"I don't understand," Nana said slowly.

"We need to go back in that room, tell them Luke won't let me Claim him, which is the truth by the way, and I'll explain to the room why I need to Claim someone. If...when Joshua offers a solution, I want us to go along with it."

"What do you think he'll offer?" she asked.

"Something that will lead me away from here and to my other potential Mate."

Luke growled from behind me.

"No one asked you," I said not looking at him. "I won't go, of course," I said to Nana.

"Will whatever you plan put you or the pack in danger?"

I gave a dry laugh. "I've been in danger since I started having those dreams. What I plan shouldn't make it worse. As far as the pack goes, that's what I'm trying to protect."

Another dream started tugging at me, and I rose to my feet, cringing at the pain in my stomach. "I swear I have the perfect plan, Nana. All I need is your support and trust."

"I would feel more comfortable if you shared your plan

first."

"Me too," Luke added. His voice was laced with concern and sprinkled with suspicion.

I was already shaking my head. "Sorry. If I do that, you'll both try talking me out of it because you don't understand everything." She opened her mouth. "And I don't have time to explain it all. We need to start this quickly. Joshua is a huge threat that can't be dealt with through reasoning or a drawn-out fight."

Nana nodded and stood. "I'll give you my support."

Luke made to follow Nana and me, but I stopped him with a raised hand. "No, Luke."

He flicked a glance at Nana. "I will keep her safe," she promised him.

My heart thumped heavily, and I fought to keep a perfectly straight face when his suspicious gaze fell on me again. "What are you planning?" he asked stepping close.

His fingers tangled in my hair, and he leaned in, nuzzling my hair aside so his lips rested near my ear. Shivers ran down my arms, and my eyes closed.

"You smell like sweet pears and cinnamon," he whispered. "The last time you smelled like this you left me at the laundromat waiting for a burger."

My insides froze and my mind told me to push him away. My arms rose to his chest, but not fast enough. Not before he did the unexpected. His tongue darted out, and he lightly licked the edge of my ear. I went stupid. Forgot how to talk. Forgot how to move. I forgot how to breathe. Darn the man.

"Are you running again, Bethi?"

I struggled to gather my wits. His questioning, boyish look

Melissa Haag

helped bring back a little clarity. He was scared, I realized. "I will come back here when I'm done," I managed to say. My internal-self was chanting "more kisses, more kisses!" at the top of its lungs so I couldn't be sure my words came out coherently.

Luke stepped back, his uncertainty clear on his face. "Watch her closely, Winifred. She's up to something."

"Of course I am," I said indignantly. "I already said that."

His lips twitched, and a full smile lit his face. It melted my insides, which made me nervous. He might not forgive me for this.

Containing my doubts, I left the apartment. Nana followed me quietly.

We let ourselves into the padded room, once again stopping conversation.

"Is everything all right?" Sam asked Nana.

She held out a chair for me. "Bethi, sit. You're looking pale again." She turned to Sam. "I'll let Bethi explain."

Clever Nana.

I gave her my best wobbly smile. It wasn't hard. All I had to do was think of Luke's reaction if my plan actually worked.

"Okay," I said with a deep breath. "Like I said, Luke found me a couple of weeks ago. I'd run away from home because of those dreams I mentioned." I met everyone's eyes briefly. Elder Joshua nodded for me to continue, so I guessed the Elders had recapped my last conversation for him. "Anyway, I wanted to run away from Luke, too, after he showed me what he was, but the dreams weren't so bad with Luke around. And he kept me safe, you know?"

They all watched me, waiting for me to get to the point.

"But he only makes the dreams better when he's next to

me. And he keeps leaving," I said with true annoyance. I took another deep breath, carefully planning my words as I flattened my palms on the table. "I don't want these dreams anymore. I don't care about puzzles or their stupid pieces. They don't make any sense and they're scary. Terrifying. I think it would help me if I Claimed someone."

I uncurled my fingers with effort. The subject annoyed me to the point that I'd fisted my hands.

"I asked Luke, but he told me I was too young. I almost had Paul convinced to let me Claim him, but Luke showed up and scared him away."

Grey gave me an indulgent smile as if to say "of course, he would scare the boy away."

"If Luke won't Claim me, I'm asking for your help to find me someone who will and to keep Luke out of it." Because I don't want him hurt, I silently added.

No one made a sound. Nana kept her face perfectly straight, but I could still see her surprise. In fact, all of their faces registered different states of shock. Joshua's also held a note of thoughtful concern.

"Does Luke know you've come to us?" he asked.

"Luke knows I'm talking to you guys, but I didn't exactly tell him why."

"I thought you wanted us to help you figure these dreams out," Sam said, finally finding his voice.

"No, I wanted to know why I was having them. After this last one, I don't care anymore. I just want them to stop. Will you help me?" I looked around the table and didn't see much approval. Nana looked like she was having an internal struggle. No doubt she was regretting her promise to support me.

"Please."

Nana sighed. "If Luke is denying your Claim, you have a right to request Introductions." She didn't sound happy about it, but she was going along with it.

Silence wrapped around the occupants of the room. I waited, keeping calm, meeting everyone's eyes. I could see the discomfort growing in Grey. Sam looked seriously troubled. Nana looked just a tad angry. I couldn't blame her. She probably felt betrayed on Luke's behalf. Joshua though, kept his eyes on the table, deep in thought.

Finally, he broke the silence. "We should consider this carefully before we move forward with anything."

Good.

"If he is waiting for her to mature," he glanced at me and gave me an apologetic smile, "then it is possible he will challenge whomever she Claims. We don't want to be reduced to chaos when there are so many other elements concerning us."

Meaning the recent attack. I kept my face neutral.

"Joshua's correct," Sam agreed. Grey nodded. They all looked relieved.

"What does that mean for me?" I asked, pushing.

Joshua sighed regretfully. "It means we too are asking for your patience. We need to ensure we are doing what is best for the pack."

Playing my role, I scowled. "Fine. But my patience is limited. I can already feel another dream gathering. I'll give you an hour to decide, or I'm going to jump on the next unMated I see and start biting."

Standing quickly, I fled out the door as if angry and almost ran into Luke. Thankfully, I'd been wearing my I'm-annoyed-and-leaving face and not my ha-ha-you-fool face. He caught my arms so I wouldn't bump into him and pulled back, his eyes searching my face. The hall was empty except for us.

"I thought you were waiting in the room," I said.

"I didn't actually think you'd come back," he commented letting go of my arms.

"I told you I would." How could a man be so annoying yet so endearing?

A corner of his mouth tilted up in a half-smile, and he threaded his fingers through mine. We walked back to the apartment in silence. Though my mouth was quiet, my mind was not. He didn't just hold my hand, he held my heart. I really started to doubt my wisdom. What a joke. Me. Wisdom.

He opened the apartment door for me. I eased onto the couch and closed my eyes.

The cushions next to me dipped as he sat beside me. His arm curved around my shoulders, and he pulled me to his side. "You look tired."

"I'm always tired." Hopefully not much longer though.

Pressed into his warm side, I relaxed and the dreams swirled. Thankfully, less than a minute later, someone knocked on the door.

Luke eased me from his side to answer it. Sam stood in the entry. "Luke, we would like to speak with you." His voice held regret. Luke glanced at me, seeking my permission to leave my side.

"I'll be fine," I assured him.

He walked out with Sam, and I waited for the main player, lightly touching the knife still strapped to my leg. As I anticipated, another knock sounded on the door.

"Come in," I called.

Joshua opened the door with a smile. "Bethi, hello." He closed the door. "We are breaking the news to Luke now. Actually, we are isolating him to give others a fair chance. We called a few candidates to the woods just outside the Compound if you would come with me."

"Perfect," I agreed, not bothering to contain my happiness. Joshua watched me closely as I stood. The stitches pulled when I tried to straighten so a cringe wasn't hard to fake. "I'm not sure I'll make it that far."

He frowned slightly, considering me before stepping close. "If you'll allow me, I'll carry you."

"Thank you."

He bent down, placed an arm behind my knees and my back, and with a quick move, he lifted me into his arms. I settled high with my arm around his shoulders.

"Joshua, I should warn you. There's another dream coming on and I'm not sure how long I'll..." I lightly sighed and dropped my head on his shoulder. I should have been in theater. "I'm not sure how long I'll be able to stay awake."

There was no dream, at least, not one that I couldn't resist. The light scent of his shaving cream filled my nose. Underneath that, I could smell the real Joshua. Woods, sky, and mud. It held no appeal to me whatsoever.

"Don't worry," he assured me, turning toward the door.

I nodded my head, the movement bringing me closer to his neck. All my attempts with Luke had taught me something. Don't dart in until you were sure he couldn't get a hand up fast enough. Joshua didn't see it coming. I ducked in and bit him hard before we made it to the door.

He gasped, a mix of pleasure and fear. I wiped my mouth on his suit jacket. Ew. His taste was worse than his smell.

The arm supporting my legs slackened, and I loosened my arms around his neck, fearing for my stitches. The blade I had strapped to my leg was trapped between us. His eyes met mine as my legs slowly slid to the floor. The arm at my back kept me pinned as he searched my face. Panic flared within me, but it was not my own. I waited patiently for him to sort through what I had just done.

"What did you do?" he finally managed. Apparently, he couldn't sort through it on his own.

"I caused you a mess of trouble," I admitted, keeping control of my emotions. I suppressed my smug joy and my own concern, giving him no indication through our link what I might be thinking. "We both know whoever you had waiting wasn't right for me. Luke would have been right if he'd been willing. I need someone strong enough to protect me. To keep me safe during the storm that's coming this way."

His gaze dipped to my mouth. His hands brushed up and down my arms. The shock of my unexpected Claim was wearing off. The calculated look crept back into his eyes. Desire flared through our link. Dangerous territory. This was the part of the plan that had caused me the most concern. I knew I'd be safe from the other Urbat now, but how did I keep myself safe from him? I'd hoped Nana wouldn't let him out of her sight.

The door burst open, and Luke strode in. Fire lit his eyes as he took in Joshua's hold on my arms. Nana, Sam, and Grey walked in behind him.

"Joshua?" Sam said as he took in the scene.

"I Claimed him," I said softly. The Elders needed to know.

All part of the plan. But watching Luke and the pain that flared in his eyes hurt. I couldn't keep the remorse from welling up within me. Joshua growled in response, and dropped his hands so he could stand in front of me.

"As an Elder, you are not permitted to Claim," Grey said with anger in his voice. "You broke your oath to hold the interest of the pack above your own interests." Grey paused, his anger giving way to confusion. "How are you still alive?"

Joshua twitched as if in pain, and his growl grew louder. The tenuous link he'd had to the werewolves had just been irrevocably severed. I held myself still. He was alive because he wasn't one of them, and wasn't bound by their rules. I'd anticipated his reaction going one of two ways. Joshua could go crazy realizing his cover was blown and try to attack the rest, or he could realize the precariousness of his dilemma.

"As you are well aware, we are not able to Claim any of these girls. She Claimed me." A low growl remained in his voice, but I felt a surge of relief that he chose to talk, not attack. "I will hold that Claim."

All eyes in the room swung to me. Luke's pain showed through his gaze.

I gave a quick nod, answering the unspoken question. I would hold my Claim to Joshua as long as he didn't try for more or try to hurt Luke. Not yet ready to get into the whole "why" of it, I eased my hand to the blade at my side. Not drawing it, but ready to as I eyed Joshua's back.

"Joshua, does this mean you are no longer able to communicate with the pack?" I asked innocently.

He turned to look at me over his shoulder, his eyes narrowing on me fractionally.

"He shouldn't even be alive," Grey restated.

"Yes, yes," I said, waving away his concern and keeping my eyes on Joshua. I still saw Grey's surprised reaction and Luke's transformation. He went from wounded ex to suspicious friend. It gave me hope for us.

Joshua's frown grew. He took a slow deep breath. His suspicion flooded me. "I feel...something from you. Not happiness exactly. You're trying to keep your emotions from me. Why?"

I answered with a small smile. "Have you told your leader what happened? You know he won't let you keep me."

Joshua's eyes flared wide, and he growled. I couldn't quite tell if the growl was at me or at the thought of losing me. I'd counted on his possessive nature and really hoped it was the latter.

"Thomas already knows," Sam's voice rang with authority.

Joshua's hands curled into fists, but I noted his nails elongating.

"Not Thomas," I said with a shake of my head. "His Urbat leader." Nana glanced down for a moment, and I had the feeling she was doing some silent communicating with Sam and Grey.

"So, Joshua, have you told him? We need to know how soon they will be coming to take me and kill you."

He roared a cry of frustration and anguish. I knew he'd just realized his inevitable death sentence from both sides. Only his connection to me kept him safe for the moment.

Luke's skin rippled in response to his outburst.

"We need to take it down a notch, guys," I said raising my hands. "This human's way too easy to break, and neither of you would like that."

Joshua struggled with himself. Grey placed a hand on Luke's shoulder. I could see the two of them having a silent conversation. Luke noticeably calmed, but he still struggled to contain his shift.

"Let's recap for everyone who doesn't know what's going on," I said softly, unsure if Joshua had thought of everything. "By Claiming you, I stripped you of your Elder privileges, blew your cover with this pack, and voided your usefulness here in the eyes of your Urbat leader. In addition, I've made you his target since he will not allow you to keep me. After all, I feel no connection with you that would help sway any decisions that I might need to make. There's really nowhere safe for you right now." Joshua straightened his stance, a sudden seriousness exploding onto his expression.

He took a slow, deep breath. "Why not just have them," he nodded at the Elders, "kill me right away? Why Claim me?"

"If they had killed you, you would have sent one last message to your leader. It probably would have started an attack and cost countless lives."

"What makes you think I didn't already send a message?" he asked softly, his eyes lightly skimming my face.

"To protect me. I'm yours, right?" His eyes softened at my words. "You don't want to lose me. Plus, you'd forfeit your life by doing so. Like I said, they won't let you keep me." I took a step back from Joshua. Luke's tremors hadn't stopped since he'd walked through the door, and I didn't want to ignite that bomb waiting to go off.

Joshua's eyes tracked me. I felt his yearning. He wanted me close. He wanted to touch me. I wondered if Luke felt for me even a fraction of what Joshua felt. If he did, how did he keep saying no?

"He underestimated you," Joshua said softly.

I knew he meant his leader. "Your kind usually does," I agreed. And still I always died.

"So how do you see this ending?"

"That depends on how many are waiting out there to meet me," I said, reminding Joshua of his original intent when he entered the room.

His lips curled. "Three."

I nodded slowly, thinking. Only three. A discreet number easy to slip in and take me. A perfect number to obliterate. I needed to keep the room at peace, and Joshua on my side for a bit longer.

Meeting Nana's eyes I said, "I don't want a Mating challenge."

Luke growled. "It is my right."

"Shush," I said, keeping my eyes on Nana.

She looked troubled by my words. I could see her weighing my safety and the pack's safety. By keeping Joshua linked to me the pack would be safe, but would I? Joshua would soon realize the only way to save himself would be to mate with me and create an unbreakable bond. Hopefully, Nana wouldn't see that just yet. Finally, she reluctantly nodded her agreement.

Luke growled, and Joshua laughed.

"Like Joshua said, I need to think about how this should end. I don't want bloodshed. That's why I Claimed Joshua. To avoid just that." I moved to touch Joshua's arm, tamping down my revulsion.

"Joshua, I'd like to meet with the Elders and figure out how we can leave here without dying."

He purred with satisfaction and in a quick move, wrapped his arms around me in a hug, pressing me tight against his body. My stitches pulled and I made a small noise. Oblivious, he leaned in and nuzzled my neck. I fought not to gag.

"Moron, you're hurting her," Luke growled, taking a step toward me.

Over Joshua's shoulder, I watched Grey clamp down on one of Luke's arms and Sam the other. They held him back as his body flexed in a constant state of shifting. I couldn't tell if his wolf form was coming or going.

"Please, Joshua. He's right. You're hurting me. I was cut recently."

Joshua still didn't pull back. His hot breath warmed my neck a second before his tongue laved it, just below the ear Luke had kissed not long ago. Joshua was marking me, wiping away Luke's scent. Not good. I could feel his desire rising again.

"Nana," I called in a slight panic.

"Joshua," Nana warned. "She is in no shape for what you're thinking. Stop now, or for her safety I will stop you."

He laughed, a rumble I felt in my own chest since we were pressed so close. But he did ease back. "Soon," he whispered, ducking down to meet my gaze. "They can't stop a Claimed pair," he promised, his hand drifting to my belly. His fingers traced the stitches through my shirt. "A few days will see us truly together."

I nodded slowly as if agreeing while trying to keep the tremors from my body. He smiled in return and released me. I couldn't look at Luke. I wanted a shower.

Nana held her hand out to me. I clasped it tightly and left the room with her. I hoped they knew to keep an eye on Joshua.

(Un)wise

He wouldn't leave without me. I'd ensured that when I Claimed him. But, I didn't want him near Luke.

Sixteen

"I don't even know where to start," Nana said, sitting across from me.

The padded room was packed. The Elders, my sisters, and I sat at the table. Emmitt, Thomas, Clay, and Luke stood.

"Who's watching Joshua?" I asked.

"Carlos," Grey answered. "He won't let Joshua leave or let any harm come to him."

I snorted. "I could care less if any harm comes to him."

"Then why did you Claim him?" Luke asked flatly. His regard hadn't left me since he'd entered the room. A glint of hurt still lingered in the depths of his gaze, but something else consumed him. Determination.

I ignored his questions knowing I'd explained myself well enough in the room. "Here's the deal. The world is not just made up of humans and werewolves. There is a third race, the Urbat. They call themselves the dogs of death and are your close cousins."

"They are the ones you can't control," Michelle added, talking to Nana.

I nodded. "Then there's us," I said, looking at Charlene,

Gabby, and Michelle. "We don't belong to any of the three groups. Werewolf, Urbat, or human. We are unique."

"Special," Nana agreed.

"We are here to maintain the balance between the three groups." Sam opened his mouth, but I quickly cut him off. "I'm not sure exactly how we're supposed to do that. We have abilities. Mine is to relive past lives—not just my past lives, but all of our past lives—through dreams. Our abilities seem to help the group we are aligned with in some way. Michelle's gift is prosperity. In past lives, she knew the locations of lost treasure, herbs with medicinal properties, how to create things to better lives. Pretty much any knowledge that could be used to create wealth. Charlene strengthens the group she's allied with and so on. I have no idea how that all plays in, but as soon as the Urbat learned of us, they began hunting us."

"If they are hunting you, why did you Claim one?" Luke asked again, maintaining a calm voice. I wondered how angry he really was.

"We return every one thousand years for a period of time. I don't know all the details of that either. But I've recalled enough of those past lives to know we always die." Meeting Luke's eyes, I finally answered him. "I Claimed him to stay alive...to buy us some time to plan."

Nana gave Luke a look before turning to me. "To plan what, dear?"

"An evacuation, to start."

"What do you mean?" Thomas asked.

"When the Urbat come, they will use the people we love to try to sway us. First, they use our families, torturing them until we do what they want. If that doesn't work, they start torturing us."

"What do they want?" Grey asked.

"For each of us to Claim one of them." My eyes darted to my sisters.

"We've already Claimed someone," Gabby pointed out. Clay rested a hand on her shoulder.

"It won't matter. A Claim can be broken by death, or simply by Claiming another. That's why I was willing to Claim Joshua."

Stunned silence held the room. Michelle gave Emmitt a panicked look. Luke's gaze didn't leave me though I refused to look at him.

"The next step is for life," I said. Luke growled a deep warning but I kept going. "Once Mated, we don't Mate again. I mean, they *could* force us to Claim another and mate, but it doesn't do any good. Our hearts stay with the first lost Mate. The new Mate holds no influence."

"Influence for what?" Sam questioned.

"For balance," I explained. "They have been after power ever since they figured out what we are. The Judgements. In the beginning, we always judged in favor of the humans. At least, that's my guess. I haven't dreamed what really happened yet. Since then, as far as I've seen, we haven't made another Judgement. I'm guessing that's why, despite the inferiority of humans in comparison to your races, they have thrived."

Sam looked thoughtful. Everyone else just looked too stunned to think much.

"The Urbat are tired of living in the shadows and want to be the dominant race for a while. The last cycle they almost had it, but one of us died. Without all of us to...do something, things will stay the way they are, with humans maintaining control," I explained. "The cycle doesn't last forever—only fifty years—so they try not to risk our lives. But they will if they must. After all, we can still be reborn again into the same cycle."

"So you're saying we need to clear the Compound because they will come for all of you and use the people here to talk you into surrendering?" Thomas asked, his disbelief evident.

"Don't doubt it. They will come. They always come," I said evenly, trying to contain my building dread. I couldn't afford for Joshua to feel that through our link. Taking a breath to ease the ache in my chest, I added in a low voice, "And death always follows." Those whispered words caught the attention of everyone in the room. Maybe death didn't need to follow this time. I held on to that possibility.

"What then? Where do we go?"

"That's the tricky part. I don't know where the pack should go, but I know where we need to go. We are missing two of our group. We need to find them."

"About this evacuation," Charlene started.

I could see she didn't want to leave. "Out of all of us, you and Michelle are the most vulnerable. Michelle's brothers need to be sent away and protected. Emmitt, if he's taken, will be a risk to both of you. They will want to break the Claim Michelle has as much as they will want to hurt Emmitt to sway you," I said to Charlene.

She glanced at her son, worry in her eyes. Emmitt gave her a smile and squeezed Michelle's hand gently. "Don't worry. We know now so we can make sure it doesn't happen."

Charlene nodded, but her fear remained.

"What are we going to do about Joshua?" Grey asked.

"Nothing. At least not yet. Oh, but I can't be left alone with him. With these stitches," I gently laid a hand over my middle, "I won't be able to fight him off."

"You said you could Claim another to break your Claim," Nana said gently. "Why wait?"

"Because I'm not done with him yet. Until the Compound is clear and we're ready to leave, I have to keep my hold on him. It's the only thing that's keeping him from reporting back to his leader."

"Are you sure about that?" Sam looked troubled.

"No, not really but it's our best chance. Now, there are three Urbat out in the woods waiting for Joshua. Gabby, can you see them?"

All eyes turned to her. She nodded hesitantly, and I reached across the table to lightly touch her hand. "We need to find them and get rid of them before people start leaving. They can't know what we're doing."

"They're not far from here. But, there are ten more scattered in the surrounding area. Nothing close enough for concern though. The rest are regrouping in the east." She paused for a moment, a frown pulling at her brow. "More are coming from the main group. I think you're right, Bethi. They're coming back."

I nodded and patted her hand. "It's good," I reassured her. "I'd be more freaked out if they weren't. Pick an Elder and a team of five to go out and hunt the three Urbat down," I directed. The ones waiting to meet Joshua and me would be the first to question our delay. "Kill them quickly and quietly so they can't communicate back to their leader. Deal with the ten on the outskirts as needed. Closest first."

Nana looked troubled.

(Un)wise

"No prisoners, Nana. Think of the families running from here with kids. Those ten prowling the outskirts will track and kill them if they get wind that this is a mass exodus. The three need to be silenced quickly without a chance for them to send word." I held everyone's attention. I could see questions still stirring, but knew we didn't have too much time.

"We need to move," I said standing. "Their leader—"

"Blake," Michelle interjected.

"Blake will be wondering why Joshua hasn't reported by now. Gabby, let us know if you see a change in their direction."

Gabby nodded.

"Nana, will you come with me to talk to Joshua?"

"I'm coming too," Luke said.

I shook my head. "No, Luke. I need him calm. Help Gabby. Clear the field so we can be done with this and I no longer need my Claim on Joshua."

His eyes held mine for a long moment before he nodded and stepped back.

"Please excuse us," Emmitt said pulling Michelle to her feet.

"Where are you going?" Nana asked concerned.

Michelle met Emmitt's gaze, and must have felt something through their link because she suddenly grinned before turning to Nana with a blush. "Cementing my Claim," she murmured.

Charlene chuckled. "If you two could wait just a bit longer, we'll watch the boys for you."

Emmitt gave a curt nod and held out Michelle's chair for her again. Michelle sat, red faced, but happy.

Gabby looked over her shoulder at Clay and shook her head. He laughed and bent to kiss the top of her head.

Seeing the room committed to the direction we needed to

take, Nana helped me up from the chair, and we left the rest to plan the evacuation.

* * * *

We could see Joshua pacing the apartment when Carlos opened the door for us. A lamp lay broken in the middle of the floor, and Carlos' lip bled. I wanted to apologize to him but knew how Joshua would take that. Joshua looked worse. His right eye had swollen shut and purple fingerprints decorated the left side of his neck. I didn't feel too badly for him.

"That took much longer than I expected," Joshua said, coming to a stop. His eyes swept over me and held malice as he watched Nana enter behind me.

"I'm sorry about that. Instead of concentrating on the problem of us, they got hung up on the fact that there's another race and that I'm not exactly human."

He barely paid attention to my words. He looked ready to fight again.

Tamping down my aversion, I walked up to him, placed my hands on his shoulders, and stood on my toes to place a chaste kiss on his cheek. The tension in his shoulders eased, and a purr rumbled in his chest.

Crisis averted, I dropped my hands, but his arms came up around me before I could step away. I let out a slow breath trying to keep any panic from welling up. I did *not* want to be in his arms.

"We need to leave here soon," Joshua said. "Our troubles are still waiting. I'm stalling as best I can."

Ah. His agitation made more sense. I could only imagine what his leader was screaming at him through their link. I nodded and tried to wear a concerned look. "I've asked that the

Elders help make our troubles go away."

He eyed me for a moment. A surge of possessiveness swept through me, then calculation. I didn't miss the hint of suspicion as he smiled slowly. "That would be ideal."

The suspicion worried me. Perhaps I was playing it up too much. "Would you mind if I took a bit more time to shower? I think I smell like a hot dog." Hot Dog? I kept my face straight while I mentally kicked myself over my random choice of smell comparisons.

He leaned in to inhale deeply. "I smell spiced pears. Delicious."

Crap. I struggled with what to do. I did not want him licking me again.

"Joshua," Nana rumbled a warning.

He reluctantly released me. "Of course. Go bathe. Winifred can fill me in."

"I'll be quick," I promised him. I just needed to wash my neck where I still felt his tongue. Suppressing a shiver, I walked away and closed myself into the bathroom.

Through the door, I heard Joshua's howl of frustration and Nana's calm tones. I stayed in the bathroom, hiding, wondering how long it would take Luke and whoever else to hunt down the three in the woods. Then, how long would it take the wolves living here to pack up and leave? I needed to do something to keep Joshua occupied until we were ready to go. He could send all the messages he wanted after that. The rest of the Urbat would still be too far away to reach us in time. I hoped.

After a few minutes, I emerged with a thoroughly scrubbed neck. Joshua's eyes tracked me as I walked the short distance to him. He'd once again been pacing.

"We're leaving," he growled at me.

"Now?" I forced myself to remain calm. "We still have your friends out there to worry about."

"Not any longer. They've been silenced. He is asking me for information. They are gathering to return. We must leave *now*."

I let out a loud sigh. "Of course. Then we need to leave." Nana sat on the chair watching us. "Is everything ready?"

"Almost," she said.

My stomach gave a sickening lurch, and a wave of dizziness hit me. A dream called, and it almost knocked me out where I stood. I struggled to breathe and stay upright.

Joshua lunged for me, worry in his eyes. Behind him, Nana rose, her expression determined. Joshua's hands gripped my arms as he steadied me. I opened my mouth to reassure them both, but only managed a wide-eyed look as Nana reached for his neck. My shocked expression was the only warning I managed to give Joshua. Nana twisted his head sharply, killing him instantly. Before his body could crumple toward me, she pulled him back.

"What did you do?" I gasped, quickly revising my thoughts that older people were nice.

"We're ready. We don't need him anymore. The families have packed and the last one is leaving. The unMated are following as escorts. Gabby has given the location of the last ten so they can be avoided. We are all that remain."

I stared down at Joshua's lifeless form and felt like crying. His death didn't bother me as much as the timing of it. I'd meant for him to live to pressure Luke to replace the Claim. Now there was no reason for Luke to give up his stubborn determination to keep me at arm's length.

"Come, Bethi," she said, lifting my bag and holding out a

hand. Lethal hands, I thought still dazed.

We walked through a quiet Compound. A sense of cold anticipation filled the halls. Doors to apartments stood open. Small things like lamps and blankets were missing. The large pieces of furniture remained. What had I started? They all trusted me. They'd listened. For the first time in all the lives I'd recalled, the people around me had run before it was too late. Did it mean things would change this time around?

Outside, the remaining cars left the parking lot in an orderly fashion. Sam stood on the porch watching it all. Three cars waited nearby with their doors open. Gabby stood near one, her eyes unfocused. Clay stood just behind her, a hand on her shoulder. They both faced the Compound.

"The Urbat have turned," she said when I stepped onto the porch. "A small group, though."

"I'm not surprised," I answered distractedly. I couldn't see Luke.

Nana nudged me aside, and I watched Carlos stride past carrying Joshua. I hadn't even known he'd been following us. He stepped off the porch and headed for the woods.

"Where's he going?" I asked. We didn't have much time if the Urbat were headed toward us.

"Taking him to the woods. Charlene put her heart into this place. Maybe they will leave it be if he's found out there," Nana said, moving past me.

She slid into the backseat of one of the cars, sandwiching two little boys in between her and Jim. Michelle and Emmitt sat in the front. I doubted they'd been given the time they wanted to cement their Claim. Emmitt started the car forward as soon as Nana closed the door.

"Sam," Gabby said, "we need to leave *now*."

Carlos emerged from the woods at a run with Luke at his side. My heart went crazy. Deep down, I'd thought he would leave without me because of what I'd done.

Sam held out his hand and helped me from the porch. He, Clay, and Gabby climbed into his truck while Luke, Carlos, Grey, and I quickly filled the remaining car. Luke kept his distance from me, leaving the space of the middle seat between us. I hugged my arm to my stomach, not so much for the stitches, but for the emotional maelstrom of doubt that lived there. We left in a hurry. Everyone followed the same road heading south. From there, cars in the caravan started taking random turn-offs.

"Does everyone know where to go?" I asked.

Grey answered. "Gabby gave everyone several safe locations where the Urbat population is low. The Urbat are mostly in the northeast so everyone will avoid that area."

"Tell Gabby we need to find somewhere safe enough to stop for a few hours. We need to plan how to get Peace before the Urbat find her."

Grey nodded but said nothing. Hopefully, he was talking to Sam.

I glanced at Luke and found him watching me. It hurt to look at him. My eyes burned, and my lips trembled. I struggled to keep it all in. I didn't think a simple apology would make up for what I'd done to him but said it anyway. He gave the barest of nods and reached across the seat to clasp my hand.

His touch, the light rumble of the tires over the road, and an already long messed up day did me in. My eyes fluttered closed, and a single thought floated to the surface before a dream pulled me under. I hate car rides.

SEVENTEEN

I woke with a gasp. Luke's hand was stroking my cheek. My head lay back against the seat.

"You all right?" he asked softly. He'd turned toward me, but he still kept his distance.

The tires still rumbled over the road as I lifted my arms. I flexed my hands and wiggled my fingers as I swallowed hard. "They cut off my fingers. One by one." I let out a shaky breath and closed my eyes again. "Can we stop for an energy drink or something?"

The car remained quiet, and I opened my eyes just in time to see Luke and Grey share a look.

"What?" I demanded looking between the two of them.

Luke picked up one of my hands and started massaging the fingers. After what had just happened to them, it felt great. But, he looked out the window while he did it without answering me.

Grey gave me a wink. "You were only out five minutes. Gabby said the Urbat seem to be tracking us. We're heading for the interstate. She'll let us know as soon as it's safe to stop."

I groaned and dropped my head back to the seat. Even with Luke holding my hand, I'd dreamt of death. It wasn't enough.

Shifting my position often and rolling the window down to let in the cold air helped, but I knew I wouldn't be able to fight off the dreams while sitting still like this.

* * * *

Five deaths later, we finally pulled into a nice hotel crawling with people. Our four vehicles parked close together. Michelle's brothers tumbled out of the car, climbing over a laughing Jim. Emmitt quickly walked around the front to open the doors for Michelle and Nana. Thomas did the same for Charlene. Clay opened the door and stood aside while Gabby slid out. She looked tired, too.

As soon as Carlos put our car in park, I flung open my door and scrambled out. My skin still crawled from the last dream. Charlene and Thomas walked ahead to book us rooms. I hurried after them.

"No credit cards," I said to Charlene, walking beside her. She nodded and approached the desk.

I waited for Michelle to enter the lobby. "How much cash do you have?"

She looked at Emmitt. "Three hundred," he said.

Shaking my head, I glanced at Gabby who had joined our group. "You said we needed to go east. We need enough cash to make it there. I don't know how deep the Urbat are into the human world. If they have any connections, they could use credit card transactions to track us."

"I have no doubt Blake could," Michelle said, keeping her voice soft. Her eyes followed Jim as he took the boys down a side hall to check out the pool. "I have someone I trust who can wire me some money."

"Good." I turned and almost ran into Luke. He caught my

arms before I could walk into him. "Sorry," I mumbled.

Just behind him, Charlene turned away from the desk. "They only had five rooms," she said, joining our group. "One is the honeymoon suite." She handed a key card to Emmitt with a smile. "The others are double queens."

She held up the remaining cards.

"Sam can room with us," Gabby quickly offered. I didn't miss Clay reaching up to soothe her back. She looked over her shoulder to give him a shy smile.

"I thought you and the boys could sleep with us, Nana," Charlene suggested. Nana agreed, and Michelle looked relieved. Her brothers would be well protected.

"Jim can join us," Grey said, looking up at Carlos. "Right, darling?" Grey teased.

Carlos stoically agreed.

Luke grabbed the remaining room card without a word. A room to ourselves. A room with two beds. Yeah, I didn't let my hopes get too high.

"Let's meet in the suite first," I suggested. "If they catch up to us, I want a plan laid out."

Five minutes later, we gathered in the suite minus Jim, the boys, and Nana. They splashed in the pool.

"I've been all over the board with my explanations. So let me be clear with what I'm trying to avoid. Dying. It's not fun," I said. "We need to stop their power trip. I don't mean just in this life and cycle but future lives and cycles, too. We need to rob them of their chance to control us in this life. We need to make their search hard and their goal nearly impossible." I did *not* want to live through another brutal death in my next life. Old age would be a new experience for me.

The thought sparked inspiration. "We need to change the game," I said with a growing smile.

"What do you have in mind?" Sam asked.

Taking a deep breath, I braced myself for the argument that I knew would ensue. "As I mentioned, there are six of us. We represent different things. Prosperity, Hope, Wisdom, Strength, Peace, and Courage. According to Gabby and Michelle, the Urbat already have one of us. Courage. They can't have *any* of us because all of us are needed to make a Judgement this cycle." I knew in my heart I spoke the truth. The world was so unbalanced it wobbled. "We can't get to Courage. There's just no way with our numbers. That's why we need to expose werewolves and Urbat to the humans."

As expected, denial broke out.

"You can't be serious," Thomas said.

"We'll be at their mercy," Sam added. "We don't go to hospitals for a reason."

"I first saw you at one," Gabby pointed out.

"I was visiting a human friend," he said, waving away the reason. "We'll end up in cages."

"No," I said, but no one listened. "Just calm down," I shouted, quieting the room.

"Hear me out. They have the advantage. There are more of them. They know what's going on, and we don't. Not fully...not yet, anyway. They've been building up connections in the human world." I looked to Michelle, and she nodded in agreement. "We need to come into the light before they do. Show the world that werewolves exist, show we're not bad, and then expose the Urbat, too. We need to show that we're different from the Urbat and that they are trying to hurt us.

"If we direct human concern toward the Urbat and not werewolves, we will have less to worry about. The Urbat won't be able to creep around trying to hunt us because the humans will be watching. Urbat won't be safe."

"Neither will we," Sam said.

"Not in your fur, you're right. You'll need to let everyone know to keep it under wraps. And the ones that can't, shouldn't go outside. But we can't expose everything until we have Peace. She takes the panic and anxiety down to almost catatonic. And Charlene can help keep everyone on the same page," I added. "Werewolves are good, Urbat are bad."

Charlene looked uncertain.

"We'll keep the initial group small," I assured her. "We need to find someone at a TV station to take us seriously enough to give us air time. We want this to be recorded at their studio to give it more credibility."

"I might know someone," Michelle offered hesitantly. "She interviewed me once."

"Perfect!" I said, excited and feeling like I was on the right track. "When we're there, Charlene will need to grab everyone in the room and keep them from thinking they should call the National Guard to make us into lab rats. Meanwhile, Peace will keep everyone in the studio from freaking out. The first impression werewolves will give is a calm and kind one. It wouldn't hurt to have a spokesperson who looks sweet and unable to snap someone's neck," I said, knowing the Elders were communicating.

Grey laughed slightly. "Winifred is not comfortable with being the spokesperson and wants me to remind you clothes don't change with us."

"We'll bring a robe," I promised. "By exposing ourselves—no pun intended—we are robbing the Urbat of their advantage. They can't hope to win against humans in an outright war. There are too many. Their technology is too advanced. A bullet in the head would kill any of the three races just the same. If we tell the world we're the good guys, and warn them to watch out for the bad guys, we're more likely to make it harder for the Urbat to win this time around."

"More likely?" Carlos questioned, speaking for the first time.

I blinked at him. "I didn't think you actually talked." He didn't answer, just continued to look at me. "Okay. Well, historically, the Urbat would find as many of the Judgements as they could, and torture us to get our obedience. But one of us always dies too late in the cycle for rebirth and stops them from obtaining their goal. So I can't promise this will work. It's never been done before."

"We agree we should find Peace before the Urbat do," Sam said slowly. "But we will need to further discuss revealing our race before we make a decision. We need to do what's best for the pack."

"Exactly," I stressed. "The pack will die as it is. It can't stay hidden. The Urbat are crazy desperate. The things they've done..." Luke's fingers threaded through mine.

"We have to stop them."

"We agree," Grey said. "We just need to think everything through."

He was right. We had time to discuss the necessity of revealing the Urbat and werewolf races to the humans. I held in a sigh and contented myself with his maybe.

"Fine. But we need to plan our next stop. I'm not sure if

traveling together is a good thing or not, but in case we get separated, we should have a place picked ahead of time."

Michelle used her phone to find another hotel a day's drive east of where we were. We all agreed on it, and she made the reservations.

Charlene excused herself and promised to bring back something to eat. When she and Thomas returned, they had one of the turkeys and several containers of the meal they'd been working on before we left the Compound.

Everyone piled food on the plates she brought. I sought her out. "I'm really sorry you didn't get to have your nice meal."

"No, Bethi. What we're doing now is much more important. For years, I've felt a...itch, I guess you'd say. Like I was supposed to be doing something, but I never could figure out what. The itch is gone now. I know what we're doing is right."

She lifted her arms and offered a hug. I went in willingly and fell into the abyss.

"Do you have Courage?" the Taupe Lady whispered from the black.

"No. They have her. But I hope to change that."

"You must have Courage," she answered. A cool hand caressed my face and, for the first time in months, I felt completely at ease and free of the terror and desperation.

"Unite," she whispered. "Before it's too late."

Someone tapped my cheek, and I struggled to stay under, but the Taupe Lady had already faded taking the serenity with her.

I lay on the ground looking up at the bottoms of everyone's plates. "Go. Away," I mumbled. I couldn't even sit up. It would kill my stomach.

"What happened?" Thomas asked. I turned my head and saw Charlene lying next to me.

"She really shouldn't touch any of us too much," I muttered. "We drain her." He frowned at me, but Charlene opened her eyes forestalling whatever he'd been about to say.

"I'm fine," she reassured him. "Just takes me a bit to pull it all back in." She turned and looked at me. "What happens when we do that? Besides draining me."

"Our abilities flare. Gabby's lights ignite with no effort on her part." Gabby's fork hit her plate in shock. "Oh, sorry," I apologized. "The dreams are chaotic and usually painful rather than helpful, but I have actually learned a bit about us. I didn't mean to say something you'd rather I didn't."

"No," she assured me. "It just keeps surprising me how much you know."

"And yet there's so much I don't."

"Do you need help up?" Luke sat on his heels beside me. He already knew the answer, but I liked that he asked first. I nodded, and he slid an arm behind my back.

Luke helped me stand, then walked me to a chair. I felt fine. Gabby followed and sat with me while Luke went to fix me a plate. Nana, Jim, and the two boys stormed the room looking for food. Emmitt caught one of the boys mid-run and lifted him into the air.

"They have a waffle maker," the boy said with a smile, wrapping his arms around Emmitt's neck.

"Really?" Emmitt looked very interested. "We'll have to beat Jim down there, then. Will you come wake us up in the morning?"

The boy nodded and started the put-me-down wiggle.

(Un)wise

Gabby distracted me from watching the happy family. "Could we ride together tomorrow?" she asked.

Luke walked over with a heaping plate. My stomach cheered for both of them, plate and man.

"Sure," I said to Gabby. "But I'm not much fun. I tend to fall asleep all the time."

"Maybe conversation will help," she offered.

I shrugged and bit into a forkful of stuffing heaven. But as I tasted it, I thought of home and had a hard time swallowing. I really wanted to call my mom. She had to be beyond crazy with worry by now. But I was too afraid I'd find out they had her, too afraid of what I'd do to try to help her. I knew I should wait until we exposed the Urbat to give her a call. My eyes fell on Nana who was speaking to Charlene. Charlene's color was coming back. She and Thomas sat on the edge of the bed eating together.

"Nana?"

She turned her head to look at me.

"Would you call my mom and let her know I'm okay?" My throat felt tight.

The room grew quiet.

"I ran away to try to save her. I don't know if it worked. I can't know if it worked," I stopped to swallow hard. "At least not until we take away their advantage. But thinking of her alone," I looked down at my Thanksgiving meal. "I just want her to know that I'm okay if she's still there."

Nana moved to me and squeezed my shoulder gently. "Of course, Bethi."

Jim brought over a piece of paper and a pencil. I wrote the number down, hesitated, and then wrote another before I handed it to Nana. "The first one is my mom's. The second one is a friend, Dani, in case my mom doesn't answer. Find out what you can. But don't tell me. Whether you reach her or not, don't tell me."

She nodded slowly, sad understanding filling her eyes. I couldn't know. I had to stay strong. I didn't think I had much left in me.

"I'm not hungry anymore," I said quietly, pushing my plate back.

"Bethi, you need to eat," Luke insisted.

"I just want to go to my room." I stood, and he followed.

He didn't put up too much of a fight about sharing a bed when we got to the room. He even pulled back the covers and took off his shirt.

I ducked into the bathroom to wash my face and brush my teeth. By then, I was ready to sleep. He watched me cross the room and held out an arm to welcome me.

"How are the stitches?" he asked.

"Fine," I murmured closing my eyes.

I woke with a stretch followed by a wince when the stitches reminded me I couldn't stretch too far. Luke's warm hand covered my stomach through my shirt; and I sighed, not opening my eyes. I'd experienced one of the best nights. I'd slept through without interruption for—I lifted my head from his chest to look at the alarm clock—fourteen hours.

"You must be starving," I said, lying back down.

"Your arm was looking good about six hours ago."

"I bet." I wasn't ready to get up yet. I sighed and closed my eyes again.

His stomach growled. I laughed and managed to sit up.

"You win. We'll go feed you."

"You, too," he said, sitting up with too much energy. "All you ate yesterday was a sandwich."

"Not true. I had a plate of pie, too."

I picked out clothes while he used the bathroom. He came out showered, fresh, and ready to eat. I shook my head and indulged in a quick shower, careful not to let the scabs around the stitches get too wet. It felt good to be so clean. When I wiped the steam from the mirror, I cringed. I hadn't been paying attention to myself. The circles under my eyes were dark again. I used the hotel hair dryer and brushed my hair until it was dry and then dressed.

Luke sat on a made bed waiting for me when I opened the door.

"Feed me," I begged.

He couldn't hide the worry that passed over his face. Standing, he threaded his fingers through mine and led me out of the room. My bag was slung over his shoulder.

We met everyone in the breakfast area. Michelle and Emmitt couldn't stop looking at or touching each other. Long looks followed by a quick kiss, a hug, or just a shoulder brush. I shook my head. I wasn't the only one. I caught Gabby's look, too. She grinned at me as Luke led me to the counter laid out with food.

He insisted I eat a bagel, eggs, sausage, and a waffle. Then he looked at me and added a bowl of cereal.

"Seriously? I'll be sick if I eat all that," I whispered as he carried the plate to the table Grey and Carlos shared.

"He'll eat what you don't," Grey said with a laugh.

I sat and started eating, asking questions between bites.

"Any news?"

"One of their sentinels must have discovered the Compound empty because they stopped grouping and have fanned out. Gabby said they are creating a net across the states, but there are holes big enough to wind our way through. It just might take a little longer," Grey answered.

Nana came up and asked about the stitches. She insisted on checking them before we left. I reluctantly agreed.

Luke used his fork to stab a piece of sausage from my plate and fed it to me with a soft command to eat.

In no time I was down to just the waffle. I had to push the plate away.

"Too much," I groaned.

Luke had the same meal I did, but twice the serving size. Still, his plate sat empty. He grabbed my waffle and finished that, too.

We shuffled the seating arrangements so Nana, Gabby, and Clay rode with us. Clay sighed when Gabby moved to sit in the backseat with Luke and me. He caught the back of her shirt before she could completely escape him and planted a kiss on her mouth before getting into the front seat.

"How you feeling?" she asked when Nana pulled out of the lot. Since we rode with Gabby, we were the lead car.

"Fine," I acknowledged. Luke's leg pressed against mine, warming me. I would probably be napping before long.

"If it's okay, I have some questions for you..." She glanced at Luke and Nana.

"It's fine with me." I'd relayed everything I thought I knew. If there was some memory lurking, some piece of information I'd failed to mention...well, it wasn't on purpose.

"You've said a lot about our abilities. I thought...I thought I was meant to find pairs."

"What do you mean?"

"When I touch people, if I'm feeling the right things, like empathy, I can transfer my power to them. Then, I get this kind of echo back from it, like ripples. When the ripple hits the right spark, it glows brighter. Does that make sense?"

Though I understood what she was saying, I'd never experienced it. "I haven't lived anything like that yet. I didn't know you could transfer your power. I wonder if the rest of us can," I said, looking out the window for a moment. Who would I want to give these dreams to? It would just be cruel. Well, maybe Luke. Maybe he would finally understand.

"When I transferred my power to Clay, my spark lit brightly. When I transferred it to Luke, your spark lit brightly. That's why I sent him. Well, part of the reason."

"You knew?" he said in a shocked tone.

"I wasn't sure. But I wasn't wrong, was I?" Gabby watched Luke closely.

Luke scowled at her.

"I could pass my power to you," she said.

She'd barely spoken the words when Clay and Luke simultaneously shouted, "No." Clay turned in his seat to give Gabby a look. It wasn't angry, but I could still see a stubborn warning there.

She and I shared a look. "It drains me," Gabby admitted. "At least, it did before I Claimed Clay." She reached forward and ran her fingers in Clay's hair. "Clay, it probably won't affect me anymore."

He shook his head. "Hands to yourself."

I could see he wouldn't be facing forward again anytime soon. She sighed and sat back.

"What's your reason for not wanting me to try?" she asked Luke.

"She's perfect the way she is," he answered vaguely and looked out the window.

Clay laughed. Gabby looked as confused as I felt, but then understanding lit her eyes.

"Have you felt the other part of my ability? The attraction I have on men?" I nodded recalling the dreams from this life. "I transfer that, too. When I transferred it to Clay," she smiled and her eyes drifted to him. He gave a tiny shake of his head as his teeth made a brilliant appearance. "Well, I Claimed him on the spot," she said.

Ah. So Luke wouldn't be able to resist me? Sign me up!

Gabby and I shared a look, but Clay kept too close of an eye on Gabby.

"I'd guessed about there being another race," Gabby said quietly. She looked at Clay sadly. "We came up here a day early because they tried challenging Clay. The men had a different color spark. While one had Clay distracted, another came in from the back. Clay heard and got there in time. But not before I saw the man." She turned and looked at me, clearly upset. "I felt it. The pull. But it felt so wrong," she whispered.

"Because for you, it was," I said. Then I looked at Clay. "To the death?"

He gave the barest shake of his head. That was a problem. But I didn't say anything more.

Eighteen

A week later we reached Georgia. We'd driven through a wicked storm and ended up a little further south than where we wanted to be. With Gabby's watchful eye, we'd avoided detection, though we'd experienced a few close calls. We'd woken one morning to a knock on our door and a quick "pack up." We'd left that hotel minutes before the Urbat reached town. They were only scouting Gabby assured us, but no one wanted to take the chance. She said their net was still spread wide. They were still trying to find us.

They had managed to catch a lone werewolf the fourth day after our departure from the Compound. The Elders immediately reached out to the man and remained mute for several hours. I shivered watching their faces and imagined the poor werewolf begging for information to give his captors as they tortured him.

Luke wrapped his arm around my shoulders and whispered words I couldn't remember afterward. He understood that I relived my own tortured pasts while the man remained in the Urbat's hands. When the Elders started speaking again, I knew his torture was over. I struggled to pull myself out of my dark memories. Luke was my anchor. He held my hand through it all, worry etched on his face.

He continued to fuss over what I ate, too. Under his care, I put on a few needed pounds and finally got more than two consecutive nights of good sleep. He started sleeping with a bag of chips next to the bed until I woke with crumbs in my hair and put a stop to his snacking.

We trudged into the lobby of yet another hotel, dripping and tired of being on the road. I was beginning to wonder if anywhere would ever feel like home again. Nana came up to me and pulled me away from Luke.

"I'd like to take out the stitches today. It was a shallow enough cut that it should be fine, but you'll need to take it easy."

I eagerly agreed. They were itching like crazy and uncomfortable. Once we had our rooms, she knocked on our door. Luke held my hand as she cut the first loop. It didn't hurt. Then, she tugged. I suffered a sharp sting on the surface as the stitch broke free from the healing skin. My stomach turned over at the queer feeling of something sliding under my skin.

"That was the easy one," Nana said. "A small one I did as a test to make sure you'd sleep through it. The next few are longer running stitches."

I didn't like the sound of that. More tugging, a little bleeding, and a lot of that under the skin crawling occurred over the next few minutes, but then she was done. I looked down at my stomach unimpressed with the new decoration on my skin. I sighed and moved to tug my shirt down.

"Not yet," she said, reaching down for a bottle. "It needs to be cleaned again." She passed the small bottle of rubbing alcohol to Luke. "I think you can take it from here."

I did not want the alcohol on all the new holes in my skin.

Most of them bled like little pinpricks. Luke watched me with a smile when I slowly tugged my shirt down.

"You heard her," he said. "Let's do this quick, and then we can grab dinner."

"I'm too sick for dinner. Let's skip it," I said, referring to the cleaning.

"Bethi, you're tougher than this," Luke said.

His gentle words made me feel like a coward. So, I made a face at him and exposed the cut. "Go on, you sadist. Inflict some more pain on your poor little human." I closed my eyes waiting for the pain, but felt nothing. Then, something brushed my forehead. A soft kiss. I smiled. He did that when he wanted to comfort me. It always worked.

A light touch of something cold on my almost healed cut elicited a gasp from me. Immediately, the antiseptic sting followed. He methodically touched each spot. I knew he had finished when he placed another kiss on my forehead.

Opening my eyes, I caught his tender look as he apologized. "I'm sorry I hurt you."

I gave a little laugh. "You didn't hurt me. I did. I'm good at that."

He helped me sit up. "But not anymore. Never again." He placed gentle fingers under my chin, forcing me to meet his gaze until I nodded.

Satisfied, he moved away from the bed and cleaned up the tissues he'd used. I stood slowly, testing my capabilities. It felt weird. It was probably in my head, but I worried the wound would pop right back open. So, though I stood straight, my movements were slow and easy like Nana had recommended.

"Since we're eating at the hotel's restaurant, it might be

better if you leave that here," he commented nodding toward the knife strapped to my thigh.

After leaving the Compound, I'd taken to wearing my knife strapped to my leg. Nana had loaned me a cute peacoat to replace Luke's shredded jacket. The new coat covered the knife whenever we stopped.

Sighing, I bent and released the clasp. I handed the bundle to Luke and watched him tuck it into our bag. When he joined me at the door, he placed another gentle kiss on my forehead. "We'll all be there," he murmured. "You won't need it."

I gave the bag a long wistful glance and left with Luke.

Down in the lobby, the others waited. The boys were being entertained by Grey and Jim doing "up-downs." The term wasn't something I associated with what they did. Each boy held the thumbs of one of the men. The men closed their hands over the boys' wrists and then started lifting and lowering them. It caused fits of giggles, but I didn't see how it could be much fun. To me, it looked like their arms would get sore. The boys', not the werewolves'. I knew the werewolves could lift like that forever.

"All set?" Nana asked.

I wrinkled my nose. "Yes. He got each one."

She smiled. "We'll get you a dessert for putting up with that."

Aden immediately begged to be let down and scampered over to my side. "Can I sit by you?" he asked sweetly. I'd watched how Jim often stole food from Aden's plate, and Aden in turn robbed whomever else sat closest to him. No doubt, he wanted my dessert. Still, I agreed.

The wait staff had already prepared a table for our large party and sat us as soon as we entered the hotel's dining room.

Luke sat on one side of me with Aden on the other. Michelle sat on Aden's other side, close to Emmitt. Jim was quick to sit across from Aden. Liam was on his other side.

Gabby claimed the spot directly across from me. Since driving together, she often took every opportunity to talk to me about her gift, trying to figure out all of its possibilities. We even found a moment free of our men where she'd offered to pass her gift to me. I'd been so tempted but knew we couldn't risk her losing her ability to see the sparks and guide our route. So, I'd regretfully declined the offer.

Talk around the table rose as everyone tried to decide what to order. It was nice not having to worry about money. Michelle's lawyer contact helped her get the funds we needed throughout our journey. No one made a fuss about using it, so I didn't either. I had enough to worry about. Besides, that's what she was meant to do.

While eyeing the baked lasagna on the menu, Gabby nudged me under the table. I looked up to see her unfocused gaze. "One of them just changed direction," she mouthed. Both Luke and Clay caught it, but no one else paid it any attention. "Maybe the rain?" she whispered hopefully, her eyes focusing again on the menu. She didn't look up again, but I could tell she monitored the progress of whoever had caught her attention. We ordered, and most of the adults conversed or entertained the children. I kept a close eye on Gabby.

She reached for Clay's hand. He wrapped both of his around hers and tilted his head. That finally caught the attention of Grey.

"What is it?" he asked softly, looking between Clay and Gabby. The table grew quiet, even the boys. Michelle hugged

Aden to her side. Jim placed a gentle hand on top Liam's head.

"Someone's changed their direction," I said.

"A complete turn," Gabby added.

"With all this rain, we should be fine," Sam assured the suddenly tense group. But we knew all it took was one of them to catch the scent and send word.

"Have any others changed?" Nana asked.

"I thought the rest looked like the same inconsistencies they've been doing since the beginning. Remember how I said it looked like a net? Several have changed directions moving toward a central point," she frowned. "They are doing that in six areas. We seem to be in the middle of one. The areas are huge though, several states. Big nets to catch little fish."

"Do we need to move?" Grey's eyes lacked their usual humor.

Gabby shook her head slowly. "I'm not as worried about their nets as much as I am the one closest to us. About a mile now."

The Elders shared a look. The waitress came to ask if we needed any refills. Jim asked for a double whiskey and two kiddie cocktails. Aden gave Jim a cautious smile.

"That's close, but with the rain, we don't think they could track us even if they were right outside the door," Nana said. Thunder boomed to punctuate her point. "Gabby, keep us updated. Sam, grab everyone's room keys and gather our things in my room. If they reach the parking lot, we'll all go there."

Sam stood and left. The waitress delivered the whiskey and kids' sodas. Jim pushed the sodas to the boys and the whiskey to Michelle. It was then I saw her pale face and worried looks at the boys.

(Un)wise

"Nana," she said. "Call Mary and Gregory. You're right. It's safer."

Nana nodded sadly. I'd wondered when she would send them away and thought her foolish for keeping them with us this long. But I did understand. How could you let go of someone you loved so much?

Michelle took a small sip, and Emmitt commented, "I guess I'm losing another shirt." It did the trick. Some color came back into her cheeks.

She leaned over and kissed the top of Aden's head and asked if they could play tic-tac-toe together. He eagerly turned over his placemat.

I could see the exact moment we were out of danger. Gabby took a deep calming breath and removed her hand from Clay's. "He's close, but stopped moving," Gabby said.

"Probably holing up out of the rain," Clay said. That man's voice did serious things to a girl's insides. Gabby caught my stare and grinned at me knowingly.

"If he clears out before check out tomorrow morning, we'll see if we can book the rooms for another night. It will give Mary and Gregory enough time to reach us," Nana spoke directly to Emmitt. Michelle continued to play with Aden but took another sip of whiskey at the news.

A few minutes later Sam rejoined us just in time for our food. I dug into my meal and looked forward to staying there another day.

* * * *

Stuffed from dinner even with Aden's help with dessert, I willingly followed everyone back to Nana's room where we all grabbed our things. The Elders agreed it would be best if they spread themselves throughout the rooms in case we needed a quick warning to leave. Grey and Carlos roomed with us, Sam stayed with Gabby and Clay, and Nana with Charlene and Thomas since their room adjoined to Michelle and Emmitt's.

Feeling awkward, I closed myself in the bathroom to get ready for bed. I washed my face, brushed my teeth, then stared at my bag. If we needed to leave in the middle of the night, I wasn't about to run out into the storm wearing sleep pants. I grabbed some clean clothes and changed. When I emerged, I saw the rest had the same idea—except for Luke. When he saw me, he smiled, pulled off his shirt, and lay back with an arm across my pillow. An open invitation to my favorite spot to sleep.

I crawled into bed and gave in to a dreamless night.

* * * *

The morning brought better news. Grey greeted me with a smile saying, "We're here for another day." Then he made the news sweeter saying, "Carlos and I are going back into our own room. It's a good thing you're a solid sleeper because he snores." He looked at Luke who grinned and seemed undisturbed by the news.

We went to breakfast and listened to everyone else's plans for the day. Michelle wanted to take the kids to a movie —early showing of course—and Nana wanted to shop for some snacks to pack in the cars for everyone. Grey claimed Carlos just wanted to watch cable all day. Carlos' only reaction to that was a long look at Grey. I had a feeling it was Grey who wanted to watch cable all day. Gabby said she had schoolwork she wanted to focus on for a few hours. I envied her belief that life would continue as normal once we found Peace. I wasn't about to tell her otherwise.

(Un)wise

Sam looked at Luke and me. "What about you two?"

"Nothing that involves driving," I said.

Sam smiled. "Well, Grey will be here if you need anything," he said, looking first at Gabby then at me. "I think I'm going to tag along with Winifred."

* * * *

Luke and I ended up walking with Emmitt and his family to the movie theater. The kids picked out a new cartoon for everyone to see. Luke and I got our own popcorn to share. It felt weird going to a movie, but Gabby had assured us there was no one close. And there wasn't anything else to do but wait until Mary and Gregory came for the kids.

So, I sat back and enjoyed the show, laughing—really laughing—for the first time since the dreams had started. Luke surprised me by cupping my chin and pulling my attention from the screen. Before I knew what he intended, his lips met mine in a kiss so mind-numbing and brief that I blinked at the screen for several minutes afterward. When I looked back at him, he watched the screen with a tiny image of the movie reflected in his eyes.

Not knowing what to think of the unexpected kiss, I went back to enjoying the movie, as I threaded my fingers through his. Every once in a while his thumb would smooth over the back of my hand.

After the show, we all walked back to the hotel. Everyone else was going to lunch, but the popcorn from the theater ruined my appetite, and I felt the tug of a dream. So, Luke and I walked back to our room.

Instead of giving into the dream, I decided to take a shower and warned Luke it would be a warm one just in case he thought

I was taking too long. I hadn't enjoyed the last time I fell asleep in a hotel bathtub.

Stripped down and letting the water run, I looked at myself in the mirror. I still desperately wanted to Claim Luke and wished I was brave enough to walk out there just as I was to try to tempt him. But I wasn't. The scars on my arms bothered me. They were from a desperate time in my life that I really didn't want to think about. The one on my stomach was just stupid. What really bothered me was my weight. I'd gained a little but not enough to look appealing, in my mind. Every time I pictured myself bare in Luke's presence, a scene from *Les Misérables*—the old one, not the new—interposed itself. It was the part where Uma Thurman pulled back the covers to offer herself as payment to her landlord. Thin and sickly, she'd disgusted him. That was what I envisioned. A grand gesture and an epic failure that would leave me crushed.

Covering myself with my arms, I ducked under the spray ready to wash away all my ugliness. It didn't work.

When I stepped out of the shower, I was the same scarred, thin me. I looked around for my bag and started to panic. I hadn't brought it in with me. Was this a self-fulfilling prophecy? I sat on the toilet on the verge of tears with a dream tapping its sharp fingers on my skull.

Why did life have to be so hard?

A knock on the door startled me.

"You all right?" Luke asked from the other side.

I quickly stood and rubbed my yet unshed tears away. "Yeah. I just forgot my bag."

"I'll get it." His voice sounded fainter, and I knew he had already walked away from the door.

(Un)wise

Making a quick I-don't-want-to-do-this face, I turned the knob and opened it a few inches to look out. He had his back to me, picking up the bag from one of the beds. When he turned and saw me, he stopped. Shame burned me as I gave him an uncertain smile, closed the door a bit further, and held out a hand, palm up. Only after I did it, did I realize I'd exposed my wrist. My eyes flew to his again. He hadn't moved.

I curled up, died, and was reborn in the fires of my anguish. Yanking the door open, I marched right up to him and pried the bag from his dead fingers.

"Just so you know, I had a boyfriend. Before the dreams started, and I went crazy," I said defensively. "It was pretty serious."

Finally, emotion broke through his shocked expression.

"But I cut ties when I realized what was coming my way. You know I'm old enough in the human world...and I know that by werewolf standards I'm old enough. When you're ready, you let me know," I said boldly, turning away from him.

He stopped me, curling his fingers loosely around my upper arms. The same arms that had a death hold on the towel and my remaining dignity.

"What are you saying?" he asked, his voice laced with a hint of a growl.

I dropped the bag and stepped toward him. "You didn't think a girl willing to cut herself, take drugs, run away from home, and hitch rides from strangers would save herself, did you?"

"Joshua?" he growled.

Giving a small laugh, I touched his jaw, tracing the ridge of it with a fingertip. "No way. He smelled like mud." Then his reaction hit me like a lightning bolt. His tense jaw, his overly focused concentration on my face...nowhere else but my face. He *wanted* to see more. My heart started beating faster, and the angry shame shrank back. Hopeful, I stood on my tiptoes.

"You smell like home," I whispered, brushing my lips against his.

He stood still, keeping his arms at his sides as I reached up and threaded my fingers in his hair. My lips traced his. Tiny tremors shook him. Then, he broke. His arms came alive and gently circled around me. He tilted his head and pressed his lips against mine. Tingles chased up and down my back. His mouth opened slightly as he planted little kisses in a trail down my neck. He nipped the tender skin there before continuing down to my collarbone.

"Tell me this is a yes," I whispered, struggling to keep my focus.

He groaned, but didn't stop. His mouth wandered back up my throat so I had to tilt my head back. He kissed his way to my lips, but before he claimed them, he pulled back to meet my eyes.

"This is a yes." He tilted his head exposing his throat.

I reached up to hold his shoulders and pull him down a bit. The towel fell to the floor. His breathing came in quick pants, matching mine. I kissed him gently, rubbing my lips on the corded muscles of his neck. Then, I bit.

He groaned and held me to him. A surge of love flooded me along with a consuming need to possess. They weren't my feelings. Not all of them, anyway. I moved on, kissing my way up his neck to his jaw. When he pulled back, a bloody smudge remained where I'd bit him, nothing else.

His lips claimed mine in a bruising kiss, and he turned us, backing me toward the bed. My heart started beating so fast I thought it would burst from my chest.

When we reached the bed, he stopped and pulled his shirt off. I knew then that we wouldn't stop at just Claiming. Anticipation flooded me. This time it was all my emotion. I smiled shyly at him and wrapped my arms around his neck.

* * * *

Snuggled against his side, I traced my fingers through the hair on his chest, content and peaceful. No dreams tugged at me. I hadn't looked at him yet. I wasn't sure if he would regret what we'd done.

"You lied," he said quietly, turning to kiss the top of my head.

"The last lie I'll be able to get away with now. Well, with you anyway." I didn't need to ask if he was mad at me. I knew he wasn't. I could feel his contentment blending with mine.

"Was there even a boyfriend?" he asked softly.

"Not a serious one," I admitted. "Still wish we would have waited for the magic eighteen?" I had to know.

He turned on his side to face me, his expression tender. "Yes," he said simply. "You are worth waiting for." His love flooded me, but I felt no regret. I leaned forward to kiss him.

"You're worth waiting for, too," I said softly. "But I didn't want to risk dying without feeling this." The connection between us grew, bursting with love and life. It wasn't just the impressions I had felt with Joshua. It was so much more. There was no room for self-doubt. With Luke, I could endure anything. Be anything. Even a Judgement.

My stomach rumbled, and a thread of concern flowed

through our link.

"Let's get dressed and eat," he said. The concern kept growing.

"What's wrong?" The depth of what he felt washed through me.

"You never eat right." He rose from the bed.

I forgot to breathe. I'd seen him in the all-n-all before, but now he was mine. I just wanted to jump on his back and pull him back under the covers with me. I wanted his touch. Needed it. I blinked as I struggled with my feelings and realized with a smile, they weren't just mine, because concern still flavored them.

"If you don't stop, we'll never feed you," he said with a smile as he strode to the bathroom.

* * * *

We met everyone downstairs for dinner. Nana glanced away from her conversation with Charlene to look at us, then did a double take. Her sudden wide smile told me she knew.

"About time he pulled his head from his—" Grey started to mutter, but a nudge from Carlos cut him off.

Four new members had joined our group. Michelle's brothers clung to two faces I recognized. Paul and Henry. They spoke to Gabby with a long time familiarity as they entertained the boys. Michelle and Emmitt spoke off to the side with Gregory and Mary. Michelle's eyes were red from barely restrained tears.

When Paul looked up and saw me hand in hand with Luke, he smiled and nudged his brother. Heat rushed to my face.

Dinner moved slowly, just the way we needed it to. Michelle agreed to let the boys go on a long holiday with Gregory and Mary. Or as the boys thought of it, with Paul and Henry. We spent the time talking about nothing important, though I caught Gabby's unfocused gaze as she constantly monitored the Urbat progress.

After dinner, we all agreed to meet in the lobby early the following morning. The next day's travel would bring us to Peace.

I went to bed eagerly and looked forward to another good night's sleep. But I didn't get what I wanted.

"Daughter," she said, standing beside the bed dressed in her usual taupe gown. "You are so blessed to have finally Claimed a Mate worthy of you."

I stood at the end of the bed, looking at Luke on his side, curled around me, his arm resting over my waist. I looked so small compared to him.

I glanced at the Taupe Lady. "I thought I only dreamt of the past."

She smiled. "This is the past. Just minutes old."

"Why am I dreaming this?"

"I'm bound to the past as much as I'm bound to the present, floating in the shadows in between. This is the only place we may speak. You must hurry to find your sisters. His anger is growing and even she won't be safe much longer. Tread carefully, loved one."

She smiled and reached out to pat Luke's bare arm. He shifted in his sleep. Then, she leaned over him to place a kiss on my sleeping-self's cheek.

I bolted upright, eyes wide, the feeling of her lips lingered on my skin. The place beside the bed was empty, but I couldn't shake the creeped out feeling.

"What is it?" Luke asked, instantly awake and sitting up with me.

I turned worried eyes to him. "I don't think I'm done dreaming, yet."

He kissed me gently, coaxed me back under the covers, and encouraged me to lay my head on his chest. He ran his fingers through my hair and rubbed my back until I relaxed again. Still, I lay awake long after he started snoring.

She was worried about Courage, I was sure of it. If she lived in the past and the present, she had to know what we planned and where we were headed. I bit my lip thinking of what Courage might be enduring despite Michelle's vision of gentle treatment.

Luke inhaled long and loud just then, his fingers twitching in my hair. I smiled at the sound before closing my eyes again. We would never need to share a room with anyone else with the noise he made.

Epilogue

The morning brought heartache for the group. We all witnessed Michelle hold back tears as she pasted on a bright smile and said goodbye to her brothers.

I glanced at Nana and wondered if she'd reached my mother. She met my gaze briefly, but her expression gave nothing away other than how she felt about the current situation.

Liam gave Emmitt a hug and asked him to watch over Michelle. Everyone heard his loud whisper. "I think she's sad we want to play with Paul and Henry."

Emmitt smiled and hugged the boy until he protested. Then, Emmitt promised to take care of Michelle, always.

"You too, you know," Luke murmured close to my ear.

Puzzled, I turned to him. His eyes looked slightly green in the morning light. He wrapped his hands around my arms and pulled me close.

"I promise to take care of you, always," he whispered just before his lips brushed against mine.

"Always is a long time for a girl who keeps coming back," I said, leaning into him.

"Forever isn't long enough," he said, enfolding me in a warm embrace and taking the kiss to the next level.

Nana cleared her throat. "All right you two. We need to travel today."

Luke pulled back with a sassy grin and clasped my hand. I needed the support after that kiss. My head spun, and my heart stuttered.

*   *   *   *

We arrived at the last hotel I hoped we'd need to stay at. Well, in our search for Peace anyway. There was still a lot of traveling and waiting to do when—if—we exposed werewolves. The Elders still hadn't given us their official decision.

"It seems like she's staying in one spot now," Gabby commented sitting on the edge of the bed in Nana's room.

"I think it would be best if just a few of us go," I said. "Gabby, since you can locate her, an Elder, and myself."

Nana looked worried about that but didn't need to comment. Gabby did for her.

"We'll need more than that. There are more Urbat here than there should be," Gabby said.

I wrinkled my nose. It was a big city. We didn't have much of a choice. We needed to be here. I understood the need to protect ourselves but didn't like how it would look to Peace. Having a large group of strangers come up to you and try to convince you to leave with them...I didn't see that going over well with her.

"What do you suggest?"

"Six of us. Grey, Carlos, Clay, you and Luke, and me. It'll give us better protection and still leave enough protection here for the rest," Gabby said.

(Un)wise

I knew she was right. "Okay."

"Sam's out driving to see what kind of place she's stopped at. When he gets back we can go." She stood and walked to Clay who waited by the door. "If it's somewhere nicer, Nana promised we can raid her suitcase."

"Absolutely," Nana agreed, hanging some of her things. Most of her wardrobe was a little more mature than I'd ever worn, but she always looked nice.

I looked down at my worn jeans and stained t-shirt. Ugh. Clothes kept you from being naked and cold; I hadn't thought about them any further than that. How had I not noticed? I looked at Luke.

"How can you—"

"What you wear doesn't matter. You are beautiful," he said, leaning in to place a tender kiss on my forehead. "Your clothes just help hide it from all the other guys out there."

Smiling, I shook my head at him. Possessive creatures.

* * * *

Four hours later, Gabby and I sat in the car with a very mulish Luke, and stoic Clay. To me Clay didn't act much different, but Gabby kept glancing at him and telling him to calm down. When she'd found out Peace was at a club, she'd insisted that we change since we needed to look like we fit in.

Nana agreed and took us both on an impromptu shopping trip that had me twitching. I didn't mind shopping. In fact, I used to love to go clothes shopping. Before the dreams. Before Urbat started hunting us. Before I had a mission to bring us all together. Now, however, the time we spent shopping and being in the open troubled me. When we walked out of the store, I sighed in relief. We had made it through without incident. And I

273

had new clean clothes.

Initially, Nana and Gabby had gravitated toward cute little party dresses that were sure to make a man's eyes melt and his tongue swell, but I'd flat out refused. If we were caught between an Urbat and Peace, I wanted to be able to run. Who ran in heels and a skirt? The movie extras that always died first! I did not want to be an extra. Neither woman could argue with my logic.

In our bags of purchased items, we both had stylish new jeans—mine hugged my thin frame in a sexy way rather than a sickly way—and very gossamer tops to go over low cut camis. Gabby went with pink over a red top, and I went with blue over a green top. My eyes stood out even more with the color combination. I even purchased makeup, surprising both Nana and Gabby that I knew how to use it. To me it was just a depressing reminder that I used to have a frivolous life. Now I had a life worth living.

Luke shifted uncomfortably beside me. He wore his own jeans and a shirt he'd borrowed from Sam. I couldn't believe how trendy Sam dressed.

When I'd stepped out of the bathroom dressed for our encounter with Peace, Luke hadn't said a word. He moved toward me, then did a slow walk around me. He'd whispered words to melt my heart.

"I can't believe you're mine."

However, he ruined it by telling me to go back and change. I squeezed his hand and gave him a quick smile. He frowned at me, his eyes dropped to my top.

"Ready?" I asked the group. Carlos and Grey were up front waiting for Gabby and me to give the word.

"She's still in there," Gabby confirmed.

"Let's go," I said with a deep breath. I struggled to contain my excitement. Five of us together again. My last memory of that was tainted with blood and battle. I hoped for more from this life.

Luke opened the door and extended a hand to help me out. Though I'd won the argument about the dresses, Gabby and I still wore trendy shoes instead of the sneakers I would have preferred. It gave me a few extra inches, which I liked when standing face to face with Luke. I gave him a quick kiss and moved out of the way so he could shut the door.

The neighborhood wasn't the best. A few blocks back we'd passed a burned-out car on the side of the road. There was no parking other than street parking. Bottles littered the sidewalk. Gabby gave me a worried glance. I didn't like it either but stepped forward anyway. I wouldn't leave until we at least met Peace.

Our low heels clicked in unison as we marched toward the club. The red door set in the brick wall of the building marked the entrance. There were no windows on the first level that I could see. I had my fake ID all ready to get in, but the door was unmanned. I began to wonder if the place was even licensed.

Luke made a small sound of disgust as he opened the door. The reek of stale booze and smoke rolled out toward us. Grey, the first one in the group, stepped in with a resigned look. I appreciated that I did not have their heightened senses as I followed. Luke held the door open for a moment longer than necessary trying to let in some fresh air, then followed the rest of us in.

A band played at one end, a mix of emo and rock. A small crowd stood in front of them dancing. The crowded bar stood opposite. The man there kept asking who was next.

Directly across from the entrance a stage sat behind a floor-to-ceiling wall of chain-link fence. Instead of band equipment, which would make sense, there were various fitness bags anchored to the ceiling off to the sides. In the center of the stage, on a huge mat that spread across the floor, a tall redhead faced off with a mountain of a man. The rest of the crowded room focused on the pair. The man's bald head glistened with sweat as they danced around each other. Both wore boxing gloves. It looked as if the fight had been going on for a while.

"That's her," Gabby said unnecessarily.

I knew her at first sight. Her rage boiled in her eyes. I was about to agree and suggest we wait at the bar, but Carlos was already pushing his way toward the fence, his skin rippling dangerously. I didn't care how drunk or high these people were, they were bound to notice.

I heard Grey swear and try to pull Carlos back. Carlos shook him off like it was nothing. That wasn't supposed to happen with an Elder.

On the stage, Peace ducked under a punch and came back with an uppercut to the man's jaw. The crowd groaned, but it was a good-natured groan. The man staggered back and shook his head. Carlos had reached the cage by then and paced back and forth in front of it, barely containing the beast.

Peace caught the movement and glanced at Carlos. Her opponent took that opportunity to swing. It connected hard, snapping her head back with the blow. This time the crowd booed, but I could barely hear it over Carlos' rage filled howl. He burst into his fur—*in front of everyone*—and crashed against the metal.

The wires bent inward, molding to the shape of his head and shoulder. A few of the brackets mounting the fence to the floor gave way. The fight on the stage stopped as the two stared at the huge beast attacking the fence. Peace looked stunned, but her opponent just stood there placidly.

"Clay, Luke," I gasped. "What do we do?" We needed to stop him. He was going to wreck everything. We needed Peace to accept us. We needed our first exposure to her and the world to be nice. "Watch for people taking video or pictures," I shouted.

Clay reached out an arm without moving, or taking his eyes off Carlos, and crushed a phone in someone's hand. Luke did the same but started working his way through the crowd, pulling me with him. People barely noticed us weaving our way through them. They were completely focused on the stage. So was I.

With a roar, Carlos charged again. Brackets popped free from the ceiling with a ping. The fence barely held on.

Peace's eyes rounded, and she took off through a side door behind the fence. Carlos' massive head swung in that direction. He paused for a moment, listened, then he took off with so much force, his claws left trenches in the wood floor.

As if that were the signal, the crowd came alive with panic and fear. Everyone flooded toward the exit. Luke wrapped his arms around me to protect me from being trampled. Clay had Gabby pinned to the wall by the door.

When the bar emptied, and the four of us stood alone with the buzz of an overturned speaker to keep us company, I met Gabby's eyes.

"What the hell was that?" I said in shock.

Author's Note

As you've notice, each girl's story overlaps...and things are just getting started. Keep reading for an excerpt from (Un)bidden, the fourth book in the Judgement of the Six series, to find out how Charlene ties into the story so far and how she might have the power to shape their future. Book five, from Peace's point of view5, (Dis)content will also tie into the scene you just read. Charlene's story, detailing how she found her way to Thomas and the amazing extent of her gift, starts when they leave the Compound. So, stay tuned.

Your continued support keeps me writing! Please consider leaving a review or telling a friend about this series.

Want to know about deals, release dates, and giveaways? Sign up for my newsletter at http://melissahaag.com/subscribe.

You can also find me on twitter and Facebook to keep up to date on what I'm working on.

Happy reading!

Melissa

(Un)bidden

J UDGEMENT of the Six:
Book 4

Melissa Haag

I left home because I didn't want to end up in a cage like a lab rat. Hitching rides, begging for cash, and sleeping on the ground got old fast. That was the only reason I braved an overgrown path to a group of buildings. I'd hoped to find a bed and a decent night's sleep. However, what I found was a place overrun by werewolves.

While on the run, Charlene finds herself surrounded by werewolves, creatures she can't control with her mind like she can humans. Their existence has her believing she's found a safe place to stay, a place where secrets are okay. However, she soon discovers she's anything but safe. Charlene must learn how to use her abilities to influence the strange new species because if she can't, the next bite she suffers might just kill her.

Read how the cycle begins, and have no doubt. Charlene's past will shape the future of the Judgements.

An excerpt from *(Un)bidden*

I sat in the soundproofed room, listening to Bethi tell us about the three races and our purpose. Her story sounded unreal, but I understood unreal. My abilities made me unreal. I studied Bethi and knew she felt it, too. The separation from the three races we were supposed to balance.

Charlene. Thomas' thoughts nudged mine back to the conversation.

"...to buy us some time to plan," Bethi said.

"To plan what, dear?" Winifred asked.

"An evacuation, to start," Bethi said.

Evacuation? My heart stopped and panic surged. An immediate sense of calm washed over me, and I knew it was Thomas.

He understood my panic. This was the only home I knew. My sanctuary for the last—how many years had it been? The only times I left were to reach the hospital in the states to give birth to my boys. I couldn't leave. It wasn't safe out there. Even after all these years, I had a sense of foreboding. If I left this place, things wouldn't end well.

"What do you mean?" he asked Bethi.

"When the Urbat come, they will use the people we love to try to sway us. First, they use our families, torturing them until we do what they want. If that doesn't work, they start torturing us."

Torment filled her gaze. What had the poor girl already endured? She so reminded me of my past self. I could only imagine how the weight of the knowledge of our past lives burdened her.

"What do they want?" Grey asked.

"For each of us to Claim one of them." Bethi's gaze darted

to Michelle, Gabby, then me.

"We've already Claimed someone," Gabby pointed out. Clay rested a hand on her shoulder.

I was glad to see the two of them had found an understanding. The first time I met Gabby, alone in the world like I'd been, I felt the need to protect her. Looking at the girls at the table, I realized I felt the same for each for them. I needed to protect them. They were unique, like me, and the Penny's of the world were still out there, waiting.

"It won't matter," Bethi said, pulling my thoughts back. "A Claim can be broken by death, or simply by Claiming another.

I was stunned by that news. By the silence in the room, so was everyone else.

"That's why I was willing to Claim Joshua."

Luke looked angry. I could only imagine how he felt knowing his destined Mate decided to Claim someone else.

"The next step is for life," Bethi said. "Once Mated, we don't Mate again. I mean, they *could* force us to Claim another and mate, but it doesn't do any good. Our hearts stay with the first lost mate. The new Mate holds no influence."

"Influence for what?" Sam asked.

"For balance," Bethi said. "They have been after power since they figured out what we were. The Judgements. In the beginning, we always judged in favor of the humans. At least, that's my guess. I haven't dreamed what really happened yet. Since then, as far as I've seen, we haven't made another Judgement. I'm guessing that's why, despite the inferiority of humans in comparison to your races, they have thrived."

Her words troubled me. It brought back memories of my first days here. While humanity thrived, these people had almost disappeared.

"The Urbat are tired of living in the shadows and want to be the dominant race for a while. The last cycle they almost had it, but one of us died. Without all of us to...do something, things will stay the way they are, with humans maintaining control," Bethi explained. "The cycle doesn't last forever—only fifty years—so they try not to risk our lives. But they will if they must. After all, we can still be reborn again into the same cycle."

"So you're saying we need to clear the Compound because they will come for all of you and use the people here to talk you into surrendering?" Thomas asked, his disbelief evident in his tone.

"Don't doubt it. They will come. They always come. And death always follows."

I considered her words and studied the fear on her face. I knew I needed to speak up, yet after all these years, I still worried what would happen when everyone discovered what I'd done.

"What then? Where do we go?" he asked.

"That's the tricky part. I don't know where the pack should go, but I know where we need to go. We are missing two of our group. We need to find them."

"About this evacuation..." How could I explain it was unnecessary? She didn't know the full extent of what I could do. No one did. Not even Thomas. I glanced at him, feeling the fear from the past grab me. Once again, he soothed me. If I spoke up, what would he do? What would he think? Would he still want to sooth me?

"Out of all of us, you and Michelle are the most vulnerable. Michelle's brothers need to be sent away and protected. Emmitt, if he's taken, will be a risk to both of you. They will want to break the Claim Michelle has as much as they will want to hurt Emmitt to sway you," she said.

I glanced at Emmitt.

He gave me a reassuring smile. "Don't worry. We know now so we can make sure it doesn't happen."

I nodded. I would stay near both my boys and make sure nothing happened. I would do whatever it took, even if it meant revealing the past.

SNEAK PEEK OF ISABELLE'S STORY

(DIS)CONTENT
Judgment of the Six: Book 5

Coming 2015

Jaw clenched, I shoved the key in the apartment building door. My skin felt too tight from all the crap I had to deal with at the office. *I should have quit like Ethan said*, I thought. *Who cares if I spend my whole life tending bar?* It would be easier, especially with the setup Ethan had.

Stopping to grab my mail from the entry, I gave a tight smile to my downstairs neighbor. Waves of annoyance rolled off him and soaked into me. My skin grew tighter. I quickly grabbed my mail and moved on before he could pull me into a friendly conversation.

My neighbors all liked me. They didn't even know me, but that didn't stop them from treating me like a close friend. As a rule, I didn't socialize with anyone in my building. It just didn't seem right. After all, I robbed them of anything negative emotion they might have. So, how could they not like me?

As a child, I'd always wanted friends. When Ethan came

along and seemed to understand me better than anyone else ever had, I gave up on having friends and settled for having a friend—singular. And Ethan was enough.

I trudged up the stairs to the second floor, opened my apartment, and stepped inside with a sigh. My eyes fell on my bag hanging from the special support the landlord had installed for me. I wanted nothing more than to start hitting it, but knew once I started, I wouldn't stop until I was drained. First mail, then change, and then dinner. After that, I could have at it.

Kicking off my flats, I sorted through the mail while walking to the kitchen. I didn't need to pay attention to where I was going. My apartment wasn't that big. The living room and kitchen flowed together with a tiny island separating them. The living room had my bag dangling from the ceiling and that was it. My bedroom had a T.V., bed, and dresser. I didn't need much.

I stopped mid-sort and stared at an envelope with a hand written address. No return address. No postage. Weird. I threw the bills to the side and set the envelope on the counter. The bills I'd write out later, the envelope I would open while I waited for food. The freezer had a nice selection of dinners waiting for me. I grabbed one at random and threw it into the microwave. While I listened to the hum of my dinner cooking, I tore open the envelope and pulled out a hand written letter.

No matter how I write this, you won't believe it. All I ask is that you don't throw this away...just consider it.

There are people looking for you. They know what you can do. They must not find you. If they do, they will hurt us both, and so many more.

Don't trust anyone. Run. Stay hidden. Our time's almost up.

I turned it over and glanced at the blank back. There was no greeting and no closing. Just an unsigned note. My eyes fell on the one sentence that truly concerned me. "They know what you can do," I murmured.

The microwave beeped. I used a magnet to stick the letter to the refrigerator and drifted to my room to change. Dressed in Spandex shorts and a tight exercise tank top, I padded out to the living room and ignored the cooling dinner that waited for me. I slipped on my gloves to protect my knuckles and started exercising my demons.

The idea that someone might know about me didn't scare me. I found it amusing. No one really knew but Ethan. My parents had their own ideas about me—how could they not after raising me? But their suspicions weren't close. They thought I exuded positive energy. I'd like to blame their hippie thoughts on their habits in the sixties and seventies, but they weren't that old. The reality of what I did wasn't that I released positive anything. It was the exact opposite it seemed.

I mostly siphoned negative emotions. But if I wanted, I could pull the positive ones too. I felt what the people around me felt. Like sampling ice cream, their emotions had different flavors letting me know their moods. Unfortunately, the siphoning wasn't voluntary. No matter how hard I tried, I couldn't completely turn it off. But, boy, could I turn it on. If I wanted, I could drain a room in two heartbeats. Taking away all that negativity made the people around me happy, but did the opposite for me. The more I siphoned, the less I felt like myself. I grew agitated, angry even. My skin tingled the more I absorbed until it felt painfully tight. The only thing that helped relieve it was physical activity.

I hit the bag, timing the back swing and setting a grueling rhythm. Who would ever think someone could do what I could do...and why would they come after me?

Good luck to whoever thought they could take me, I thought. I'd leave them on the floor with a gap-toothed smile.

APPENDIX

The Judgements:

- Hope— Gabby, recently reluctant Mate to Clay [*Book 1: Hope(less)*]
- Prosperity — Michelle, Mate to Emmitt, son of Charlene [*Book 2: (Mis)fortune*]
- Wisdom — Bethi, Mate to Luke [*Book 3: (Un)wise*]
- Strength — Charlene, Emmitt's mother, Mate to the werewolf leader Thomas [*Book 4: (Un)bidden*]
- Peace — Isabelle [*Book 5, anticipated release 2015*]
- Courage — Olivia [*Book 6, anticipated release 2016*]

The lights Gabby sees:

- Werewolf — Blue center with a green halo
- Urbat — Blue center with a grey halo
- Human — Yellow center with a green halo
- The Judgements:
  - Charlene — Yellow with a red halo
  - Gabby — Yellow with an orange halo
  - Michelle — Yellow with a blue halo
  - Bethi — Yellow with a purple halo
  - (Peace) — Yellow with a white halo
  - (Courage) — Yellow with a brown halo

Touch

By Melissa Haag

Tessa longs for freedom...
A touch. That's all it takes for Tessa to know her future with a boy. Her mom tells her she needs to choose her best option before she turns seventeen. Problem is, she sees all her "options" dying before they turn thirty. That may have worked for the last fourteen generations of women in her family tree, but Tessa can't choose and condemn someone to an early grave.

An unfortunate incident at Tessa's school starts a chain of events that reveals Morik, a centuries old chaos demon.

Morik won't stop looking for her...
Hidden from the world, he has waited for his chance. Desperate for a purpose, he struck a deal. The time has come to collect.

An excerpt from *Touch*

Light from the hallway spilled onto the bed where I lay curled on my side. My blonde hair spread on my pillow like a halo. Brian, silhouetted by the light, stood unsteadily in the doorway. Sweeping a hand through his light brown hair, he sighed, turned off the light, and made a noisy attempt at creeping into the room. I could smell the alcohol and perfume on him. We both knew I wasn't asleep, but neither of us spoke. Down the hall, our daughter slept oblivious to her father's infidelity and, later, his alcohol induced death.

Standing in the senior hallway of Middlelyn High School, I dipped my shoulder, shrugging off Brian's warm hand and the remnants of the vision.

"Tessa?" he said. He stood close to me, waiting for my answer.

Revulsion filled me as the bitter tang of stale alcohol lingered in my nose. Turning my deep brown gaze on him, I fit a stiff smile on my lips and answered his question with a lie.

"A movie and dinner would be great, but I'm not allowed to date. Sorry, Brian."

He didn't seem to hear me. He shifted his stance and tucked his rejected hand into the front pocket of his fashionably worn jeans.

"I could come over and maybe help with homework or something."

He spoke quietly so the animated conversations pouring from the kids flowing around us muted his suggestion. The school secretary's voice blared over the intercom system, droning through the end of the day announcements, and joining the symphony of noise. None of it registered as I studied Brian's expectant face.

"Brian, I have to be honest. I don't trust you or your sudden interest. What's up? Really."

When I first moved to Middlelyn a few weeks ago, the boys asked me out based on genuine interest. Blonde hair, deep brown eyes, a trim figure, and oval face with straight teeth, I passed as attractive. Add to that the fact I didn't grow up with any of them and witness their awkward stages of puberty, or they mine, and I stood out even more. Fresh meat.

However, after rejecting most of the boys in my grade, the requests had tapered off and I'd been labeled a prude. Just one of many labels I now carried. The sudden interest of Brian, one of the most sought-after boys of the senior class because of his messy light brown hair, chiseled classic features, bold blue eyes, and a buff body, didn't fit.

He flashed his cocky I'm-hot-and-you're-not grin. "Fifty bucks for the first one to get you on a date. Say yes and I'll split it with you."

Hurt, I turned away and stacked the textbooks into my locker. He didn't leave, confident the money would tempt me.

In a school this size, everyone knew where I lived and that my family didn't have much money. He probably didn't even realize how cruel his words sounded. Just a game to them. It annoyed me how callous boys could be. Then again, I'd witnessed girls acting just as bad. In fact, I'd been one of those girls a time or two. I didn't like being *that* girl, but sometimes, I didn't have a better choice.

"Wow. So tempting," I said still facing the locker. "But if I take half, it won't leave much for the booze you're thinking about buying."

Glancing his way, I caught his startled look before he schooled his features. I immediately regretted my temper. Annoyed or not, I should have kept my thoughts to myself.

"You're a freak," he said as if just now understanding the rumors circulating about me.

I hated the rumors, but couldn't claim them untrue. My mouth often got me into trouble. Might as well finish with flare.

"Yep, and the freak thanks you for asking her on a date, Brian."

Grabbing my jacket and bag, I closed the locker door with a metallic clang and walked away, merging with the steady stream of passing students.

The vision of my life with Brian remained consistent with most of my visions. Not horrible, but not better either.

Making my way through the halls, I ignored my schoolmates and their careful avoidance of the pariah—me. I tried to keep what I saw to myself, but sometimes details slipped because I believed I had some choice, some ability to influence the outcome. The rumors about me seeing someone's death started to circulate not long ago.

The recent vision had been clear. Date Brian and he drinks himself to death. But what if I didn't date him? I didn't know if he'd live any longer. Given his reaction, I'd guessed accurately about his current drinking habits. Would my rejection or comment about his drinking change anything? Despite his callous attitude, I hoped it would.

I pushed open one of the main doors and viewed the line of waiting buses. Their exhaust tainted the clean, cool fall air. I headed toward the end of the line and boarded my bus, taking the steps two at a time. The warmth was welcome.

The driver, using her mirror to watch the trouble underway in the back of the bus, ignored me as I sat near the front with the younger kids. They were less irritating. Less irritating made the forty-minute bus ride tolerable. Lunch long gone, my stomach rumbled as I thought of the lengthy ride.

The flow of kids leaving the school slowed, and the first bus in line pulled away. The rest of the line slowly followed.

At sixteen, taking the bus sucked. I had my license, but no car. I had no job to pay for one. No job because I lived so far out of town I needed a car to get a job. My aunt, great-great aunt, great grandmother, my mom and I all lived together, pooling resources—only my mom and Aunt had jobs. With all that pooling, we still didn't have any extra money for even the crappiest of cars for me.

The little boy next to me tapped my arm and asked me to tie his shoe. I smiled at him and showed him how to make bunny ears out of the laces. Boys were cute at this age, before they learned to care what their peers thought of them. At one of the first few stops, I moved to let him out. After that, I stared out the window and watched the trees pass in a blur of brown.

When the bus emptied of a few of the more obnoxious older kids, I pulled out my homework to pass the time. Despite the long ride, I usually beat my mom and aunt home. It worked out well, though. With my homework done, I could help out a little. The quiet time spent making dinner with Gran and great Aunt Danielle made my night.

Two minutes after finishing my last math problem, the bus slowed for my stop. Bag slung over my shoulder, I stood near the driver and waited for the door to open. Gravel crunched under my feet as I stepped down, and a crisp breeze swept past.

As the bus pulled away, I tucked my hands into my coat and moved to the mailbox. My one true chore in winter. I held the mail under one arm and returned my hand to my pocket. The air that had felt cool and refreshing after school now just felt chilly.

Eyeing the distance to the house, I wondered not for the first time, how we would manage to shovel our long driveway. Naked trees and long dormant grass crowded the narrow drive.

Minute hills and valleys in the gravel made for a bumpy ride or a slow walk. A challenge to navigate with a shovel. But the house made up for the driveway.

From a distance, the faded green paint that coated the wood siding of the two-story farmhouse didn't look bad. Up close, you could see the crackled pattern in the paint that stubbornly clung to the old boards. Other than being drafty and needing paint, the house remained in good shape, and low rent made it worthwhile.

I spotted my great grandma waiting for me on the porch and hurried my steps. Her stark white hair stood out against the green paint behind her as she rocked slowly in an old wicker chair. She had no jacket on, just a blanket wrapped around her shoulders.

In her early seventies, though she looked the grandmotherly part, she didn't always act like it. Her life had been hard early on, especially after the death of her daughter, my grandmother. It had taken its toll. She told me repeatedly that my birth had breathed life back into the family.

I climbed the steps. "Gran, it's getting too cold to sit and watch for me."

She laughed away my concern. "The cold won't be what kills me. How does spaghetti sound for dinner?"

"Great." I helped her from the chair, and we both went inside.

It wasn't much warmer indoors, but I still peeled off my jacket before I followed her to the kitchen. I knew the small cheery room would warm up as soon as we started cooking.

I moved to the butcher's block, and she went to the pantry.

"Anything interesting happen at school today?" she asked, returning with an onion for me to peel and chop. She set it on the board and drifted to the stove.

"Brian asked me out. Touched me. With me, he'd be a drunk and a cheat until the day he dies."

"Any kids?" Gran asked absently, moving the empty pot from the stovetop to the sink.

The image of a sweet, cherub face invaded my mind, and I suffered a pang of loss. The visions, along with their emotional attachments, stayed with me for a few days. When I recalled details, it all felt real.

Gran set the pot full of water on the stove and pulled out another pan, jarring me from the fake memory.

"One." I grabbed some garlic to mince while she prepped the sauté pan with oil.

"Hold out for at least two."

I didn't bother answering. That's what they—my mother, aunts, and grandma—all said. Not, "Hold out for a guy you like who will live to see his hair turn white," or "Wait for the right one. Someone who makes your toes curl." No. Instead, their suggestions all revolved around holding out to make the best of a horrible fate. After all, they'd all done the same.

Understanding their stance didn't stop their answers from frustrating me. I didn't want to make the best of things. I wanted life to go easy on us all for a little while.

I could feel her eyes on me while I chopped in silence.

"Tessa, honey, you know we want you to be happy. We've all tried to find what happiness we could. When you lose your man, you'll at least have your daughters. That's why we say to wait."

The onions and the garlic made my eyes water so when I answered, I sniffled a little. "I know, Gran. I just don't understand why this is happening to us."

"All we have is what is in Belinda's book," she said sadly before turning to pour the noodles into the boiling water.

Belinda, the first of our line, had created an unpretentious, small book that detailed the basics of her life. She had passed it down to her daughters, and they had passed it down to theirs. The book had followed her line from mother to daughter, giving us a few slivers of knowledge.

All women of our line have a gift; with a single touch, we see a glimpse of our future. The touch only works on men. The gift manifests on our twelfth birthday. We have until our seventeenth birthday to choose a boy. The choice is binding. Once we choose, the gift disappears.

Reading the first few pages of the book, a person might think fate favored us with such a wonderful gift. To see our potential future with any man we touched, who wouldn't want that? Avoid the cheaters and the unmotivated and search for the one who could make a girl truly happy. However, if a person kept reading, they would understand the depth of our misfortune. The one we choose dies young. Always. If we're lucky, we'll have a daughter or two before that time. Always daughters, never sons.

Belinda's book left so much for us to guess. What would happen if we didn't choose? Neither she nor any of her descendants ever noted an answer. Only that we *must* choose.

In the back of the book, Belinda started a family tree of sorts. Mothers noted the birth of their daughters by entering their name. Many branches just stopped. Like great Aunt Danielle's, Gran's twin. She never had a daughter. No one ever talked about her choice. My mom warned me at an early age not to bring it up. Mostly, Aunt Danielle sat quietly on the chair in the corner of the living room, her haunted eyes staring off into space. I suspected she lost a daughter long ago along with her husband, but I never asked.

Aunt Grace, my mother's sister, chose a man who wouldn't

give her children. Unlike Aunt Danielle, Aunt Grace spoke about it once when just the two of us were home. She hadn't wanted to condemn her child to our shared fate, the visions and forced choice. But after helping to raise me, she regretted her choice. Only one branch remained active in the book. My mother's. Everything rested on me now. I'd have no cousin to share the burden when I reached their age.

Gran and I worked in silence. The smell of fresh basil, plucked from the herb pot in the kitchen window, filled the room. Water bubbled on the stove, heating the kitchen. Gran added the chopped ingredients into the frying pan, and I moved to sit at the table. I buttered bread, cut each slice in half, and set them to the side. I enjoyed working in the kitchen, mostly liking the warmth and light.

"Looks like it will be dark early tonight," she said, glancing at the cloud-laden sky through the window by the sink. "Homework done?"

"Yeah." I loved summer and its long hours of daylight. I was able to do so much in summer. However, winter sucked almost as much as the bus ride from school because of its short days.

Only in winter did I truly resent the rules in Belinda's book. Actually, not all the rules. Mostly just the one that stated those with the gift had to be home before dark. No explanation why. Just simple instructions to secure the house before the sun sunk below the horizon and a note that shutters worked best to block out the night.

Mom and Aunt Grace arrived home just as Gran and I put supper on the table. As usual, Aunt Danielle didn't join us, preferring her solitary chair. She took her meals when she felt like it. No one seemed overly worried about her. As Gran's identical twin, I supposed they would worry if she started to look thinner than Gran.

After supper, we all got ready for bed. I had priority on the shower since I wouldn't wake before seven. Another lovely rule. To protect the daughters from the night, we slept until the sun's first ray crested the horizon. In winter, it made it a tight race to get to school on time.

Mom knocked on the door. "Fifteen minutes until dusk. We're starting now."

"Okay," I called back, turning off the water.

In late fall through early spring, the monotonous events of my short days made me want to scream. Get up, race to school. Do homework while riding the bus home. Make dinner with grandma, eat, and get ready for bed. No time remained for anything else.

I hurried to pull on my pajamas; fleece lounge pants and a cami. The material stuck on my damp skin a few times. When I rushed out the bathroom door, I felt slightly twisted.

The tightly closed shutters blocked out the fading light and cast most of the house into darkness. Using my hand as an anchor on the hallway wall, I moved to the living room where everyone waited. The one time of day Aunt Danielle actually joined in.

They sat on their heels in a small circle on the living room floor. Their quiet murmurs filled the house. Each spoke the words from Belinda's book. Words of protection.

Outside, I could feel the sun setting and a cold scary presence growing. I stepped between Mom and Gran to stand in the middle. As one, they rose and reached their right hands toward me. Their fingertips brushed my bare arms and lethargy set in, cocooning me in safety. Their quiet words stopped.

"Sleep tight, Tess," my mom whispered, wrapping an arm around my shoulders.

She led me to my room. I struggled to keep my eyelids open

so I didn't run into my bed. Waking up with a bruised shin made me grumpy.

Yep, I hated winter, weirdly induced sleep, and boys who died after committing their lives to me.

Printed in Great Britain
by Amazon.co.uk, Ltd.,
Marston Gate.